SUSPENSION

Suspe

nsion

A Novel

ROBERT
WESTFIELD

HARPER ● PERENNIAL

NEW YORK ● LONDON ● TORONTO ● SYDNEY

HARPER ● PERENNIAL

P.S.™ is a trademark of HarperCollins Publishers.

HarperCollins books may be purchased for educational, business, or sales promotional use. For information please write: Special Markets Department, HarperCollins Publishers, 10 East 53rd Street, New York, NY 10022.

FIRST EDITION

Designed by Jamie Kerner-Scott

Library of Congress Cataloging-in-Publication Data

Westfield, Robert.
   Suspension : a novel / Robert Westfield.—1st ed.
     p. cm.
   ISBN-10: 0-06-074137-6
   ISBN-13: 978-0-06-074137-2
    1. New York (NY)—Fiction.   I. Title.

PS3623.E849S87 2006
813'.6—dc22   2005055003

06 07 08 09 10 WBC/RRD 10 9 8 7 6 5 4 3 2 1

For Mr. Troiano,
and all the teachers like him

The fact remains that getting people right is not what living is all about. . . . It's getting them wrong that is living, getting them wrong and wrong and wrong and then, on careful reconsideration, getting them wrong again.

—Philip Roth, *American Pastoral*

SUSPENSION

NOVEMBER 2001

JUST UNTIL THE SWELLING goes down. That was how long I intended to stay home. Until I could see out of my left eye, until my lower lip closed up. Until all the cuts scabbed over and faded into pale scars. Until I could bend the joints in the two small fingers of my left hand without feeling pain shoot up to my neck. Once the physical injuries healed, though, I still had the anxiety, the guilt, the shame, and then the creeping realization that *not* leaving my apartment was easier than I expected. It was on a Saturday morning in August, with my palms scraped raw, my two fingers in a splint, and my knees taped in bloody bandages, that I slowly pulled myself up the two steep flights to my small one-bedroom in Hell's Kitchen, closed the door behind me, and quietly turned the locks—click, clack, click—and it wasn't until November that anyone mentioned my absence. That person was Sonia Obolensky, my friend and tormentor.

I should point out that I used to be thrilled by Sonia's blazing tirades. I listened to her rants and watched her shake her fists as if I were sitting in the front row at the opening of the Moscow Art Theater's American tour. Whenever she ripped her blondish hair loose in an explosive moment of ferocity, her tiny teeth gnashing the air, her blue eyes swelling out of their sockets, I wanted to stand up and cheer, invoke endless curtain calls, and throw long-stemmed roses at her petite feet. By that November, however, I suspected that I'd endured the full repertoire and wondered when she would take her show to Chicago and free up the theater for something new.

I still did my best as a friend. When she was fired from her coat-check job at Orso and came to me in tears of rage, I told her I was glad she lost the job. I was honestly relieved that rainy days could now pass by without gleeful squeals of "Umbrellas, umbrellas!" That Sonia would find such euphoria from a few extra wrinkled dollars pressed into her hand while she stood for hours in a box stuffed with dripping trench coats and the suffocating smell of wet wool made me uneasy. As one of the first Americans Sonia met, I felt responsible for all of her setbacks, so it was with increasing frustration that I watched her bounce through a never-ending series of very odd jobs. At times I used humor to help her climb back up on her troika, but making a joke about Sonia's life was a game of Russian roulette.

Sonia had been fired from her eighty-sixth job in the city and was trying her hands at massage; the thought occurred to me, as I lay naked, smeared in oil, and wrapped in a sheet on her folding table, that she was now literally inches away from turning tricks. In hindsight, I should not have voiced the observation. I felt her fingers freeze on my thigh. Then her palm slapped my back. She began noisily packing up her assorted oils and rubbing manuals, leaving my left leg untouched and my right one overworked. Already on edge, I was now lopsided and greasy, unprepared for what she said next.

"And you're mean and spiteful!"

"Sonia, I'm sorry. You know it was just a joke." I was still face-down on the table, my face in the rubber doughnut. "Please do my left leg."

"No! Absolutely no!"

I stared for a few moments at the faded blue carpeting three feet below me. The massage, I knew, was a lost cause, but I still had a chance of letting her fire burn out if I could deprive her of added fuel.

She moved on without my help. "And your apartment stinks and you're lazy."

"My apartment stinks?"

"It has no air. You never leave. You stay here twenty-four and seven."

I sat up, tying my sheet in a knot around my waist, and said, "Twenty-four-seven. No *and*." This was a sore point between us, and the only thing I could think of to distract her.

"Twenty-four AND seven!" she retaliated. "You never leave."

"What do you mean I never leave?" I tried to laugh it off.

"And what do I mean? You never leave this place. What are you doing here? You mockery me but what do you do?"

"What?" was the best I could muster. I added, "Where?"

"Here! What are you doing here? This stinky room?"

"It does not stink."

"Like one thousand socks! What are you doing? Tell me."

"I am thinking!" I blurted out. Sonia laughed and spat out something in Russian. I made a show of wiping my face of her spray, sliding two fingers firmly over the contours of cheek and chin. She wasn't shaken. I modified my answer: "I'm writing."

"O, Mr. Twain, Dostoevsky!"

"Stop spitting on me."

"Present me your work, so grand."

I had nothing to present her, since I wasn't a writer and only said so because it was a marginally better answer than "I am thinking." Sonia waited. She looked down, her arms folded, her jaw clenched. The residual oil from her hands spotted her bright orange T-shirt. The air was pulsating, I could hear the second hand ticking on her watch. I opened my mouth and then closed it, exhaling through my nose. The silence was uncomfortable but speech was impossible. My throat was contracting.

"Well?" asked Sonia.

"Well, what?"

"Where is your grand think-piece?"

"I'm not showing you. You can read it when it's published."

She held her oily hands up in front of her, palms forward, then back, and then forward again, to remind me of the full extent of her labor-filled life.

"How do you make money?" she asked.

"I have the same job I've always had."

"And you don't go to job!"

"I work from home."

"And they let you do this? How is this thing possible?"

What to tell her so that she wouldn't erupt? When my ever-accommodating boss, whose own attendance record was patchy at best, learned that I was a victim of a brutal street attack, she gave me "plenty of room to recoup" and allowed me to submit my projects via e-mail. Then, a month later, just uttering words *September eleventh* allowed virtually anyone to work from home. I was given further deadlines and kept on a perpetual payroll without a single question asked.

I didn't want to get into this with Sonia, so I just said, "I'm lucky, I guess," and the curtain went up.

Sonia's performance began with a loud cough and increased in volume for the ten minutes she held the stage. Bouncing from wall to wall in my tiny living room, the back of her right hand slapping the palm of her left, she cataloged her struggles and described how much more severe her life was. Mine, according to her, was "easy and dumb"; my reactions to the downward turns of fate were encapsulated in a Russian word whose meaning she had never taught me but I could infer was deeply offensive from the harsh *k* sounds. (The Russian language has a system of slang unrivaled in its guttural depravity.) I wouldn't survive a day in the former Soviet Union, she concluded, and I should be thankful for everything I had: a full-time job and free massage.

I couldn't tell her that I expected to lose that source of income any day, or even begin to explain the terror of opening the door and stepping out into the hall, much less onto the street. I wasn't able to tell her how I'd pleaded with the postman to climb the stairs every day or with the superintendent to haul down the trash. I said nothing, because I couldn't describe it to someone who still had a naive faith in humanity. After folding up her table in loud claps, Sonia threw my front door open. I felt the intrusion of the city and held my breath as the engines roared and the citizens cried.

Before she slammed the door, she turned to spit: "And you get over! As I! Get out of your tomb!" With that, the tanks withdrew. I turned the three locks with relief. Click, clack, click. I was left alone, just as I liked it, inside my five-hundred-square-foot apartment, with a front door painted the same canary yellow as the living room so that, when closed, the door disappeared into the wall. The room was sealed off and safe. From the windows facing north and south, I could touch the brick of the other nineteenth-century tenement buildings on either side of mine. This made me feel more secure, even though at least one of these three decrepit buildings was leaning. My bedroom, and the cubicle I called an office, had views of Ninth Avenue, but I hadn't looked out recently. I pulled down the blinds after seeing refrigerated trucks passing by on their way to Ground Zero and hadn't peeked through since the city initiated a shuttle service to take family members of the missing to a local pier from the sidewalk two floors below.

Wrapped in a sheet, dripping in oil, I sat on the couch and waited for Sonia's voice, still vibrating within the walls, to simmer and completely dissolve. My tomb! What did she know? The history of civilization is peopled by loners removing themselves from the crazed buzzing of society. Virginia Woolf understood the need for a room of one's own; Emily Dickinson rarely left her house in Amherst; Marcel Proust soundproofed the walls of his study with cork; Thomas Merton moved into a strict Trappist monastery for almost thirty years. In my solitude, I was in good company. Was Walden a tomb? Weren't Thoreau's most valued contemplations a product of time apart from the maddening crowd? I was getting fired up—a little too late for Sonia, but she'd be back. (There would be others as well. My mother and sister were now living only twenty blocks away from me.) Now that the accusation had been made, my retreat was no longer a secret and I needed a defense. I didn't want to find myself choked up again.

I gathered up my sheet and barreled into my box of an office. I started turning pages of *Bartlett's* until I found a quote I could use the next time someone questioned my isolation. I would smile and tell them, "As Thomas De Quincey once famously put it: 'No man ever will unfold the capacities of his own intellect who does not at least checker his life with solitude.'" I sat back and relished the perfection of the sentiment. Of course, I had never read Thomas De Quincey. For all I knew, he was being ironic; I vaguely remembered he smoked opium. In any event, the sentence did articulate a passionate conviction of mine. I wasn't actually attempting to unfold the capacities of my own intellect, but I could always start. I copied it out and pinned the note card to my bulletin board. The only word in the De Quincey quote that gave me pause was *checker*, because it implied periods of sociability in the future, and I could not conceive of those. What could possibly draw me back into the violent, hateful throng?

I MET **SONIA THREE YEARS** earlier, before the color-coded terror alerts and anthrax scares, when the dot-com bubble was still inflating and I was comfortable in my role. It was a time of great stability, without a sign of the naked person shivering in front of Sonia as she berated him in his own home. I had recently begun working for one of the largest educational testing services in the country, creating the multiple-choice exams that would be shipped to auditoriums and cafeterias nationwide as a means of ranking college hopefuls. I would take a list of correct answers and supply four false alternatives, which made me a guardian of the truth and also an author of the fabrication. I loved the game of it, concealing the right answer in a thicket of could-be's. Some people can fill out crosswords or play Scrabble for hours; I was able to fill pages and pages crafting these brainteasers. That sense of accomplishment and pride in my work might explain the confidence with which I bounced along Morningside Heights beneath a cloudless September sky.

Riverside Church offered English classes for newly arrived immigrants and arranged exchange programs with various foreign language departments at Columbia University. The immigrants, desperate to learn English in order to assimilate and survive in the metropolis, were tutored by Americans, who, in turn, used the opportunity to practice their accents and grammar with the mythologized *native speaker*. I had graduated from Columbia four years earlier but was auditing an introductory Russian course a former classmate was teaching. It was a good opportunity to learn a language for free, and I signed up for the exchange as a way to accelerate my basic communication skills.

In the church's basement—a dark cafeteria smelling of fried potatoes—I found my assigned partner sitting alone at a twelve-foot-long table wearing the red beret mentioned in the note that set up the rendezvous. I asked if she was Sonia. She nodded, threw the beret to the side, as if she couldn't wait to get rid of it, and immediately asked if we could meet Mondays through Saturdays from one to four. Warned by the office administrator in the Russian department that the immigrants inhaled time, I politely explained that I lived downtown, had a job and other commitments and could only meet for one hour twice a week. She, in turn, had obviously been warned by her office administrator that the Americans were lazy and far less committed.

To dispense of it early, Sonia began the session in Russian. She asked my name, and I happily replied, "*Menya zavoot* Andy Green." Then she asked me how many years I had been studying her language. I misheard and thought she'd asked how many students were in the program.

"*Sto.*"

"*Sto?*" Her eyes bulged.

"Roughly. Maybe. Ninety?" I retreated to English that quickly.

"And one hundred years you study Russian language?"

"Oh, no." I laughed. "Apparently not." Sonia repeated her question in Russian. When she heard my answer of *three weeks*, she pulled her lips into her mouth. After a deep breath, she began to ask me simple questions about the color of my shirt and the location of the bathroom, newsstand, and grocery store. I ignored the first question—what was the Russian word for *teal*?—told her the newsstand was on the street, and asked her to repeat the word for bathroom.

"And I do not know why you come. And you do not know Russian language!" She had raised her voice within five minutes of meeting me, and though this speech couldn't compare to the performances that would follow in years to come, the fury was daunting. Her glottal stops bounced through a room that was empty except for a native Hindi speaker who angrily flipped through a dictionary. There was nothing more she could do for me in Russian until I studied a few more chapters, so we switched to her English lesson. Suddenly I was the teacher and she was the student, and since I hadn't appreciated the feeling of vulnerability, I relished the authority.

"I've already noticed that you seem to be overly fond of conjunctions. You tend to begin your sentences with *and.*"

"No. This is okay. This is no problemo."

"Actually it is a problem and you should also know that *problemo* is not English."

"And my teacher she tells me *no problemo.*"

"Well, she's wrong."

"*Nyet.* I do not think."

"She's adding a Spanish *o* to the end. It's fine, it's just not English."

"And it's fine. Yes."

"No. No, it's not really fine."

"And you just say *fine*."

"I take it back."

"You what?"

"You can say *problemo*, but it's not technically correct and you wouldn't want to say it in a job interview."

"And what is *teknilly*?"

"*Technically*? Um. Just don't use *problemo* in a job interview."

"Listen, American. And I will not job interview. I am singer. That is what. I want to sing and chatter in American, okay? Thank you."

"Chatter?"

"To my owdience."

"Owdience? Oh, audience."

"And that is what I say."

"No, you said *owdience*, which sounds as if you've been hurt. *Awwwdience*. Before we start I just want to get back to your conjunction problem."

"And this is no problemo."

I gave up. "So you're a singer?" She acknowledged her victory with a nod and then spoke of her plans for becoming a cabaret star in New York and then a national sensation. A national cabaret sensation? I couldn't think of an example. She asked me to help define a list of words that had recently stumped her. It was strange for me to look at a vocabulary list without having to improvise other choices. "Most of these words only come up in Cole Porter songs," I told her. "No one says *de-lovely*."

Near the end of our first meeting—her mind on citizenship—Sonia asked point-black: "And do you have girlfriend?"

I answered by correcting her: "Do you have *a* girlfriend?"

"Of course not."

"Of course not what? Oh, I see. I meant the *a*."

"A what?"

"Never mind."

"Never what?"

"Never mind."

"Now stop this!" She slapped the table. "Do you have girlfriend?"

"No. I don't." I had only recently begun admitting to complete strangers my reasons for not having a girlfriend, but I still felt as if I had to explain and justify my lifestyle to any and all who asked. So, I began: "Let's have one brand-new word a week."

"Wickywackywoo."

"Pardon?"

"And this is my word."

"That's not really a word."

"And it's in *Nagasaki*."

"What?"

She sang something about *tobaccy* and women who *wicky wacky woo*.

I smiled at the melody but then said, "No. I'll pick the word. Let's try *sexuality*. This is how it's spelled." Sonia looked quizzically at the three-by-five index card I slid across the table. I tried to define it but did what came naturally to someone whose job was to confuse test-takers from Tallahassee to Spokane: I avoided clarity, speaking faster than she could possibly follow and using words she couldn't possibly understand.

I was underestimating her; she was listening very closely and would years later throw this speech back in my face.

"Some people will have you believe that sexuality applies merely to orientation, but it's much more complicated, entwined in individual histories, biologies, and associations. Each person's sexuality is unique, an emotional fingerprint. Not only does it apply to the gender, or genders, with which you find yourself infatuated but also to the type of person, the activity, the positions, the mode of dress, the dynamic you're aspiring to. Do you like to control the situation or be at someone else's whim? Do you prefer privacy or exposure? Someone older, younger, or a contemporary? The visual aspect or the tactile? The moment itself or the anticipation leading up to it? Or the memory? The reality or the fantasy? Is the sexual act itself the entire equation or are you more interested in the way you relate to the person out of the bed? Sexuality refers to how one relates to other members of the human race. Now all of this can and does shift over time and from place to place, but to inquire about someone's sexuality is to ask a question that may not be answerable in words because the question itself goes so much deeper than I think . . . we can . . . be prepared to understand."

Sonia dropped her eyelids. "Do you have girlfriend?"

"No. I'm gay." Would I have to define this? Would I have to draw a picture on an index card? Fortunately, not. She knew the word and surprised me by grinning maniacally. I expected her to be disappointed, but she was thrilled, because despite my attempts to dispel her outmoded stereotypes and superficial assumptions, when she heard I was gay, it meant only one thing: this immigrant from St. Petersburg with dreams of a career in cabaret had found her first American fan.

● ● ●

SONIA BECAME AN ex-coat-check-girl-giving-deep-tissue-massage because there was a limited audience for altos with thick Russian accents singing "All God's Chillun Got Rhythm." I, however, was an enthusiastic member of that audience. My mother, who scolded her children for laughing the way others scold theirs for screaming on the bus, couldn't fathom my response—*Aren't you her friend, Andrew? Does she know you're giggling at her?* I never bothered to explain. Most of the regulars fell for the comic side of Sonia's act, though she claimed that there was nothing funny about it and often asked me why people were laughing.

"I think it's because your childhood memories are so disturbing."

"No, they are not! And I am not to changing my act."

"Please don't."

On the day after New Year's in 2001, Sonia called me at work. Since she didn't have a computer, I was in charge of an e-mail list that could alert over three hundred people to any appearance she wanted publicized.

"And I am singing to the angel." My busy hand transcribed her words on my notepad to decipher what she meant. I crossed out the *And*, which after two years she was still using extraneously. Spitefully. "I am singing to the angel." I underlined *angel* and scrambled for a word she could have mispronounced.

I asked, "You're singing for an agent?"

"*Nyet! Da poshli oni* to their devil mothers! This is better. The angel is coming. And I am singing to the angel." She explained that a patron of the arts had arrived on the cabaret scene earlier that season. Coming from nowhere, it seemed, stepping out of a drizzly fog and into the cozy rooms of piano tinkles, this man had financed the shows of two or three relatively unknown performers. Rumor had it that he was planning to produce a CD for one of them. Sonia learned through a friend that the man she called the angel was going to wing his way into her gig that Thursday. My job was to aggressively recruit an audience who would surround the angel and clap in his ear.

"I want him thinking I am big underground sensation. Then he will be pulling me over ground."

"Resurrecting you," I suggested.

"Stop your games."

"Sorry."

"And I must fire Bob now and hire someone new." Sonia hung up. Bob was Sonia's accompanist whom she had fired fifteen or twenty times in the past two years. I was relieved to see him at the piano when I arrived at the show that Thursday. Bob could improvise anything and was never fazed by Sonia's eruptions on- or off-stage. She tried to banter, but he rarely said more than a word or two. Once, when Sonia prefaced a song by describing a childhood of eczema and breadlines, she turned to Bob and asked if he had similar stories. Tickling the ivories, Bob, who was educated at boarding schools in Connecticut, smiled nostalgically and answered, "Oh, absolutely."

The Moonbeam Room, a narrow windowless space with a make-shift stage at one end and a bar running along a wall at the other, was packed. Fifty people. Patrons sat in folding wooden chairs around cocktail tables adorned with votives and miniature placards listing the house martinis. I found my seat with two friends from work, one of whom had heard us speak of the song stylings of Sonia Obolensky and was eager to experience them in person. As the two of them talked about office politics, which I felt never affected me, I turned from the table and scanned the crowd for the angel.

This took all of three seconds. Sonia didn't draw a wealthy crowd. Most of the people who came to her performances had worked with her at one time or another, so I couldn't miss the very handsome man sitting two tables away wearing an Italian suit and drinking champagne. The bottle was in ice on the table. This was not a man who offered customers free samples of goat cheese at the Amish Market or who paraded along Sixth Avenue dressed as a giant roll of Advantix film. His tousled brown hair and sculpted chin made him look like one of those young aristocrats in the society pages who escorted socialites like Nan Kemper to gala performances at the New York Philharmonic. He sat with his legs crossed, taking in the room, gently pressing and lifting his fingertips, one by one, against the cold glass of his champagne flute, as if he were playing the instrument and had control over the movement of each tiny bubble of air.

I watched him and wondered how I could persuade someone like this to fall in love with Sonia's act. Suddenly, the angel-aristocrat's head turned and his blue eyes cut through the room to connect with mine. He smiled and I panicked. I quickly looked into my lap. I knew it was clumsy, so I looked up and smiled, but it was too little, too late. His attention was elsewhere. There was a nervous stirring in my stomach, which felt less like butterflies and more like dirty pigeons pecking for seed. I turned back to my friends and pretended to be absorbed by conjecture about the late lunches of our office manager.

Five minutes after the hour, wearing a brand-new black cocktail dress, Sonia Obolensky appeared on stage and climbed up onto her stool as the audience politely applauded her entrance. Bob began to play the introduction to her opening number. Sonia pulled the microphone off the stand and said, "And love can sometimes be tricky thing. Ask my mother. Once I am finding her in front yard throwing rocks at man she say is my father. I will now sing "Why Was I Born?"" There are few performers who can get such a big laugh that quickly, but Sonia didn't want to be one of them. As she sang, she regarded the audience with more than a touch of hostility, which carried through and strengthened the entire set. When Sonia, glaring at us all, noisily replaced the microphone after forty-five minutes and two encores, she exited to wild applause. My novitiate from work whispered: "She's fucking brilliant!"

I peeked to my left to see if the angel agreed and was gratified to see him smiling. He was slowly shaking his head as though he could not quite believe what he had just heard. This was a normal response. Watching Sonia's act was like standing on a sidewalk looking at a body whose limbs were twisted and akimbo—either you were witnessing a flexible street performer whose contortions had you reaching for your wallet or you were staring at a body that had just been flung through the windshield of a speeding bus. I considered it my job to convince this man that he was experiencing the former. He again turned and smiled and I again, like a complete jackass, turned away.

I had trouble making eye contact when I was a teenager but gained confidence midway through college, when my acne finally cleared up, muscle began to form on my bones, and I discovered a haircut that fit my face. After that, people began to gaze in my direction and rarely made me nervous. I could usually walk up to strangers, striking up conversations without the slightest bit of awkwardness.

I had planned to approach the angel's table after the performance, to introduce myself and ask his opinion or to talk loudly with friends sitting nearby about how stellar Sonia's performance was. Now that the show was over, I found myself staring into the votive flame at my table and feeling completely intimidated. I was unable to work the room because he'd smiled at me. What would Sonia say? My friends from work finished their drinks and raced off to catch a late movie, leaving me alone at the table.

"That was a unique show, wasn't it?" The angel was standing next to me, a hand in his pocket, the other holding his champagne. I stuttered something in agreement and moved to stand up but then changed my mind, leaning back and trying to replicate his earlier pose of ease. I crossed my legs and placed my fingers around my empty glass of wine. It felt uncomfortable to me and surely must have looked that way.

In an attempt to explain away my earlier stares, I said, "It's always interesting to see how newcomers take to her show. I've been looking around the room to gauge audience reaction." I couldn't tell if he believed that or not.

He asked, "You've seen her before then?"

"Many times. I'm kind of her manager," I lied.

"Wonderful!" He extended his hand and introduced himself as Brad Willet.

"Andy Green." I shook his hand and held it a couple of seconds longer than what was professional, but he held his grip as well. I remembered I was there for Sonia. I stood up and instantly knew that that was the wrong decision. "So you enjoyed the show?"

"I did. I think I did. Her choices are unusual."

"Each one is very deliberate." The truth was that Sonia chose songs that she simply liked: some of them were songs that she and her grandfather used to sing at his piano and they often did not translate.

"She seems so earnest, but she can't be serious," Brad commented. "At first I thought it was an Andy Kaufman type of stunt, but she can definitely sing. A few of her higher notes can sound a touch shrill, but her lower register is lovely." So was his, I thought to myself, a kind of rich baritone a spokesman for a tropical getaway might have. "The performance as a whole is so funny, though. Do you know who she reminds me of?"

"Who?" I looked forward to passing this on to Sonia.

"Gilda Radner."

"That's a new one." I wouldn't pass this on to Sonia, but I appreciated the comparison.

"Is Sonia really Russian?"

"Yes."

"What about her stories? Are they real? The one about the rash . . . ?"

"Well, I don't want to give away the mystery. Let's just say she's a rather complicated artist." He seemed pleased with that. Because of the clutter of chairs and tables, we were standing in close-up. I guessed he was in his mid-thirties. I could make out the suggestion of wrinkles, but they were the best kind, laugh lines around the eyes.

"She's certainly amusing," he said. Then he added, "More amusing than mangoes."

"More amusing than mangoes?" I repeated uncertainly, but Brad was sipping his champagne and leaning over the table to study a photograph of Old New York that hung on the wall. I would learn this was a technique of his. Brad frequently quoted the American songbook and the Broadway musical without ever referencing them. The words came off somehow as his own, which made his language seem more vibrant than others. The lyricists of the past century were his composite Cyrano to the world's Roxane.

In the front of the room, near the stage, Bob was trying to get past someone without being seen, so I assumed Sonia was the tiny person being embraced by several audience members.

"Here comes Sonia now," I announced.

"Wonderful. I need to use the restroom, but I'd love to buy the two of you a drink."

"One each?" I asked without thinking.

Brad laughed, and I watched as he threaded his way toward the staircase to the basement. When he turned his head in my direction, I actually waved at him. Like an eleven-year-old girl.

● ● ●

BRAD WILLET ENDED UP buying us each a number of drinks. The Moonbeam Room was empty except for two waitresses, a manager, and the three of us huddled around Brad's small table. Sonia was on her best behavior, moved as I was by the attention of a man who surely had better places to go. There were a few awkward moments, though. The first thing Sonia said when she shook Brad's hand was, "I am sorry of all the hyenas tonight." Noticing Brad's perplexed stare, I laughed out loud. Brad laughed with me; Sonia grinned, figuring that there was a reason behind my madness. The other moment was when Brad gripped my shoulder and toasted Sonia for hiring such a handsome manager. I was forced to admit that I wasn't technically her manager before Sonia could refute my position, so she took it upon herself to refute the adjective: "And he's not so handsome." Fearing an explosion, I wanted to whisper to Sonia to play along, but the compliments, mysterious or not, were compliments, and since Brad was lavishing praise, she didn't need to bellow at anything.

"She's not one of your idols?" Brad asked Sonia near the end of the evening.

"No," she answered.

"Really?"

"I do not even know this Gilda Radner."

"That's hard to believe."

"And if you want me to say so, yes, she is my idol."

"You're just saying that."

"Yes, I say this."

"If you don't mind me asking, who are some of your idols?"

"I do not know if I am having these idols."

"Everyone has an idol."

"And do you?"

Brad took a sip of champagne and considered the flipped question: "Yes. Yes, I do. I'd say my idol is J. D. Rockefeller Jr."

"I didn't know he sang," I joked.

Sonia scolded me. "And of course he sang! Everyone knows this."

Brad told Sonia she was hilarious. "He's an idol of mine in philanthropy."

"And what is this word?" Sonia asked. "I do not know this."

"Well, it's an outdated concept."

"You know this word?" Sonia pointed at me. "He plays with words every day."

"Do you?"

I briefly explained my job to Brad, who seemed startled that someone made a living that way. I turned to Sonia and told her that since the word came from the Greek, the Russian equivalent probably sounded very similar.

"*Feelantropia!* Yes, yes!"

"It comes from the Greek?" Brad asked me.

"Loving people or a love of people . . ."

"Interesting."

"Always look for the root word," I said. Hearing myself, I placed my glass of alcohol on the table and sat on my hands.

"And so J. D. is your idol in this?"

"J. D. Junior, yes. He gave away what his father made. Not everything, of course, but the father was the great monopolist and the son was the great philanthropist. I recently read that Junior gave ten times more to charity, in today's currency, than any other individual in American history."

"And good for him! An angel."

"There are so many programs on television now advising you how to best invest your money in order to make more money—there are even channels dedicated to that—and the rest of television is telling you where to spend it. Where's the channel or the program advising you how to best donate your money?"

"PBS is always wanting it," Sonia said.

"My father used to say what everyone seems to be spouting now: 'Take care of yourself and you'll mysteriously help other people.' I say: 'Take care of other people and you'll mysteriously help yourself.' I believe that money is like fertilizer . . ."

"Fertilizer?" I asked.

"It's no good unless it's spread around, encouraging young things to grow."

"That's *Hello, Dolly!*" Sonia piped up and Brad nodded.

"To be part of the solution. You can either give to this world or take from it. You, Sonia, happen to give."

"Thank you."

"You make us laugh."

"You also have a beautiful voice," I quickly added.

"Of course. You come on stage to make people happy, not to hurt them." He looked up and chewed his lower lip in concentration. "So much of what we do does hurt, doesn't it?" Sonia and I both nodded our heads slowly. "We need to look at our actions with vigilance, but so few of us do. We make excuses. We commit atrocities, or sit by as they happen, and our only justification is that *we have to pay our rent* or *everyone has to make a living.*"

I doubted Sonia was paying attention to any of this. She was more interested in the earlier conversation, in which she and Brad had mapped out a strategy for the next few months. There were phone calls she needed to make, contacts to meet; she was going to type up her song list and send Brad a bio. I also started losing interest in the content of this speech, because it was delivered through two perfect rows of the whitest teeth I had ever seen. I certainly wasn't ready for him to stare me down and ask me how I slept at night.

"On my side," I answered honestly.

"I'm referring to your job."

"What about it?"

"It seems to me that while some people spend their time helping troubled teens, you spend your time *making* them."

"Hm," I said, suddenly desperate for coffee.

"You're employed to confuse high school students. I mean, isn't that your job?" I took a deep breath and then ended up shaking my head. What was he talking about? He didn't seem to be accusing me. His tone was that of a doctor quietly asking me to describe my symptoms. "You help institutions of higher learning eliminate applicants. You do this by leading the applicants to rub their pencil points in the wrong circles."

"Most of what I do is really clerical; the multiple choice is just a part of it . . ."

"Your job is to prevent aspiring college students from achieving a perfect test score by draining their confidence. You're not helping students; you're weeding them out."

"I hadn't thought of it that way."

"I don't mean to pick on you." I felt his hand squeeze my knee. "You don't feel cornered, do you?"

"No, no, not at all."

"I'm glad."

Sonia brought the talk back to her corner: "And do you think Bob upstages me?"

I tuned them out. In the years working at my job I never thought about its ethical implications. Maybe Brad was right: the multiple choice exams weren't just puzzles to amuse myself; they were traps I was setting for innocent minds. I was an obfuscator. I was hired to choose words that sounded or looked right, create analogies so weirdly related they were bound to be the answers, and convince unsuspecting kids that the above passage's chief concern was (b) when the real concern was obviously (d). For these acts of academic sabotage I collected paychecks every other Thursday. Not Friday. The company's motto: Always keep them guessing.

While mulling this over, feeling strangely like a Nazi collaborator, I missed the critical turn in the conversation—something about miserable childhoods—that gave Sonia the idea that she could share something of mine, which she'd promised never to tell a single soul. I did not talk about my mother to many people, certainly not to anyone who seemed to be flirting by calling me handsome or squeezing my knee, so I was jarred to hear Sonia say, "At least my mother never tries to kill me. Like Andy's."

"What?" both Brad and I asked.

"When he is small baby," she said. "Andy's mother killed him. Almost." I slid her glass of wine across my body and blocked it with my elbow.

"What does she mean?" Brad asked me.

I didn't want to answer, but I didn't want to seem evasive, so I blurted, "When I was about a year old, my mother." Eye contact became difficult again, but Brad was waiting. "Tried to drown me."

"Really?"

"She didn't though. So that's the end of that."

"Why would she want to drown you?"

"Oh, you will see." Sonia laughed.

I wanted to knock her off her chair. Brad repeated his question.

"I honestly don't know. It was a tough time for her. It was a few weeks after my father's funeral and she'd just found out she was pregnant with my sister."

"Maybe it was an accident."

"No. I had to live with my grandparents in Trenton until I was three."

"What about your sister?"

"She did too. She was snatched from the delivery room."

"What was wrong with your mother?"

"I don't know. We don't talk about it. It was her dark period. Her missing years. On Easter Sunday, when I was three, she showed up at the house and we went home with her."

"How's your relationship with her now?"

"Better."

"I would hope so." Brad smiled.

"My mother's my mother. We regard each other warily." I tried to change the subject. "So why are you so interested in cabaret?"

"Because life is a cabaret, old chum," he answered quickly. "Where does your mother live now?"

"My mother and sister live in southern Maryland. Where I grew up."

"Except for those years in Trenton."

"Except for those."

"Did she ever remarry?"

"Not really." He looked confused. "I mean no." I decided not to tell him that my mother was married to Jesus.

Brad kept up his interrogation for another five minutes. How did your father die? Did anything ever happen to your sister? Did your mother go through counseling? Was your mother on medication? I gave up very little. At least he wasn't devoting any more of his attention to my evil work.

Sonia didn't bother stifling a loud yawn. Two hours had passed since the end of her show and she was crashing. You could never turn Sonia off; you just had to wait until the batteries died down.

"It's getting late. Let's get our star home," Brad said. "We can all share a cab. Where do you live, Sonia?"

"Brooklyn."

"We'll drop you off first. Let me pay here so they can close up."

We were going to share a cab and the first stop would be Brooklyn? You don't drop someone off in Brooklyn. You give them cash and wave good-bye from the curb.

"And you live close," Sonia said to me once Brad was out of earshot. "Why are you inside our cab?"

"I'm along for the ride."

"And the angel I am thinking is gay."

"I have the same hunch."

She took my hands: "Maybe he is both our angels." In the cab she gave me a meaningful glance when Brad sat between us.

After the driver's grumbling about a trip to Brooklyn, the taxi lurched forward, scattered a group of jaywalkers, and accelerated through the yellow traffic light. Sonia and Brad shared their opinions on a few cabaret spaces we passed in midtown before they began holding hands and singing a song with sophisticated lyrics I'd never heard before. I tilted my left leg into Brad, pressing my jeans against his Italian suit, and sat back for the ride. My twenties were almost over. I was able to count four significant relationships, though none longer than a year. The first was after college with a woman, one last disastrous and mangled attempt at heterosexuality, followed by a succession of young men who started off as everything I ever wanted and ended up as learning experiences to avoid in the future. I was looking forward to my thirties. The crowds in the theater district seemed to shimmer along with the glass flecks that made the sidewalks sparkle. Every pedestrian had just seen the greatest single performance of their lifetime or they had gotten engaged or it was their birthday or they had been generously tipped. A drunken bachelorette party wearing streamers around their heads danced on the island between the Virgin and Kodak signs as if the New Year's ball were still dropping. The throngs were instantly replaced by empty office buildings as we drove south of Forty-second, airborne for a moment after hitting a bump. There were no more flashing advertising lights, just crosswalk signals that blinked for no one. Steam rose through the manhole covers. By this point, Sonia and Brad were harmonizing to "Moon River," and I actually felt tears on my cheeks, which I discreetly wiped from Macy's to Little Korea. I leaned my head against my window to admire the passing view of electronic shops, stores for wholesale perfume and watches, places to pick up earrings, sunglasses, and souvenirs. During the day, these several blocks were bustling with shoppers, office workers, and men from around the world pulling unwieldy carts, stacked high with boxes, around the ubiquitous hotdog stands, but the metal gates were now locked and the place was deserted. I tried to see the tops of the turn-of-the-century buildings with their elaborate decorations: ornately carved columns and arches, mansarded roofs and cupolas. At Madison Square we curved around an old general's monument and glided past the Flatiron. I rarely saw how things in the city connected because I usually took the subway. After a few more blocks down Broadway's sleeping spine, I was surprised and excited by the busy nightlife in Union Square, which was far less touristy than the last pocket of energy twenty-five blocks north. I watched some kids lose their skateboards in midair as we made our own quick turns and shifted into one another. Somewhere between Grace Church and Kmart, Brad and Sonia began with the lyrics "Start spreading the news," and I joined in, as did the driver, an Egyptian in a Yankees cap. The four of us sped south of Houston, singing together, through the cast-iron canyon and then down Canal Street, where the shops were closed and the garbage cans spilled out onto the street. We hit the finale halfway over the Manhattan Bridge, holding the last note for a good, loud fifteen seconds. We applauded ourselves; Brad had his arms around the two of us and complimented the driver.

"Isn't that gorgeous?" Brad said, looking past me to the illuminated Brooklyn Bridge. The three of us agreed. "I try to walk over it a few times a year. I think it's the most beautiful thing in New York." I casually mentioned that I'd never made the crossing. Brad was horrified. "Are you serious?"

"I walked over the George Washington once."

"The Brooklyn is completely different from any other bridge in the world."

"I fully intend to walk it one day." He nodded and I added, "I will cross it on my knees."

"That's the spirit."

We hit a pothole as we left the bridge and began cruising up Flatbush. I started feeling a bit of champagne-induced car sickness. Our driver was on a post-performance high and now seemed to be conducting music with the steering wheel, so I was glad that Sonia had moved to a sublet near Prospect Park, which was closer than her last place. I leaned my face against the cold glass and tried to take in an avenue I had never seen aboveground. Sonia pointed out Junior's where she ate her first piece of cheesecake and the Brooklyn Academy of Music where Enrico Caruso suffered a throat hemorrhage that ended his career. She offered this piece of history whenever anyone mentioned the Brooklyn Academy of Music. As if to check on the health of her own voice, Sonia hummed the rest of the way; I got dizzier as we slipped through trees, around the giant stone arch, up the parkway past the library, U-turning in front of the floodlit

Brooklyn Museum, and back down the service road to an abrupt stop that made me close my eyes and take deep breaths. Brad walked Sonia to the front door. When I opened my eyes, I saw Brad give Sonia her bag and place his hands on her small shoulders. Her glowing face was tilted upward, and whatever he was telling her, she had never heard a better lullaby. Sonia entered the building, and Brad returned to the car.

"Brooklyn Bridge, please. Take Cadman Plaza West to Fulton."

"Is that where you live?" I asked.

"I live in Chelsea. We're going to walk over that bridge now."

"Right now? It's January. It's after eleven o'clock."

"It's not so cold and not too late," he said.

It's one of those nights, I thought to myself. Just go along for the ride and see where you end up.

"Cadman Plaza West to Fulton," I repeated, and in less than ten minutes, Brad was telling our driver to keep the change and our driver was telling us to be careful. It felt good to be in the cold air. Soon we were stepping onto the elevated walkway above the traffic, the fabled promenade that gave certain pedestrians the same pleasure as standing at the rim of the Grand Canyon. I always appreciated the bridge as a landmark, but close up, at long last, in the wind and under the night sky, I saw it for the marvel it was—thousands of tons of steel and miles of wire twisted into cords and then into cables; steel wrapped around steel, steel pulling at steel, holding so much weight, activity, and history in suspension above the river. I could feel the tension in every direction: the anchorage on Brooklyn strenuously pulling its cables, engaged in a tug-of-war against the opposite shore of Manhattan, where its anchorage had been pulling just as forcefully for over a hundred years; and the pull between the tops of the stone towers and the span where we were walking. As we moved farther into the webwork, it was conceivable that not only had Brooklyn and Manhattan been connected by the structure, this "harp and altar of the fury fused," but so had every landmass and human life as well.

It was louder than I expected. The winds were strong, there was a steady stream of cars speeding in both directions below us. I don't remember anyone else on our level of the bridge. No cyclists, no pedestrians, no muggers lurking in the shadows. We reached the center where the span rose its highest, where the cables dipped their lowest, and stopped to take in the view to the south and west: the Watchtower and the giant Eagle clock; the Brooklyn Heights Esplanade above another expressway dotted with headlights; the Verrazano-Narrows Bridge and Governor's Island; Liberty presiding over the harbor; Ellis Island with the fanciful rooftops; and the massive Twin Towers looming over everything.

I leaned against the rail, having a difficult time keeping my balance, woozy from the champagne or giddy perhaps from the unplanned romance of being alone with such a debonair man on a giant bridge under a dark sky. I wasn't sure now if I was angry or grateful that Sonia blurted out something as personal as my near-death experience as a baby, which Brad didn't bring up again but which somehow set an intimate tone for the rest of our conversation. We talked about New York mainly, about where we grew up— Brad was from New Jersey—and how we made our way to the city. We were both amazed that life here could be so overwhelming and still so natural and familiar. Books, songs, movies, and television made New York the world's hometown. The clock at Grand Central, the lions in front of the library, the United Nations, Fifth and Park Avenues, Wall Street, the Waldorf, the Plaza, car horns, the paintings at the Metropolitan and the MoMA, the horse carriages in Central Park, the Empire State Building, the Russian Tea Room, Rockefeller Center—these were familiar to millions of people, though understood in a kind of jumble that needed to be rearranged upon arrival. Brad, for example, had thought Harlem was one of the boroughs, and I had thought a knish was an elected official.

Brad told me that when he moved into Manhattan, his most significant hurdle was a lifelong fear of heights, which he conquered over the course of several weekends by repeatedly crossing the bridges. I asked him if he was afraid of anything else; suddenly the lights on the towers, span, and walkway went out, and he answered, "Darkness." We both laughed. The wind was getting colder, but it made the night all the more exhilarating and gave us the sensation that we were trespassing. I told him how happy I was that he was helping Sonia. He just smiled and looked out over the water.

"If you don't mind my asking, where did the money for your foundation come from?"

"I don't mind. My father."

"Oil like the Rockefellers?"

"No."

"Steel?"

"Cardboard. My family made their fortune manufacturing cardboard."

"Cardboard?"

"There are all sorts of ways to get rich." He said this as a sad fact of reality.

"So when did you start the foundation?"

"I was organizing for a couple of years, but I didn't really begin until last fall."

"Why do you have a foundation?"

Brad was surprised at the question. "What do you mean?"

"I mean, what's your mission?"

Looking out over the harbor, he said with all sincerity, full of the night, the alcohol, the bridge, and the chill, "To help illuminate the world. Because there is so much pain and need in this city alone, so much willful stupidity and anger. Choices are made and too many people choose to perpetuate the misery every day. You can help people or you can hurt them. You can be part of the solution or part of the problem. It's simplistic but it's true. You can build bridges or walls. You can love or you can hate. You can fight or you can dance."

Brad looked at me as if this was a duet and it was my turn to sing. I took the Statue of Liberty as my cue: "You can free or enslave. Enlighten or enshroud." I felt a bit dorky, but it was one of those nights and I felt he would judge me if I didn't try to match his enthusiasm. I looked over to Ellis Island: "Welcome or spurn, admit or reject, embrace or expel." I was warming up. Twin Towers: "Build into the sky or burrow into the ground." South Street Seaport: "Establish trade or lay an embargo." I knew that was pushing it and stopped myself.

Brad joined back in, moving close. "Give. Or take."

"Donate. Or hoard."

"Heal. Or injure."

"Trust. Or fear."

"Your place? Or mine?"

BRAD INTRODUCED ME TO many new experiences after the bridge. The February twenty-second performance of *Samson and Delilah* at the Met, for example, marked my first opera that didn't require binoculars. We were seated in the center orchestra a mere fifteen rows from the stage. Brad was reading the synopsis in his program, but I was too distracted, gawking at the audience and wondering where I would be if I had bought my own ticket—probably high above the chandeliers, still climbing the stairs, being led by a sherpa. What would I be wearing? Probably a sports jacket and a nice pair of slacks. Definitely not a navy blue double-breasted Italian silk suit with square-toed, rope-laced, hand-stitched leather shoes. I knew what Sonia would say if she saw me.

My relationship with Brad Willet was not hard for her to understand; as she had recently put it: "You have wined and dined on

Mulligan stew and never wished for turkey. And now turkey is all you are wanting."

"He's not that rich," I said. "He lives in a modest two-bedroom in a building on Seventh Avenue." Sonia dropped her eyelids—she had seen the doorman and the Art Deco interior. It was never easy to argue with her eyelids, so I just said, "It's not about the money."

"And it is always about the money," Sonia said. "Listen. I don't care. What is good for you is good for me. Do you like this life? These taxis everywhere and these free dinners? Of course you are liking this life. You are the woman and he is the rich husband."

"For the last time: I am not the woman."

"Is he the woman?"

"No one is a woman, and this is not about the money."

I was drawn to passionate people. Brad loved to brighten people's days and I loved to watch their faces light up, this illumination in the darkness, which is how he always spoke, whether tipsy on a bridge or not. Brad overestimated my enthusiasm for cabaret—once a month was plenty for me—but I accepted every invitation anyway, meeting him at clubs or restaurants a few times a week so that I could be near his contagious idealism. I felt optimistic and strangely safe whenever he was complimenting someone and offering his assistance. He started by asking them about their careers and their dreams, a line of questioning that helped him analyze how he could most effectively be of service. Sometimes we met with only one or two people; other times we were surrounded in post-theater bars where everyone seemed to know him and he would throw his arms around several sets of shoulders, encouraging the hopeful and the disenchanted. Brad could make anyone feel like he was the most important person in the world, and no one walked away from him without looking happier. Or from me, for that matter. Brad never actually introduced me as his boy-friend, but everyone knew who I was. People would pull me aside for tête-à-têtes and share personal feelings they assumed I would pass on to Brad. I secretly enjoyed the attention. It also gave me a chance to hear others sing Brad's praises, which made me feel even more fortu-nate, though I did cringe when one of his singers whispered how lucky I was to have found him. With her hands wrapped around my elbow, she whispered, "It must be like dating Gandhi."

A very well dressed elderly couple moved into our row. They both sat down and began getting comfortable. The husband handed his wife her program, and she opened her purse and pulled out a roll of mints, using her manicured pink thumbnail to cut two mints free from the foil before offering him one. He thanked her and reminded her to turn off her cell phone. She said that it was already off; he doubted that. She pulled the phone halfway out of her purse, saw that she was wrong, and without any further recrimination from him, pressed the OFF button. She smiled at me, began opening her program while looking at the giant gold curtain only fifteen rows in front of us. She asked her husband if he remembered what was so special about the curtain. He answered that it was the largest tab curtain in the entire world. She laughed quietly. The exchange was obviously a long tradition in their opera going. I felt a pang of envy. Not for the routine but because they had such clearly delineated roles. He was in charge of the programs until they sat down; she dis-pensed the mints.

"And why is he liking you so much?" Sonia had asked.

"It hasn't even been two months. I'm not thinking about it."

"You lie! And tell me, American: how many times do you go to your gym?"

"A few times a week." Six, actually.

"Keep young and beautiful," she sang.

"I like to be healthy."

"And your teeth are whiter."

"It must be the lighting," I said with indifference, but I was secretly glad to hear that the toothpaste was working.

"And this?" She handed me a plastic bag from Duane Reade with ten CDs I'd requested from her collection of old standards. I may have been leading Brad on a little—borrowing music from Sonia and reading biographical articles on composers and performers so that I could drop bits of my reading into our conversation as if I had grown up with the knowledge—but I hoped that his passion for me didn't have too much to do with my fraudulent passion for cabaret.

"You see it is always like this. One person has the money and one person does all the work. And it is life and it is love: one person is paying and one person is working."

"It's not about the money."

"Keep the sex alive," Sonia warned. "Or this relationship is doomed."

Fortunately, that was not a worry, because the bedroom was the one place where I knew who I was and what I wanted, without having to be chronically grateful. I didn't have to fake a thing during sex; the nakedness leveled us somehow and let me forget that he was heir to a cardboard fortune and I had a single mother who worked as a secretary at a suburban middle school.

On the evening of the opera, before I knew we had tickets, I was lying beside Brad in his bed, watching the shadows on the wall slowly thicken as the sun began to fade. Brad sighed contentedly and ran a hand across his chest. I thought how refreshing it would be to nap. To sleep for an hour, wake up, order in, have more sex, and sleep through the night. I closed my eyes, rolled onto my back, and slid one of my legs through his. I drifted off easily, but then woke up when the radio alarm suddenly started describing the effects of a lane closure on the Cross Bronx Expressway. I felt Brad on top of me, turning off the alarm and announcing that we had to get up and shower.

I almost groaned—another night, another piano bar.

"I have a surprise for you," he said with the same face he used when doling out gifts. "I'm taking you to the Met."

"The museum?"

"The opera."

"Do you know someone in the cast?"

"What do you mean?"

"It's not for your foundation?"

"No. It's purely social. It's our night. Just the two of us."

"Oh." That was a different matter entirely.

"Don't you want to go?"

"I do. Definitely." I knew a bit about opera; I had a few anecdotes, an untapped resource of stories to share. "Which opera is it?"

"*Samson and Delilah.*"

"Oh, good. That's such a sweet story." He laughed, squeezed my leg between the two of his. "Hey! I don't have anything to wear." The clothes I wore from work were in a wrinkled pile in the living room.

"Of course you do. I have three closets full of clothes for you to wear."

"Your clothes? They won't fit me." I imagined they were all tailored to the centimeter, and only Brad could wear them.

"Why not? We have the same build." That was true; he just had better posture.

"What about shoes?" I asked. We held our feet side by side.

"A perfect ten," Brad said, kicking my foot and jumping out of bed. "You see, everything's coming up roses!"

Thirty minutes later, after a hot shower, I was standing in front of a full-length mirror decked out in one of his sharpest suits, amazed at how perfectly it fit. He stood behind me and we looked at each other's reflection.

"There's something very Alfred Hitchcock about this," I said. "I hope there won't be any foul play when we get to the opera. Do you promise not to throw me off?"

"Throw you off?" he asked genuinely confused. "Off of what?"

"The balcony," I said, thinking that was obvious. The opera equaled balcony.

"No balcony. We'll be downstairs." We were from two different worlds. Sonia was right: this relationship was doomed. This dread kept me preoccupied during the cab ride and the walk to our seats.

I was still lost in my thoughts when Brad, closing his program, grinned and said, "They have an ad for shampoo in here. Very clever, don't you think?"

"Why?" I tried to catch his meaning.

"It's a program for *Samson and Delilah.*" He smiled. "What are you thinking about?"

How rich you are and how little control I have in this dynamic.

I improvised, "That it's strange to be spending a night without helping someone. We're not taking anyone out for drinks or dinner . . ." I caught myself—Brad paid for all the food and beverages. "I'm sorry, I didn't mean *we.*"

"That's fine. I like that you said that. Go on."

"I was wondering if there was anyone in New York whom we could help tonight." I turned in my seat and pointed upward. "Do you see that balcony up there? The one way, way up there? Next to the ceiling? There are hundreds of people sitting up there."

"Say it isn't so."

"I'm afraid it is. They can't even see the stage. Though I guess that doesn't really matter because it takes so long for the sound to reach them they're still listening to last night's opera. It's very sad."

"At least they have a good view of the gold ceiling."

"From up there, the ceiling looks aluminum—don't laugh—and the seats are plastic like at a stadium. It's not funny. We have to do something for them."

He tapped my knee with his program. "Do you know what I love most about you?"

I tilted my head, waiting for the answer, pretending that I'd never worried about that very question. Suddenly the conductor entered the orchestra, the spotlight found him, and the audience of four thousand began to applaud.

"Quick!" I said. "What do you love most about me?"

Brad laughed. "I'll tell you at intermission." I grabbed one of his hands.

"Tell me while they're clapping."

He leaned into my shoulder, brought his mouth to my ear, and said over the noise, "I love that you care, Andy. I love how supportive you are to all the people we do take out. I love how you help Sonia with her mailing list and how you help her with her English." The conductor was going to turn and raise the baton any second; the couple in the row behind would shush us. "I'm happy I found a partner in crime, and you can say *we* whenever you like."

The conductor faced his orchestra and the applause died down.

That would do for now, I thought as the overture began and ours ended; after two months, I would take "partner in crime." I could work with that. As far as which of us would dispense the mints and remind the other about his cell phone, I could be patient. I sat back comfortably in the soft suit and waited for the largest tab curtain in the entire world to rise into the air.

● ● ●

OVER THE COURSE OF the next month, Brad kept referring to me as an ally in his crusade; sooner or later, I was going to have to do more than merely echo him.

One evening, Brad and I sat with three friends, laughing over red wine at a window table in a French restaurant on Ninth Avenue. The table was round, but Brad was at the head of it. I sat on his right-hand side. On Brad's left was Sonia. Brad was financing her upcoming cabaret evening at the Firebird along with her first CD, which she was going to record as soon as the arrangements were completed by Bob, who was notoriously slow and possibly a drug addict.

To the left of Sonia sat her new boyfriend, Porfiry, an ex-gymnast she met at a midtown gym where she worked briefly as a receptionist and where he was a trainer and agitator. After Porfiry urged Sonia to demand higher wages and then forced her to quit "to maintain her dignity," he visited her apartment, where the two railed against the filthy pig of a club manager, the voracious recruitment of members, the incessant corporate push for profit, and the criminal markup in the retail store. They did Stoli shots, slapped each other around, and fucked all over the floor.

Last at the table was Rod Hamilton, a tour guide whom Sonia met a year earlier when she worked briefly as a roamer for a student travel company. Roamers gathered tour groups from the various Broadway theaters and escorted them back to the hotels they were unlikely to ever find after one of Disney's musical extravaganzas. Sonia lost this job because she lost so many of her groups. She too easily disappeared into the crowds of Times Square, no matter how high she held up her sign, and since she never bothered to glance behind her, she frequently arrived in the hotel lobby, without a single tourist in tow. Rod rescued a flock of eighth-graders from Tennessee, who had seen *The Lion King* and were standing huddled close together on Forty-ninth and Seventh. He returned them to the hotel and tracked down Sonia who was muttering Russian obscenities on Eighth Avenue. She took her sign and ripped the school mascot into pieces. She was an immigrant who spoke limited English when she arrived, but still she found her way around. What was the matter with these people? By the time she was fired two weeks later, Sonia loathed tourists and loved to hear the kinds of derogatory stories Rod was now sharing with the table over our fourth bottle of red wine.

"So I meet the teacher the next morning, and you should realize that some of these hotels are pretty foul. I meet the teacher and she tells me how sickening her room is."

"I bet they charge one thousand dollars a night," Porfiry interrupted, a constant social critic.

Rod continued. "She found a used condom under the bed and brown streaks that looked like feces smeared on the wall." Everyone at the table grimaced. "Disgusting, right? So I ask her what it turned out to be, and she answers: 'I don't know, but it tasted like chocolate.'"

We all cried out and then broke into more laughter.

Porfiry said, "This is why Americans are so fat."

Brad asked, "Rod, where do you find these people?"

"Most of them aren't bad."

"And they are all like this!" Sonia interjected.

"That's not what I mean," said Brad. "How do you find your clients? Or how do they find you?"

Rod explained, "I freelance for a few companies. Student travel, senior citizens, corporate incentive. I also give private tours for families, couples . . ."

"Do you advertise? Do you market yourself at all?"

"I have business cards and there's strong word-of-mouth."

"Do you have a Web site?"

"No."

"Would you like to attract more business?"

"I do fairly well, but there's always room for growth."

We all need a little boost. I could hear it coming.

"How about an award?" Brad offered. Rod looked puzzled. Brad mentioned that he had been meaning to host a night at a local theater to recognize valuable members of the community. He could give Rod free publicity by establishing an award for the city's top guide, the most knowledgeable, entertaining guide on the island of Manhattan. A veritable institution.

"And it's good for résumé," said Sonia, an authority on the subject.

"There are so many awards now," Rod said.

"This would be different. More traditional. Rather than give forty awards to forty people and have them talk for ten seconds each, we can choose four recipients and then hold up their merits to the audience for fifteen, twenty minutes."

"It's not my thing."

"You're just being modest. I'm thinking of it as a *This Is Your Life* sort of segment. How did these recipients get to be such remarkable, dynamic social contributors? We can show the people behind our stars, the lives that led to this moment. The wind beneath the wings."

Rod snorted at this.

When Brad proposed something, he disliked interruptions and despised negativity.

He shook his head at Rod and insisted, "You'll just show up. My foundation will do the research. It will be the best thirty minutes of your life."

"*Thirty* minutes! Why would I . . .?"

"You love New York, right from Yonkers on down to the bay, and you pass on that love of the city to thousands of visitors from all over the world. You are New York for most of these people and that . . ."

"I'm not interested."

"Why wouldn't you be interested?" Brad asked. "I've been thinking about this reception for a month or two and awarding a rep of the tour industry makes for a well-rounded evening."

Rod opened his mouth to say something but poured some wine into it instead. Brad was accustomed to some semblance of gratitude. He turned to look out the window onto the post-theater traffic bound for the Lincoln Tunnel. Silence consumed the table. I was desperate for the laughter to resume, feeling like a hostess of a cocktail party where someone had just shouted *Bullshit!*

"I have an idea for the foundation." I started the wheels in motion. Brad looked at me.

"And what?" Sonia asked, since no one else was responding. Even after so much wine and two and a half years, her *and* still bugged me.

I continued. "Scholarships." I explained that I wanted to give scholarships to high school students who had done poorly on their standardized tests. I wanted to reward those who might feel they'd been set back by the testing process. Maybe they didn't make their dream school or lost out on grant money because their scores were lower than they should have been.

"Where would you start?" Brad asked me.

"In this neighborhood, I think. With the guidance counselors."

"A great idea," he replied. The enthusiasm returned to the table. "How much?"

"How much what? Money? Oh, two scholarships, let's say, of twenty-five hundred each?"

"How about two scholarships, let's say, of five thousand each?" There were smiles everywhere. His passion was contagious. "Maybe even ten thousand dollars each."

Crisis averted, and I had my very own project.

● ● ●

THINGS BEGAN TO SHIFT. By the spring, I was convinced that Brad's desire to help others emitted some sort of scent, because the denizens of the cabaret world surrounded him like a pack of wolves. I could not believe how brazen they were or how irritating with their tired anecdotes, their vulnerable egos needing constant stroking, their insulated, petty little dreams. Their ad hoc singalongs drove

me especially crazy with everyone gathered around a piano compet-
ing to hit the highest note or sustain it the longest or belt it the loudest. I often had to remind myself that if I admired Brad's willingness
to help people, shouldn't I try to emulate him? I couldn't bring myself to rave over every performer—I already had one Sonia in my
life—but I could concentrate on improving the world in my own
way. I threw myself into the task of finding two worthy recipients of
my scholarship, and through these efforts, I earned an entire evening alone with Brad for the first time since the opera.

May had come by the time we met in a cozy, unpopulated café
in the West Village to read through the applications for the ten final-
ists of the scholarships and to select the two winners. I was enjoying
the intimacy, though Brad seemed edgy—there were performances
happening throughout the city and he was stuck in a hole-in-the-
wall listening to a Vivaldi CD. This annoyed me, but I continued to
focus on the task at hand. When the pool was narrowed to four, we
decided to take a break, order a couple more cappuccinos, and chat
about the presentation ceremony. That naturally reminded me of
the new certificate design, which I'd drafted that afternoon at work.
I pulled it delicately out of the folder and presented it to him. His
shoulders rose into his neck.

"What is this?" he asked. I took the paper back and looked it over
for a typo.

"What's what?" Brad bobbed his head from shoulder to shoulder
as if giving me time to figure it out myself. "I don't know, Brad."

"I think the name of the scholarship is peculiar."

"I think it's funny. AGAS. Which means the Andy Green Academic Scholarships, but it really stands for the Andy Green Apologetic Scholarships. Is it too bland?"

"Where's the money coming from?"

"Oh. Well, from your foundation, but it says that right here."

"In a reduced font."

"I'll make it bigger. It's just a rough draft."

"Sure." He took a sip, removed the foam on his upper lip with his lower one. "Why, though, would the scholarship be in your name?"

"Well." I heard a strain of sarcasm in the three syllables it took me to say that word. "I came up with the idea. I designed the logo and letterhead. I chose the five public schools and met with the guidance counselors. I created the application and interviewed the forty students. I narrowed them down to ten . . ."

"Yes, and I'm giving twenty thousand dollars . . ."

"Hm." Strange behavior from an ally.

"Besides also paying for our dinners and drinks and cab rides . . ."

"Slow down! I've tried to pay many, many times . . ."

"When was the last time?"

"Well, I'll be paying for these cappuccinos, that's for sure." I looked back at the applications but couldn't stop myself from asking: "Why is this so important to you?"

He countered: "Why is it important to you?" I wasn't sure. Maybe I was tired of being the anonymity seated on Brad's right, of being told where to meet, what to wear, what flowers to buy for whatever diva we were feeding that night. I was also getting sick of people calling me "Brad's boyfriend" or "Brad's partner" or "Brad's companion" when I had a name.

"What is going on here?" I asked.

"I just like to see credit where credit is due."

I smiled before rolling my eyes, biting into a cookie, and laughing.

He stiffened and his lips parted. "Why is that funny?"

I chewed for a few seconds, hoping I would calm down, but after I swallowed, I said, "Wanting credit where credit is due. I'm surprised to hear that coming from someone who plagiarizes musicals and passes them off as his own." He pretended to be baffled. "Brad. You constantly quote song lyrics as if they were your words. You can't deny you do that. It's very weird."

"I assume everyone understands the reference."

"Most of them are obscure. Not everyone speaks Broadway as fluently as you do." He bristled, and I backtracked. "It's not that important. I'm sorry. You don't use footnotes, so what?"

"Then why did you bring it up?"

"I guess because I too like to see credit where credit is due."

"What are you getting at?" he asked suspiciously.

"Nothing," I answered honestly.

"Nothing?" His eyes narrowed. There was a brief confusion on both our parts, and the conversation could have gone in either direction.

Brad said, "Let's not fight. Call the scholarships what you want. It doesn't matter."

"It obviously does. The Brad Willet Scholarships."

"The Andy Green Apologetic Scholarships is fine."

"I'll give the foundation a larger font."

"Fine."

"Then why don't you pick the two winners?"

"No, you pick."

"Come on. Please." I took his hand, which was gripping the table top. "Are we still in the fight?"

"No. We're not fighting. The two on top are the winners."

"That's a little too random."

"Life is a little too random," he said, and then added, "That's not a quote."

"No, but you're still mad."

"No, I'm not. I'm choosing the top two, because all four candidates are wonderful kids and there's no other way to decide."

"Fine. Then the scholarships go to Karl Johnson and Angela Cho."

"To Karl Johnson and Angela Cho." Brad smiled his customary smile and we toasted our winners.

This clumsy argument tainted the scholarships for the moment, but I was able to sit beside two separate guidance counselors the following week and make two high school seniors very happy. Karl Johnson actually jumped in the air, clapped twice before landing, and wrapped his arms around me and my chair, hugging us both. He called his mother and let me hear her screams over the phone. Angela Cho cried and said, "Thank you so much for believing in me." It was the best day of the entire process.

The worst was when I had to tell the students that the scholarships were no longer available.

● ● ●

IN THE FIRST FEW days of June, Sonia Obolensky shocked the world of cabaret by severing her ties with the angel. A week before recording her CD, she suddenly and adamantly refused his philanthropy in a tearful Restaurant Row bar scene. When I heard about this, not from either of them but from a gossipy acquaintance, I called Brad and was surprised when he didn't call back. Five days of subsequent phone calls went unanswered. Calls to his cell phone went straight to voice mail. I called Sonia and asked her about the evening on Restaurant Row. She assured me that they hadn't spoken of me. My name hadn't come up at all. The discussion was exclusively about her career. When I asked why in the world she would turn down Brad's charity, she told me that there were many reasons, without specifying one. She gave me the most basic outline of their conversation and told me that Brad, visibly hurt—ingratitude sharper than the serpent's tooth—stood up when she finished and went straight out the door, not saying good-bye or picking up the check. He went straight out the door and then what? Was there a screeching of tires? Was he hit by a truck? Why wasn't he returning my calls? Sonia had no idea.

I took the subway down to Chelsea to talk to Brad in person, but I didn't even make it past the front desk. As soon as I walked in, the concierge said, "Mr. Green," and ducked quickly behind the counter. I looked behind me, half-expecting to see a man with a gun, and then stepped up to the desk.

"Hi, Mike."

"You can't go up there," his voice sounded.

"He's not in?"

"He's out of town. Didn't you know?" He stood up, the better to observe me, and placed a plastic Rite Aid bag on the desk between us. There was an older couple sitting on the sofa six feet away from the desk. They looked like they were waiting for a son or daughter to come downstairs and join them for lunch. A gift-wrapped box, holding a shirt or a sweater, was on the woman's lap. As they waited, they watched the two of us at the desk.

"He can't be. He would have told me if he was leaving town." I discerned in Mike's thin lips the slightest smirk. He had always been polite and friendly to me, but his new demeanor hinted that I wasn't a guest of a tenant anymore, so unless I was suddenly the UPS man, the door was behind me. I wondered if he was just trying to head me off at the pass. "Perhaps he's back. Can you call up?"

"No." He was playing the role of the gatekeeper to the hilt. Maybe he was trying to show the couple on the sofa how safe their child was in this building.

"Then I'll just go up and knock."

"I'm afraid you can't."

"Why not? I'm in the book."

From a drawer under the desk, Mike pulled out the overstuffed black binder and flipped to Brad's apartment number before swiveling the book around so that I could better see it. I could feel the parents watching my face. I saw what was once my page marred by an oversized X made by the ink of a blue Magic Marker. Written at the top of the page was No *admittance*.

"No admittance? Why?"

"I don't know," Mike said, shrugging his shoulders and shaking his head at the dissolution of yet another Chelsea romance. He began turning his wedding band with his thumb—unconsciously, I assumed. How many years had Mike—middle-aged, balding, chubby, heterosexual Mike—worked in this building? How many inebriated, overly dramatic tiffs had he witnessed in the lobby? How many tricks and escorts had he directed upstairs?

"Why?" I asked again, turned now to the parents who sat with downcast eyes. The woman straightened the bow on the giftbox. There had been no sign at all that this was coming. Was Brad Willet breaking it off with me?

"If you have any copies of the keys on you . . ." Mike said, interrupting my thoughts. He had opened a cabinet where keys hung from hooks. Line after line of failed romances dangled in front of me.

"He never gave me a key," I admitted quietly and hated the meek sound of my voice. I also hated the phrasing. I could have said *I never asked for a key* or *I never needed a key*, but the power in this relationship, from the start to what appeared the finish, was always in Brad's hands. I spoke up for myself just once and it was all over. *He never gave me a key.*

"This is yours," Mike said and pointed at the bag. Inside were three of my CDs, a book, a magazine, my toothbrush, contact lens solution. Adhered to the front of the magazine was a large Post-it, which read, *Andy, I'm sorry . . . it was just one of those things. Brad.* The lobby was deathly quiet. As I was trying to think of something I could claim was missing in order to demand access to the apartment, the birthday boy and a friend/lover/roommate walked out of the elevator. The parents jumped to their feet and there were hugs and hands shaken. Only Mike paid me any attention. If a pause needed to be filled at lunch, my tiny scene would be turned into a sad little anecdote; otherwise, they had a birthday to celebrate. I leaned over the desk. "Is he really out of town? Could you call up, because this isn't right . . ."

"He is out of town."

"Do you know when he'll be back?"

"If I did . . . I couldn't. I'm sorry." I slipped out of the building before the cheerful party of four so that I wouldn't have to dance around them on the sidewalk.

I stumbled aimlessly through Chelsea. Several times my legs were too wobbly to walk. I took breaks and sat on stoops. This was all too abrupt. There was nothing, aside from our fight in the café, to explain why he would end our relationship through a doorman and another quote from the American songbook. It didn't seem possible that I could have misread our relationship this drastically, but maybe we were ready to topple for weeks and I was just too blind to see it. I felt like I was in the middle of a multiple choice test and had just learned that the test booklet and my answer sheet didn't correspond. With forty questions left, I had run out of bubbles. I had believed in something that wasn't true, and now that it was gone I was having a hard time keeping my balance.

I tried to make one last contact with him through e-mail: "What about the scholarship money? Or is that too just one of those crazy things?!?!" There was no response, which made me angrier, because my life was not the only one he was dumping.

Karl Johnson was eighteen. He graduated fifth in his class. He was the vice president of the student council, sang in the chorus, and played guard on the basketball team. He was voted friendliest by his fellow seniors and won the biology award from the science department. His mother raised him alone after the death of his father in an electrical fire when Karl was only five. His personal statement dealing with panic described what he felt when confronted with those moments that *tell the world who you are and what you are capable of.* Angela Cho wanted to become a teacher of any subject but math. She played the trumpet and gave the morning announcements. Her principal himself wrote her letter of recommendation, and her biggest disappointment was finding out she was turned down by Carnegie Mellon where her boyfriend was a sophomore. When she learned she was the recipient of the $10,000 scholarship that would help her family pay for her education at Vassar, she mumbled *thankyouthankyouthankyou* and wept.

● ● ●

I BEGAN WITHDRAWING FROM my life after I shattered their dreams. I still commuted to work and did my own shopping, but I spent more and more time in my apartment, ignoring phone calls, particularly any from Sonia Obolensky. I had come to feel that her break with Brad led somehow to his break with me. I was also piqued that Sonia was still part of a couple. In late June, when one of her messages announced that she had broken it off with the trainer/agitator, schadenfreude allowed me to forgive her, and we went for a walk in Central Park.

At Turtle Pond, I finally learned that Sonia's act of career suicide was also part sabotage. Her break with the angel, she told me, was brought on by Porfiry who was convinced that money gained somewhere meant money lost somewhere else. Repulsed by the way Brad flaunted his fortune, Porfiry, after weeks of diatribes, gave Sonia an ultimatum, threatening to leave her if she recorded one note with the foundation's dirty money.

Sonia impressively chucked a stone halfway across the pond and threw herself onto her back in the grass, telling me that soon after she had chosen Porfiry, she realized she had made the wrong choice.

"And I am a whore," Sonia said.

"No, you're not," I said. "You didn't choose the money. You chose the sex. You're just a slut." It was a good day and Sonia laughed. We both did. The cool breeze that afternoon was fresh but not as refreshing as hearing of someone else's misery. I preferred to dwell on her failed relationship rather than mine. We worked on her version of their final moments.

"It was at night," she said. "During sex . . ."

". . . during a sweaty floor exercise with your gymnast . . ."

". . . when I am realizing I do not want this every night."

"That you'd rather be singing of love than being pounded by a few inches of it."

"YES! Exactly this!"

"What a horrible discovery after you'd rejected the greatest caba-ret patron in recent history."

"I am panicking. I throw myself into the act. My new act. This is my new act. I cannot look at his eyes. Why am I sacrificing? This man? This sex?"

"You didn't love Porfiry!"

"I didn't love Porfiry! I jumped off him and took that . . . thing in my hand."

"That poor excuse for a microphone."

"And who can hear me through this? I am thinking this."

"What applause will that ever bring you?"

"And this was what I chose? This is what I chose! Every song I ever sang . . ."

". . . now look what was in your mouth."

". . . every job I ever endure . . ."

". . . and now it's all blow." With a broad smile, Sonia screamed and then threw her hands over her face. She began to moan and she told me about Russia. Her grandfather taught her to sight-read when she was only four, and they sang duets at every holiday until his death. Sonia told me that at the airport, when she was leaving Rus-sia, her mother cried, reached under Sonia's shirt, and dug her fin-gernails into her back so that she would physically be with her daughter a little longer. Sonia didn't cry until later, halfway over the

Atlantic, when she rubbed her back and felt no trace of the half-moon marks. She told me that the sun was orange on the skyline when that first subway train came out of Brooklyn to cross the Manhattan Bridge and she mentally wrote her first letter home. She had only been a week away from recording her CD. One week!

Sonia and I were sitting up on the grass. I had my arm around her. We had each of us in our own separate ways scorned the greatest patron alive, and it didn't seem easily remedied.

All of her grief, frustration, and fury went into that last bout with Porfiry, and as she slammed her forehead against his rock-hard abs, practically giving herself a concussion, she heard him moaning and groaning with pleasure. When he reached the final notes, the crescendo of screams that brought knocking from walls, floor, and ceiling, she realized that she had given her voice to him and she didn't know how to get it back.

"'Get out and do not return,' I say to him and he just cries 'why, why, why, why . . .'"

I DRAGGED MYSELF HOME ONE day in July to find nineteen messages on my answering machine. A quick scan of the Caller ID confirmed they were all from the same source: Ruby Green. Even though I always returned the phone calls from my family, my mother still felt she needed to tell my machine exactly what she wanted me to call her about. I deliberately set my machine to record messages up to a minute only, which usually discouraged her from leaving more than eight. The fact that she had called nineteen times meant that her most recent humiliation was unprecedented.

I didn't know if I had the emotional strength to sit through all nineteen messages, but it was always safer to find out what I was getting into before calling her back. I opened a bottle of beer and took a drink before sitting down to listen. The home in southern Maryland I rarely visited had apparently become a bleak landscape of drunk driving, chemotherapy, and unwanted pregnancies, and my mother related these sordid events with her highly honed skills of compression, able to pick up precisely where she left off at the start of each new message.

I pressed PLAY.

"Well, no one's pressing charges." A sigh followed. "That's the good news."

My sister was having an affair with a married man who happened to be her manager at the Petey Pepperoni, a theme restaurant where, according to Ruby, children ate pizza and played arcade games while the fathers drank beer and swapped wives. Beth had taken a job as a waitress there the previous December and was soon having sex with her boss in the parking lot.

"I hope you're not laughing at this," my mother ended message two. I had to laugh—it was the only way not to be submerged in the depths where she always threatened to push me. I was always amused and inspired by my sister. Sprouting kinky red hair from a slightly misshapen head, her cheeks mildly pocked from an adolescence of greasy skin worsened by abuse of cosmetics, Beth never considered herself anything but ravishing. She moved gracefully through life, as if perpetually on camera, the paparazzi concealed in the bushes. She tossed her hair and posed sultrily for family photos as if she were a supermodel who'd taken to wearing denim skirts and rayon blouses too tight for her frame. After seeing the latest Julia Roberts movie, Beth would say "Isn't she sweet?" in a slightly patronizing tone, as if Julia had been a last-minute replacement after Beth pulled out of the role. In high school, she brazenly entered herself into the beauty pageant at the county fair without a shred of inhibition. Such confidence made my job as an older brother very easy—I never had to defend her from insults, because she never heeded them.

Our mother, on the other hand, often disapproved of Beth's hair-styles and clothing purchases. She thought Beth deliberately attracted mortification to the family by dressing like a "slutty clown." To Ruby, the Charles County Beauty Pageant was a mockery—because of the area's tobacco-growing history, the winner was crowned Miss Nicotina—like something out of Revelations, and she prayed the world would end before her daughter walked down the runway. Next to what had happened this week, however, the Miss Nicotina debacle and my coming out of the closet were photoworthy memories that my mother could order in various sizes and mail to our grandparents.

Beth had the good sense to dissolve her "love affair" before it wrecked a marriage she had "no wish to dismantle." There would be no more hand jobs in Reed D'Carloff's Plymouth Volare. She would accept no more gold-plated jewelry. When she arrived the next day at work, fully prepared for the awkwardness but willing to console him over their mutual loss, she saw that Reed was already flirting with a newly hired busgirl, a senior from McDonough High. They were both giggling as he filled ketchup bottles and she braided his ponytail. Had Beth been forgotten that quickly? She was on the wrong side of twenty-five, but she was still young and beautiful. Her day was about to get worse. On the chart that designated the duties of the staff—she was always a server—she located her name opposite *Petey Pepperoni*. After seven months of working at this restaurant, with seniority on her side and regulars who asked to be seated at her table, she was now expected to dress up as the restaurant's giant rat and stand outside the entrance in the corridor, greeting mall shop-pers with sample menus. Outraged, Beth wrestled herself into the smelly costume, pulling the suspenders over her furry shoulders before pulling the rat's head over her own. Clutching a ten-dollar bill, the ever-smiling Petey Pepperoni stomped through the kitchen and restaurant and marched halfway down the length of the mall into a store that sold tag board and black Magic Markers. The cashier's monotony was broken by selling these items to a giant rodent and then watching the rodent use his oversized paws to fill both sides with block lettering. For the next twenty minutes, Petey Pepperoni paced back and forth in the main entrance corridor to the mall, holding a sign which, on one side, read: THE REAL RAT IS INSIDE THE RESTAURANT. When Reed came out to put an end to Beth's activism, he saw that the sign's flip side read: WATCH YOUR CHILDREN, THE MANAGER LIKES 'EM YOUNG!!! Reed lunged at the tag board. There was a chase before Beth was tackled. The ensuing fisticuffs between the manager and the rat made the *Maryland Independent*. A crowd gathered and took sides. When Petey's head was ripped off and rolled to a stop at the feet of an eight-year-old boy, the crowd gasped at the sight of the red hair. The boy broke the silence by saying with quiet disillusionment: "Petey's a girl." Reed rolled on top, trying to push the sign out of Beth's grip. Beth grabbed Reed's braided ponytail and yanked him off. She sprung to her oversized rat feet and began kicking her soon-to-be ex-manager, to the alarm of the crowd. Without the giant smiling head, this light amusement had become an ugly, violent altercation, with an obviously sordid redneck backstory that could only end with mall security.

It wasn't the first time I was grateful to Beth for being my sister. Without her deflection, how would I have survived my childhood? Then there came a surprise in the middle of the seventeenth message.

I could hear Ruby speaking with Beth who had just come home. The phone was hung up.

Message eighteen: "Well, your sister's engaged. Call us."

Message nineteen: "Not to her supervisor. To some magician, apparently."

I finished my beer. Engaged? I slowly peeled off the label and scratched at the glue. Good for her, I thought. I closed my eyes, leaned back in my chair, put my feet up on the desk. I was twenty-nine and saw a future littered with relationships that ended abruptly and without explanation.

When I finally called, my mother answered breathlessly, "Oh, Andrew! I was so worried."

"Why?"

"You didn't call."

"I was at work."

With all seeming sincerity, she said, "I thought maybe you were down at the docks with the rough traders."

I waited a few seconds. "I dropped the phone, sorry, I didn't catch that."

"I said I thought you were down . . ."

"Beth is getting married?"

"I can't even think about that right now. I have to calm down. Whenever you don't return my calls, I imagine you've been strangled by some anonymous sexual partner."

"Mm-hm." She had performed this sketch before. From experience, I knew that she was ready with a response to anything I might say, so the best strategy was to wait it out until I had the opportunity to steal the offensive. I let her finish her routine, while I took another beer out of the refrigerator. "So Beth was fired?"

"In the most mortifying way imaginable." She moaned, "Oh, Andrew. What are we going to do?"

"Nothing. Beth isn't traumatized, is she?"

"Of course she isn't."

"Then she'll bounce back. She'll get a new job—you said yourself there were no charges."

"It was in the papers."

I told her that was a nice touch. "You have one paper and it's a biweekly."

"Which is worse. The news lingers longer here."

"I think the whole thing's a little funny actually."

"It's not funny." She was adamant.

"Why not?"

"Because it just happened."

"Nonetheless. She was dressed in a rat suit . . ."

"A mouse suit, Andrew, please. Don't make it worse."

"A giant ratlike mouse suit."

"What am I going to do on Sunday? How can I face my congregation?"

Here was my chance to take the offensive: "I wouldn't worry what they think, Mother. These are people who believe that the only person on the entire planet who had a boat was Noah."

"Andrew."

"Or that out of five thousand people only one boy packed a lunch."

There was a pause: "I'm sorry, I dropped the phone."

I pushed my advantage: "Hopefully they'll mind their own business, Mother, unless . . ." I let it float. "Unless they're really devout, in which case they'll persecute you."

"Please don't joke about our lives."

"Beth doesn't care, Mom. Why should you?"

"You have no idea. You're eight hundred miles away. You've forgotten what it's like to live in a small community where there's such a thing as a reputation. This isn't New York City where you can have sex on the sidewalk at two in the afternoon."

"Doesn't Beth's engagement make you happy?"

"Her engagement? To a man she just met? He's an amateur magician from Texas . . ."

"First of all, I did not *just* meet Peter" came a voice on the line to set the record straight.

"How long have you been on that phone?" my mother asked.

"I've been dating Peter since February."

"You were having trysts with your supervisor until last week."

"Which is when I got engaged," Beth said. "Hi, Andy."

"Congratulations," I told her.

"Thank you. I'm glad someone's happy for me."

"I'm sorry, Beth. I've just never had a child of mine incarcerated by the police."

"You still haven't. It was mall security. They gave me coffee and magazines to read."

I asked, "Hey, Beth? Did they take your pawprints?"

At the sound of Beth's guffaw, our mother slammed the phone into its cradle three times in quick succession.

When she was off the line, my sister instantly asked if I would give her away. "I will not walk down the aisle with her." I didn't reply, surprised at the idea of giving my sister away. She continued to plan. "I think I'm going to make her a flower girl. Wouldn't that be funny? With Angie's three-year-old. They'll wear matching pink dresses that stop at the knee. Oh, I'm writing this down."

"How far are you into planning this?"

"Far enough. We're going to be married this fall."

"Why so soon?"

"No, I'm not pregnant!" she groaned, as if reaching the end of a tedious press junket.

"I didn't think you were." I thought she'd prefer a prolonged period of saying *fiancé*. "Doesn't planning a wedding take months and months?"

"We're not getting married at the Plaza. We're getting married at the church and having the reception at the firehouse."

"The firehouse?"

"Yes. The one off 210. They move all the trucks out of the garage and set up tables and chairs. We're not going to have tablecloths, because dinner's going to be a crab feast, so we'll just cover the tables with newspaper. Or brown paper if we want to go for classy. Marty's brother is going to be the deejay, because he does all the proms in the county, and we might make it an eighties night. What do you think?"

I could only reply, "That's so depressing."

"What's depressing?"

How to answer that? Everything was depressing.

"Nothing, I'm sorry," I said. "I was looking through some mail." Beth resumed outlining her wedding plans and I tried to concentrate and sound supportive until I hung up. At that point, I wondered how many days she would expect me to be nearby. Would it be possible to take the train down that morning and leave early that evening before the line dancing? Would I be expected to live at home in the days leading up to the ceremony or host any of the prewedding events? Would I have to take her fiancé out and give him a man-of-the-house kind of talking-to?

It turned out I would meet Peter sooner than anticipated. Two weeks later, my mother left another series of messages, informing me that Peter was coming to New York for a weekend in August to drum up some business at a conference, and I was expected not only to meet him for dinner but to be charming.

Message six: "It's just dinner, you don't have to take him to the Empire State Building or anything, and Andrew: I need you to do your best to hit it off, because it means so much to Beth. She isn't getting any younger."

Message seven: "Neither are you."

There was an indentation of the DELETE button in my thumb after I purged my machine of my mother's mind games.

● ● ●

AUGUST 10, 2001: the day I've lived over and over.

It's an extremely hot Friday, and my office manager releases us all before lunch. Some of my coworkers invite me to see a movie; others invite me to go to the planetarium. I decline both invites. No one minds, because I've withdrawn in the past few months and they're all bored with my moods. I come straight home. I am taking a nap that afternoon, to store up energy for this dinner with my impending brother-in-law, when the phone rings. I let the machine pick it up. A concierge from the Sheraton hotel informs me that a package has been left for me by a Brad Willet. Two months have passed since I last saw Brad. It's too hot to walk over to the hotel. Though I am curious. Is this a long-overdue letter of apology and explanation? Or another CD of mine? Why wouldn't he just mail it? I call Peter's room and leave a message asking him to pick up the package for me. *The Sheraton is next to your hotel; it's a good place to leave your business cards; it's on the way to dinner.* Peter drops by the hotel a couple of hours before dinner and calls me to let me know that there is no package. I'm shocked at his accent: my sister's marrying a hillbilly. I ask him if he spoke to the right person. He says of course, but there's no package. Maybe Brad changed his mind or he realized that whatever he was returning to me actually belonged to someone else—another idiot who was probably about to get dumped by a concierge at the Sheraton. Why should I care? I thank Peter and fib: *I'm looking forward to dinner.*

"Pick a card, any card."

With these words, my sister's fiancé greets me four seconds after I enter the restaurant. Since there are only the two of us at the table, I have no choice but to obey. I peruse the deck, drawn open like a fan, select at random a plastic-coated rectangle, slip it out, memorize it with a nod of complicity, and replace it in the tightly closed stack. I act astonished and clap a few times when the seven of diamonds reappears at the top of the deck after a series of shuffles and finger taps. That is the first of many feats, however, and within twenty minutes I've labored through the entire cycle of appropriate responses—smiling; shaking my head; laughing; whistling; lifting my brow and saying *wow;* muttering *unbelievable;* asking where the dealer learned that one; and making the shamefully inane suggestion that Peter get a job in Vegas. The next twenty minutes I spend testing a new series of responses—opening my menu; offering to buy the dealer a drink; yawning; and rubbing my card-pulling fingers as if they were now cramped and incapacitated. If I knew this grand illusionist at all, I would say: "Put those away, you're boring the shit out of me." This is something I cannot do, since both my mother and sister, at home hundreds of miles away, have stressed how important it is that Peter and I like each other, so after we order our dinners, I continue to play along—only now I have to hand Peter my wallet, my keys, my pack of Certs; I have to think of a number between one and four thousand; I have to cut my egg roll into three parts and guess which of the shuffled tea-cups holds the center section. The waitstaff at The Great Wok give the magician a round of applause when he turns two chopsticks into ten.

At the sight of the three silver hoops Peter pulls out of his satchel, I taste pork braised in stomach acid. I smile, pretend not to notice them, and crack open my fortune cookie, which is X-rated: *Happiness is eating pussy.* I spear a pineapple cube with a toothpick and ponder the ancient wisdom. Is this why I'm so sad? Peter can't find his fortune. The cookie is empty. "Wait a second, wait just one second." It's behind my ear. *The future is in your scrotum.* For once, Peter is silenced, accustomed to the Chinese takeouts found in food courts. While his eyes scan the slip of paper for a typo, I imagine with a shiver the entire generation of nephews and nieces in black capes and rabbit-filled top hats that Peter's scrotum is sure to yield.

I stare at Peter and think to myself that maybe I loathe magicians because of our affinity. We both make our living entering the minds of others in order to deceive them. A magician's so-called feats come with a running commentary of what he assumes we, his audiences, are thinking. The magician speaks our thoughts aloud. "You're guessing there's a wire. Let's use this hoop to rule that out." The entire trick lies in the bewildering of our thought processes. Our befuddled minds are what constitute a magic show. Otherwise, the magician would just say: "Here's the false panel. Right here." Or he would warn us: "You're looking in the wrong place. Keep your eye on my right hand." What a different world it would be if the magician performed his tricks while giving voice to his internal monologue. What a different world it would be if I were able to inform the test-takers right up front, in the directions, that the correct answer would always be italicized. Honesty, announcing to the world where you're coming from and what you've done and plan to do, would render obsolete both magic shows and standardized testing. Thankfully, we're condemned to trust the wrong hand of the magician and choose the answer that "sounds right."

These musings and an air conditioner set to ARCTIC make it easy for me to decline another round of drinks. I perform my own conjuring act: with my index finger and thumb, I scribble nonsense in the air, and in moments the check arrives. I thank the waiters and move toward the exit before Peter can demonstrate the sleight of hand with the coins. I hear the laughter and the Cantonese behind me. When the door, a glass-and-steel contraption, won't open onto the street, I strongly suspect my future brother-in-law. I feel anxious. The restaurant is an icebox, and I'm trapped inside it. I'll have to pull Peter's finger or pick one key out of twenty. For my life, I throw myself against the door and pop the frigid suction of the room, falling out into the ovens of August. I almost black out. By the time Peter joins me thirty seconds later, I'm sweating.

"Whoo-whee, it's hot out here," he says. "Is this why they call it Hell's Kitchen?" I don't answer. I'm too busy struggling to breathe. "Now where's my hotel from here?"

"It's a few blocks that way . . ."

"Hey! Why don't you walk me and we can stop at that Sheraton and you can see for yourself that package isn't there."

"We don't have to do that. I believe you."

"Come on. It was crowded when I went and my person was kinda distracted."

"Okay. Fine. Let's go to the Sheraton." I wish I had never said it. I should have put Peter in a cab and put a cap on the night—hands would have been shaken, a wave at the curb, a wedding invitation in the mail. Instead, we walk together through the hot breezes of Tenth Avenue and pockets of summer stench, eggs hard-boiled in urine. Peter finally tells me how he and my sister met: on the stage in the foyer at the mall in Maryland, she volunteered and he cut her head off. I notice his accent is thickening and I wonder where in Texas one has to live to grow up with that kind of drawl. As I listen, more and more of my shirt sticks to my back. My armpits are dripping; my feet are slippery. The soles of my sandals pick up warm tar from the street and leave prints on the sidewalk.

On Forty-seventh Street, I think of Brad Willet. Brad always preferred the quiet, deserted side streets, which he thought were more romantic. I feel peculiar walking with someone else down this street after dinner and am surprised at myself. I should be over Brad by now, shouldn't I? As we near whichever new gay bar has replaced Citron 47, four men look me over and then turn their eyes to Peter, who abruptly smiles and says "Howdy." The address, far too direct and unexpected, joins all four men into one startled bond, their sultry reserve now as pierced as their nipples. Each scurries and scrambles to speak, say something, by which time Peter is two steps past them all.

I can see how someone might find Peter attractive, how, in fact, most might: blond hair cut short, a strong jaw cleanly shaven, and pine-green eyes I'd probably admire if I didn't know that they belonged to such a dorky magician. The promotional brochures Peter has been dumping all over Manhattan prove just how goofy he is. The photographs of him squinting and pursing his lips in an effort to look mysterious aren't nearly as inept as the stage name he's taken and printed in a font size of thirty-six—following in the footsteps of another celebrated illusionist who adopted the name of a beloved Dickens character, Peter has begun billing himself as Bob Cratchit.

We turn up Ninth Avenue and walk to Fifty-first, another side street lined with pear trees and shadows. No one is holding anyone's hand tonight, so why does it happen? Do we touch shoulders? Are we walking too close? Does he pat my back? There is absolutely no sexual energy between me and Peter—just the odor of beer-drenched garbage baking in the street—but two strangers (having followed us from Forty-seventh? or the restaurant?) see two men walking together in a neighborhood recently overrun with rainbow flags, cosmo happy hours, and Broadway chorus boys who have always lived on the West Side but have recently far exceeded their quota.

The men step up from behind, and under, it seems. Too close. Heat on the back of the neck, weight between the shoulder blades. Hands push me into the street and others swing Peter by his satchel into the black iron cage protecting one of the pear trees. We are past the nervous-laughter portion of the conflict. I'm already on my sweaty knees, now scraped and bleeding. I'm hugging the bumper of a massive SUV docked at the curb. My last physical fight was in the sixth grade, and my body doesn't remember what to do. As I wait for myself to participate in the urgent reality of the moment, my shoulder is kicked into my neck. I fall into the street, which is empty of traffic, strangely desolate. My left hand is tingling; the gravel underneath it is hot and soft, like clay.

The other man is holding my sister's fiancé by the neck and the top of his head, knocking that head against the cage. "Take that."

His head strikes twice, three times, four. Peter makes pained, explosive whimpers. The man above me hits me in the mouth. I feel a tooth slide through my lower lip. I can't take my eyes off Peter, who gets kneed between the legs, and so a fist connects with my face again. My eye. I look down at the street. My head is bouncing between a fist and the SUV's bumper. I cover my head with my arms. I hear a popping sound and something hits the ground. I peek behind me. Both men are with Peter, whose face is drenched in blood. His head bangs against the cage five, six, seven times. He's not making any more sounds. They're holding him up. They let him fall. He drops without muscle into a pile. My body recalls how to move . . . and I run away.

I run to Eighth Avenue, without bending my knees, which I can feel are ripped open. My heart's pumping too fast. I pass restaurants where I can get help but I keep on. I pass people but keep on. I am not in control of my legs. Am I running to the police precinct? I stop at Fifty-third, remember my sister, turn, and hobble back. The air is thick, almost drinkable but for its dieseled filth. Over the taxis tearing uptown, I can hear my heels squishing with sweat in the leather. The men were kicking Peter as I left. I'm going to shout and take them by surprise. I feel suddenly convinced that I'm going to kill them. I'm going to tear their arms from their shoulders. Rip their bodies into meaty chunks. Stomp them into the pavement. I see the blue and red flashing lights a half block away and move directly into the colors.

A car and two cops on the curb: one on the radio, one leaning over Peter's body. No one in the back seat. No one in handcuffs against a wall. Where did they go? What did they look like? No specifics. They were just two young professionals, in office clothes.

Business casual. Would we be living in a safer world if we still dressed up? I'm embarrassed by how loudly the ambulance wails when it arrives. All the radios, the lights, the audience: West-Siders in between bars, curious, gathering. Two Dominicans in kitchen whites and checkered pants, holding dirty rags, arms crossed. A story to tell their wives if they don't forget all about it on the subway home.

I sit on the sidewalk. A few feet from Peter and the tree. A paramedic grips my legs, and I cover my knees. The two smaller fingers of my left hand look strange. I realize they're broken. I turn my face away. The paramedic hastily shifts his attention to Peter, who seems to be in critical condition. I only have a black eye and a cut lip. I keep looking at the ground. Bloody shoeprints and crumbs of dog shit smeared into the ridged cement. Brown plants in the box holding the tree. Chips of white enamel lying on the sidewalk like shards of pottery. My tongue feels around my mouth. Peter's teeth are on the ground, not mine. I can barely look at Peter. His feet point in opposite directions. His legs, limp and sweaty on the ground beside me. He's not aligned. His torso banks to the left, his stomach upturned in a wet T-shirt. I can't look above his chest where the two men are working with concentration. I see his chest inflate and know he's alive.

I look away. I need to concentrate on something else. I stare up at the tree. The leaves, toplit by a streetlamp, are green with a white glow; the black branches frame the dark sky in different shapes. Two-thirds of the way down the trunk are the blunt iron spikes that poke outward at the top of the cage, a cage made of sixteen vertical bars, braced horizontally three times—at the ankle, the knee, and the chest. The cage is wet but otherwise unbreached, protecting the tree that seems completely safe and more secure than any of us.

● ● ●

A NEUROLOGICAL INTENSIVE CARE unit is imbued with such dehumanizing horror that I would rather be a patient there than a visitor. Most of the patients are comatose, at least, and don't have to witness the hospital's full-blown tour showing the rest of us how close we are to death and how pathetically frail our bodies are. It's better not to know that such a place exists. When I entered the ICU, my eyes had to adjust to the darkness. The brightest light, ahead and to my right, belonged to the nurse's station, a U-shaped desk from where the unit was monitored and where three staff members were filling out forms. Starting on my left and surrounding the nurse's station on three sides were the separate doorless rooms where the patients lay. The first room: an ancient Chinese woman. Connected to machines, her head was bald and stapled shut. I quickly looked to the floor. Against my will, I peeked into the second room where a teenage black boy lay, his enormous feet dried and cracked. A white tube led from his mouth to something I didn't wish to scrutinize. The third room held a small middle-aged Puerto Rican woman (I knew her family from the waiting room), who seemed to be crushed by the weight of the cables snaking all over her chest and stomach. The IV drip caught my eye. I scanned all the places where her body was pierced. I spun to my right and weakly groaned at the desk.

A nurse who was explaining why she would leave her husband for one night under Brad Pitt turned professional and looked up at my face. She didn't cringe at all. My black eye and cut lip looked like mere scratches in a neuro-ICU. I whispered why I'd been sent inside. She pointed to a corner unit. A man named Eugene escorted me past the other bodies. Cables from machines were plugged into cords and wires were hooked to metallic stickers pressed against hair and skin. Plastic pipes from ventilators covered mouths and noses, extending the lungs to the bedside. Clear bags holding fluid with waste down below and nutrients up above bonded with the body via tiny transparent tubes with needles on the ends to jab tender veins under sensitive skin. The bodies were taped, sewn, stapled, glued, like second-grade art projects fecklessly thrown together, signed on the clipboards at the foot of the beds. Cancers, burns, fevers, and blows to the head. I thought of the electricity these brains were misfiring, the distorted dreams.

Peter's machines were on his left, his bags of fluid on his right. I took peeks up the body toward the head. His hair was gone. Black, wiry stitches and bruises. Purple welts. His left eye: dark, cut, and swollen. Nose broken, bandaged with thick white cotton squares. Abrasions on his face. Was his jaw broken, too? There were metal stickers tagged all over his chest, stomach, and arms. The tangled webs of cords and cables hung off the bed. I saw urine and blood leak through a plastic tube and mix in the attached bag.

I hurried away from the body, past the nurses' station and through the doors to the hallway, where the stomach acid I'd tasted the night before poured out of my mouth. In five body-heaving retches, I dumped everything out of my gut. Tears and sweat mingled on my cheeks. I couldn't stop coughing. Because I skidded on the floor, my knees under the bandages were bleeding again. I saw what they had done: those two warped, motherfucking asshole bigots—the kind that tie boys to fences in frozen weather in Wyoming and drag men behind trucks in West Virginia—beat the life out of a man who was doing nothing but walking back to his hotel. The body in that bed was not alive. *I killed him, I killed my sister's fiancé* was the thought spinning in my head as I blacked out.

• • •

I WAS SITTING IN a wheelchair in a hallway when a nurse came to tell me that my family had arrived. My sister was in with Peter, who was still clinging to life. My mother was in the waiting room. She wanted to see me. There was no other choice for me—I didn't want to go into Peter's room again. I slowly stood up. I could feel the cotton bandages pulling at my knees, which now were sore, stiff, and aching. As I waddled toward my mother, I felt a strong wave of déjà vu. From another hospital, decades earlier.

I wasn't even a year old the day my father died. I didn't remember this, but I had been told the story enough times to think that I did. I was in the arms of my babysitter, Sally, who had just seen someone write the time of death on a clipboard. I was crying, and she came out into the hallway where she found my mother frantically checking door numbers and moving in our direction. As soon as my mother saw the look on Sally's face, she stopped and leaned against the wall. Sally walked up to her, saying how sorry she was, and placed me in her arms. For years, this was the crucial moment for me: What kind of person places a helpless infant in the arms of a woman so recently widowed? For years I imagined myself as that baby in the cradle of my mother's trembling forearms, my tender skull just three feet above the hard floor.

Now I felt something else as I walked toward my mother: I was once again the one who made it. I was the survivor. I was guilty: for choosing the restaurant; for picking the time for dinner; for not putting Peter in a cab; for walking with him down Fifty-first Street toward the Sheraton; for living in New York; for being gay; for breaking only two fingers. It was my fault. Both times. First, Ruby's husband, now Beth's fiancé. I was the one who pulled through, but I felt certain that if either of them had the choice . . .

Ruby was seated in one of the well-worn vinyl chairs, fretfully rubbing her arms. Her dark red hair was cut short, and she seemed overdressed as if she'd come to the city for a weekend of shopping. She stood up when she saw me. Something in her eyes let me know that she was reliving that day in 1973 more vividly than I was, but that quickly gave way to a look of concern as she noticed the bandages, the splint, the swollen eye, the cut lip, the dried vomit stains on my shirt.

She hugged me by squeezing my shoulders, and her care not to bruise me made me feel more injured. Neither of us spoke. She looked over my face and body. Once she determined that the most severe injuries were easily remedied by time, her lips settled into a tight line, and I felt a pang of fear: she was going to make me feel worse.

She said, "I knew this would happen."

"How could you know?"

"This is exactly why I never wanted you to move to New York. This is why I didn't want you to live in a place called Hell's Kitchen. This is why I didn't want you to be . . ." She stopped herself. Didn't want me to be gay? Or didn't want me to be, period? "What happened, Andrew?"

"I told you on the phone. I don't know anything more."

"Have they been arrested?"

"I don't know."

"What do the police think? Why do they think these men . . . ?"

"I don't know."

She whispered, "Did you tell the police you were gay? Do they think the two of you are gay?"

"Why are you asking that? What does that matter?"

"Because if they think you're gay, they won't do anything to help. It's not worth their time. Don't look at me that way. That's what they think. Not me. Everyone knows this. Did you tell them Peter was engaged to your sister?"

"I told them he was my brother-in-law."

"I wonder if that will ever be true now." She clenched her fists. "He wasn't even here two full days, Andrew. I hate New York!"

"It's not New York," I said and felt suddenly inclined to say more. I wanted to hit her where *she* lived, I wanted to blame my mother's church. The Baptists indoctrinated prejudice, sang hymns and held boycotts for the destruction of the "unsaved" who were outside their flock. Members of their congregations attacked gay men and the rest defended the beatings, because Jesus, they were sure, wouldn't mind a little bloodshed in the crusade to keep men from holding hands. If Jesus and his apostles walked in robes through the Bible Belt today, helping others and being sensitive, they would have to pull out every miracle they knew to keep from getting the shit beaten out of them. I didn't voice any of this; there was no way to shift the blame from myself.

"You go in. See Peter. I need to check him out of his hotel."

"No, you don't," my mother said. "We can just call and explain."

"I need to do something."

"Come with me and see Peter."

"They won't let us all inside."

"That's not true."

"Go on. Please. I'll be back in an hour or so. We'll have a late lunch."

Outside, the hot afternoon air was stagnant. People were talking on cell phones, carrying grocery bags, waiting for a bus. Only an occasional pedestrian glanced at my face. Didn't they know what had happened? I studied them as I walked slowly to the hotel. They all seemed so brittle. Pull a string from his T-shirt collar and his head would fall off. Shake her hand and the staples would pop out of her wrist. People had hearts, smaller than grapefruits, filling and draining with blood, received and transmitted through the tiniest of tubes—how could blood pour out of such minuscule veins, as it did the previous night, and saturate a sidewalk? A woman shook her head and I thought she would crack her own skull. The body was so delicate and yet no one seemed to be paying any attention to it. Their brains were busy planning lunches, returning calls, reading ads, hailing cabs, buying papers, playing the lottery. So much was stored in these poorly protected eggshells with hair. They should all be wearing helmets, I thought, they should all be walking very carefully, hands out in front at all times. But instead these fragile antiques spent a good deal of their time kicking each other, punching, biting, scratching, stabbing, shooting. . . . What was wrong with them? They were all insane. Their brains had already been damaged. I made a concerted effort not to walk too closely past any of them.

I had Peter's key and wallet, a letter from the hospital. A security guard and a bellman stood by inside the room as I packed up Peter's dirty clothes, toothbrush, shampoo, and the ridiculous promotional brochures of Bob Cratchit. On the table next to the bed was my phone number scrawled on an envelope. Peter had no idea where pressing those seven digits would take him. I threw the envelope away, purged the room of evidence. At the front desk, there were five charges. Four phone calls and an adult movie. It was difficult for me not to picture Peter masturbating alone in a hotel room, but it was also difficult for me, after having seen Peter in the ICU, to believe that it had ever been possible. The woman behind the desk, upset by my face, stepped away to ask her supervisor if she could waive the charges due to the circumstances, but I just placed the money on the desk, ignored the stares, and walked out of the hotel with Peter's bag and magic trunk.

I didn't go back to the hospital for lunch with my mother and sister. I couldn't stay outside any longer. I was shaking and exhausted, more vulnerable than I'd ever felt. I walked down Fifty-second and made it to my building. With my palms scraped raw, my knees taped in bloody bandages, I slowly pulled myself up the two steep flights, closed the door behind me and quietly turned the locks, resolving not to leave again until the swelling went down. It was August eleventh, and since I wouldn't leave until the following March, this is where I would be a month later, when the sirens brought me to my window and I watched Ninth Avenue, completely shocked and disoriented, as all of Manhattan walked north.

MY APARTMENT WAS A refuge, not a tomb. I could breathe
there, but whenever my mind ventured out of doors—to a
wintertime walk over the Brooklyn Bridge or a Chelsea lobby or a
wet sidewalk on Fifty-first Street—I felt sick. Painting my front door
yellow so that it would blend into the living room comforted me.
The one drawback was that, even if I expected a delivery, I still
jumped at the sound of someone knocking on what I considered a
wall. There was a day in particular, a week or two after Sonia's abu-
sive massage, when the outside world demanded continual access to
my home.

I woke up to suspicious noises on the staircase in the hallway. I
kept my head motionless, one eye buried in the pillow, the other
staring across the living room at the door. I listened carefully and
could make out the squeak of rubber soles, a cough, and whispers.

There were twelve apartments in the building. Nine were occupied by the same Ecuadorian family. The tenth apartment was home to a frail French woman whose son, a heroin dealer, was jailed in the spring after rolling up an overdosed client in his mother's rug and dumping the corpse in the train tracks beyond Tenth Avenue. The eleventh apartment was, I suspected, a hideout for a cell of Al Qaeda terrorists. On the other side of the door, the voices got louder. I held my breath. I waited. Were they coming for me? Who were they and what did they want? I heard a metallic jangling and then a key skitter into its warren. The neighbors going into their apartment. I closed my eyes, taking in deep breaths of air. I thought that everyone in my building probably feared the sounds of the hallway; you could feel the relief whenever a knock turned out to be the exterminator or UPS rather than the police or FBI.

I drifted into a half-sleep state, hearing footsteps again, and losing the sense of who I was. I didn't understand what I feared or why I'd become one of those men throughout history, holding his breath and waiting for the fist to connect with his door. I felt like I was hiding in an unrented flat in downtown Warsaw, in the cellar of a clapboard house on the Underground Railroad, or in the attic of a warehouse annex in Amsterdam. Had secret police come to take me away? Was I an undesirable, an enemy of Pinochet, Nero, Palmer, or the pope? I hear the boots on the staircase, the horses being tied to the post in the front, the cane tapping at the false wall. I will lose the life I've been protecting. I'll be dragged screaming to torture or execution, prison or public humiliation. They know I'm in here and they won't go away.

I sat up in my bed. This was not a dream. A palm was slapping my yellow wall. I rolled out of the bed and hit the floor. The lock of the building's door on Ninth Avenue was broken—breaking the lock was easier for many of the residents than it was to make a copy of their keys—so anyone off the street could just walk up the two flights to my front door without ever buzzing my intercom. I stayed beside my bed on all fours for a few more seconds before finding my land legs and slowly stumbling toward the now agitated fist. I braced myself for the worst and asked who was there.

"It's your mother" came the horrifying reply.

Ruby and Beth had been staying in my aunt's rarely used, rent-stabilized apartment on the Upper West Side, where they wheeled Peter in September after he was released from the hospital. I assumed they would have moved back to DC, a city with several world-class hospitals, but his doctors and physical therapists were here, they told me. My sister had cast herself in the role of a lifetime, complete with the cinematic backdrop of New York, nursing her fiancé down an extremely long and arduous road to recovery. My mother had opted to nurse the rest of the city, having found some purpose in the relief work. The Board of Education had given her a leave of absence, and her church in Maryland was bankrolling her missionary work on the grieving island of Manhattan.

I opened the door long enough to admit Ruby and then shut the door quickly behind her. After securing the locks, I turned to face her. This was not my mother's first visit since August, but this was the first one without a warning. I chose not to say anything; I wanted her to lead the conversation. Why was she here? I just needed a clue and I could adapt accordingly. Unfortunately, she shared my strategy.

She had the advantage when it came to armor. I was wearing only boxer shorts while Ruby wore layers of blue denim and black wool, complete with leather gloves and construction boots. She looked as if she had already fought a couple of battles and was raring to make another charge. Her red hair was pulled back, exposing her forehead, which glistened with oil. She looked like too much a madwoman to be en route to a volunteer job. I realized she had worked the night shift and was now on her way home.

I furtively peeked at the clock on the cable box to determine where I would be if I were still commuting. Not necessarily at work yet, but certainly not half-naked, pre-shower, pre–orange juice. The office was opening late today, due to fire-alarm testing, I rapidly decided in case she questioned me.

"How's it outside?" I spoke first.

She pulled her hands out of her tight gloves, looking down at her boots, answering, "The people honest with themselves are still working through their misery and fear. The others are trying to put it all behind them. They're trying to put on a happy face for the holidays, but it'll come crashing down on them in the New Year."

"I meant, does it look like it's going to rain?" Ruby shook her head, either to indicate that the sky was clear or that the subject was not worth her attention. My mouth was dry from sleep and from nerves, so I walked past her into the kitchen and quickly filled a glass of water for myself. I didn't offer her anything, because I didn't want her to stay. Behind me, I could hear her drop her gloves on the kitchen table and remove her coat. When I looked around, she was measuring the table with her arms, stepping back, studying it, moving in for more arm measurements.

"What are you up to?"

"Just thinking. What are you doing for Thanksgiving?" I hesitated too long. I had no idea how many days there were between now and Thanksgiving. Was it this Thursday or next? What was today? She hopped on the delay. "Nothing. Good. You'll host. We'll cook. This table is big enough for a buffet, but we'll have to sit in the living room. Do you have any trays?" I didn't answer, as my mind was scrambling for an out. "Well? Do you have any trays?"

"What kind of trays?"

"TV trays. For our plates. So that we don't have to eat from our laps." I shook my head. "Do you have a card table?"

"A card table? No!" I took another big sip of water, swallowed, heard my heart beginning to pound. "Who's coming to this dinner?"

"Your family, a fellow volunteer or two, Peter . . ."

"Peter can't climb the stairs. It's two flights. The staircase is too steep."

"You're right." Ruby frowned. "Then we'll have Thanksgiving at our place."

"That's a much better idea."

"Do you suddenly remember other plans?" she asked me, and I could read in her eyes that I'd fallen into some trap. I sipped at my water. "Were you invited to another fabulous dinner? Or are you going to promise to be there and then not show up?"

"I don't know what you mean," I said and threw the rest of my water into the sink.

"No? It's what you've done for three months. Business trips, crosstown traffic, late hours at the office. What else? A friend's birthday party, an emergency dental procedure. Peter's hospital is ten blocks from this apartment, and you never visited."

"The visiting hours were not . . . I tried to."

"You never tried to, Andrew. You were available if Beth or I came to you . . ." She stopped abruptly. "Our favorite act of yours by the way . . ."

"What act?"

"When we came here, you were always pulling your shoes off. As if you'd just gotten in. Once I was outside waiting for Beth for ten minutes. When we came up, you were taking your shoes off and told us you'd just gotten home. I didn't see you pass me on the street."

"I must not have seen you either."

"Andrew, please. At first, we let you rest. We understood you were tired, you were upset, but you haven't been outside your apartment in months."

This was my opportunity. My mother was the first person after Sonia to make the accusation for which I was now prepared. I had my defense ready to go, but wavered now that I was facing another inquisitor who, having spent the months feeding and cleaning a severely beaten future son-in-law, was unlikely to empathize with me. Denial still seemed the best route: "Of course I leave my apartment."

"We're not stupid, Andrew. You're not fooling anyone. Not your family, not your friends. Sonia and I spoke about this weeks ago."

"What? We need to establish some boundaries. Sonia's in my address book; she's a person from my New York life."

"How tidy it would be if we all lived in separate worlds."

"It's an issue of privacy."

"You gave us her phone number."

"When?"

"When we were looking for a nurse. She helps with Peter." I vaguely remembered this, a misguided attempt to get off the phone with my mother.

"I need to get ready for work. We're opening late, because of fire alarms." The excuse sounded false as I said it, but I needed to put on some clothes. I was too exposed. I had to cover my nipples and gird my loins. As I walked into my bedroom, she casually observed that my navel wasn't getting any smaller and then echoed her stupid theory that its size was a result of my having spent an extra three weeks cowering in her womb.

I pulled a shirt out of the dresser and took deep breaths. I wanted to convince her that I had been outside, that all was fine and that she was free to leave and go home, but when I opened my bedroom door, dressed for the office, Ruby was standing right in front of me.

"I was hoping to take you out for breakfast, Andrew."

I changed the subject. "My name is Andy." This was an ancient argument. Andy was a nickname and one that represented for her a life not taken as seriously as it should be taken. She was flabbergasted to learn that Andy was not only what I called myself but how I signed my checks. *Is that even legal?* This morning though, because we had been through this all before, she ignored my attempt at distraction and repeated her invitation.

"It just so happens I've already eaten breakfast," I answered. She walked into the kitchen and I followed her.

"There aren't any breakfast dishes in the sink. Only your water glass."

"I've washed, dried, and put them away."

From the roll of paper towels above the sink, she tore off three sheets and began to wipe the entire sink dry. I felt a chill as I watched her rub at the metal. This was not just obsessive-compulsive behavior. My mother did not like a wet sink, and since a performance of *Macbeth* in high school, I understood this was a gesture closely tied to Lady M's midnight scouring.

Point-blank, she suddenly asked, "Who brings you your groceries?"

"No one. I shop every few days."

"Sonia and I were trying to figure it out."

"Trying to figure it out? What am I, a parlor game?!"

"Your mailman brings you your mail. Sonia observed that herself."

"I have to get to work." She smiled, crossed her arms, and leaned against the sink.

"I'll walk you out," she offered. "You do know it's Saturday." She shook her head, amazed at how pathetic I was. "It smells in here." She spotted something on the refrigerator, and before I could stop her, she pounced, sending the magnet clattering to the floor and hungrily reading the page. The grocery store's phone number was listed on the piece of paper, as were the numbers for the laundry, the pharmacy, the video store, and several restaurants.

"I forgot that New York delivers everything. Isn't it expensive?" I didn't say anything. I stood by the refrigerator and hoped she would leave. "Your sister is feeding her fiancé oatmeal as we speak. It's probably dribbling down his chin as you stand here patronizing us. He can barely speak, Andrew. What happened that night?"

"I've told you."

"Two men just walked up behind you?" I nodded. "So then who are you hiding from? Who do you think is after you? Is it money? Do you owe them money? Was it drug-related?"

"Drugs?! Mother. I'd never seen them. I don't know them."

"Then why did they attack you?"

"Because that's what bigots do. They pick two men walking side by side and then they try to kill them."

"For what reason?"

"Because people are evil." I used her lingo.

"I don't accept that, Andrew."

"The Devil entered the bodies of those poor sweet souls and turned their hearts from Jesus. The Devil set them on a rampage. Or maybe Jesus, who apparently hates homosexuals . . ."

"Jesus does not hate homosexuals."

"That's what your church says."

"It says no such thing." She waved me away and sat at the table. Placing both hands flat on the surface, she looked directly in front of her, and assuming the air of a great detective, she repeated my story out loud, every detail she'd squeezed out of me since August, before she proclaimed: "It doesn't add up."

"It adds up."

"Then why aren't you leaving your apartment? You know something else. You're afraid. Of what? Of whom?"

"The world is not that complicated. It isn't a mystery, it's a gay bashing."

"Why didn't they call you any names? Besides, Peter's not gay. Why would they think he was? Were the two of you kissing?" I opened my mouth to tell her we were doing more than kissing, but she saw the look in my eye. "Don't make a joke! If you went outside, you'd know people aren't joking as much nowadays. Would you like to see Peter, Andrew? You wouldn't be joking if you saw Peter!"

How could she say that? I saw Peter. I saw Peter every day. I saw Peter's blood and urine rushing into a plastic bag. I saw his shaved scalp, his broken jaw. I heard his whimpers and the sounds of his skull thumping against iron bars. Every day.

I opened the refrigerator and pulled out a carton of orange juice.

I poured my mother a glass, placed it in front of her, and changed the subject by asking how her volunteer work was going. She took my hand before I could withdraw. She looked into my eyes and squeezed my fingers. Then she took a long drink of the juice before looking down at her knuckles, which were scraped pink. Quietly, she began to praise the construction workers at Ground Zero, "the unsung heroes," who were working in noxious air on unstable ground amid countless explosions, toppling walls, and jagged glass and steel. She capped this off with a complaint against the bureaucracy of OSHA, which was forcing the men to wear masks that hindered their view, and which was prohibiting propane heaters in the tents just in time for winter.

"Despite it all, the boys keep on." I realized that we hadn't changed the subject. This was all for me, her way of showing me what some men did as others hid inside their apartments, but I didn't rise to her challenge. "The Lord is there, Andy. I know you don't like hearing that, but the Lord is there. He's everywhere we need him to be. I'm going to leave you with that thought." I didn't respond. Ruby drained her glass and said she had to get back to the apartment to help with Peter. I scurried for her coat.

At the door, she told me she wouldn't be hosting a Thanksgiving dinner. She would be volunteering instead.

"When do you sleep?" I asked.

She smiled, her hand on my cheek. "I'd feel guilty for the luxury." She opened the door and a frozen wind blasted in over the tundra, the floor buckled, and the room filled with screams and the rubbery stench of an electrical fire. The next moment the door was closed, she was gone, and I was alone in my canary-yellow room. I peeked through the peephole and watched my mother reach the staircase and disappear down it, watched the floor eat her body in ten-inch chunks. I kept peeking through the door into the narrow, dim hallway. A wet strand of mop was curled like a noodle on a filthy brown tile that used to be green. The super always left a piece of mop behind to prove that he was fulfilling his weekly job requirement, as if the vinegary smell of the water he used wasn't proof enough.

I fell onto my couch. Exhausted. Conversations were really beginning to take it out of me—all the work projecting and decoding, concealing, confirming, dispelling, urging, resisting, making faces, and moving the mouth. It was difficult enough talking to the mailman who'd gotten more chatty over the past month, but it was impossible to interact with my mother.

A fist slammed against my door. I gasped so quickly I gagged. Tentatively, I stood up, consulted the peephole, and opened the door. I stepped to the side as Sonia barreled in with her massage table and duffel bag. She ordered me to undress. I watched as she assembled her table and began arranging her condiments. The room shrunk in the presence of her table and her personality. I did what I was told, wrapping myself in a sheet in the bedroom. When I returned, I had one question for Sonia.

"When did you talk to my mother about your little theory?"

"I will not argue with you, Andrew."

"Andrew?! Andrew?"

"I talked to your mother when I see your sister and her patient."

"Fiancé."

"Patient. He is terrible. They need much help. I am coming now to say apologies. For how you argued and how wrong you are. And it is not my concerning. You want to live in stinky apartment and dope around, that is your concerning. It is not mine, this thing. I don't have money, so I must work at this massage. I must practice so I must come here and work your back. And so I am sorry. You have terrible life."

I thanked her for her kind and gracious apology.

"And hold on to your sheet. I try to make apologies yesterday to Brad Willet. I want him to know I changed my mind long time ago. I see my CD and I see years of massage and I think I have nothing to lose. Nothing! I call, say sorry, I make CD. Or I call, say sorry, and hang up. Nothing to lose. His phone is not there anymore, so I go to his apartment. I am to be in person."

I sat on the arm of the couch and waited for what she had to say.

"And Brad Willet does not live anymore in that 6B."

"He moved?"

"Yes. I think he moves out of city. And that is why I don't see him. Since June he is gone. Marta Sanders does not see him. Andrea Burns does not see him. He is not at cabaret, he is not at theater. In summer people ask me where Brad Willet is and I am not thinking much. Then 9/11 no one is knowing where anyone is. Last night I come to do shots with many who know him. One says Brad is in Finland."

"Finland? Why would he be in Finland?"

She shrugged, "We were drinking shots. And there are rumors. Natalie, you know, the very pretty singer who is very fat, she tells me you died on 9/11. I say this is not true. I know Andy is living. He is just crazy."

"Thanks."

"And Brad is not here. No one is seeing him. Months. He is not in the Big Apple. Whatever it is, he is gone. Maybe he is in Finland. Again we are on other sides of ocean. But I am not going to try cabaret in Helsinki. Get on your stomach."

I obeyed, and Sonia began to knead my back. What this information meant to me was that, if I stepped outside, I wasn't going to run
into Brad Willet on the street. I wasn't sure if I was relieved or disappointed.

"And I do not know why your body is so tight. You don't see or do
things. In my body you would know tight. You have no reason for
tight."

I told Sonia that I doubted any of her future clients would appreciate having their stress levels compared with hers. They prefer sym-
pathy and expect their masseuse will believe in their pain and rub,
squeeze, and knuckle that pain away.

"And this game they are playing, what am I getting?"

"Money, Sonia. It's a job. That's why you're doing it."

"Money! Money, money, money, always money."

"As well as the satisfaction that you've helped another human
being."

"Okay, okay, I try this."

"Good."

After a few moments, she said, "I want Porfiry to die painful,
painful death."

"That's not soothing, Sonia."

"And I am just not in good mood." She told me that on the way
over she passed the firehouse that lost the most men on the eleventh.
She said there were still flowers, bunting and signs, letters, and pictures covering the walls. She said that theatergoers on their way to
the matinees were stopping and taking photographs of the firemen.
"With jelly eyes." Then she said she walked by a phone booth and
saw a MISSING flyer. November, and they were still being taped at
eye level. Did the tapers still think their loved one was just missing?

Sonia stopped inexplicably to take the flyer in. There were two photos of a smiling young woman—in socks in front of a Christmas tree
and on a motorboat with a drink in her hand. Sonia considered it
questionable to advertise the loved one "boozing up," but then
cringed when she saw in the girl's eyes how much fun she was having. How much fun she had once had. Sonia leaned into the flyer
and read the type beneath the photo. She and the girl had been born
on the exact same day. Sonia was alive and the girl with the drink
was MISSING. Sonia stood on the sidewalk and cried.

Sonia massaged in silence for a few minutes, but inevitably spoke
again. She told me that sometimes she felt that she was massaging
the island of Manhattan itself. In this case, Central Park would run
up the lower spine, Ground Zero would be in the left Achilles ten-
don. I thought this site-specific shiatsu was a terrible idea. I was
afraid Sonia would poke my emotion with her thumb.

My mind always went right back to the two boys in the subway
showing pictures of their mother to the news camera. The reporter
kept badgering the oldest, trying to get him to talk about the last
conversation he had with his mom. The boy admitted they'd had a
fight that morning, and he began to sob. The reporter pushed him
out of the way, pulled the younger boy closer, and asked, "What were
the last words your mom said to *you*?" Where were those boys now?
How would all these people make it through? On the afternoon of
the eleventh, I heard my next-door neighbors with their extended
Ecuadorian family cheer uproariously, and I couldn't fathom why anyone in their right minds would be cheering until the mailman told
me a week later that they had all been waiting for the girl who went
to school near the towers; she walked all the way home, and what I
had heard was her family screaming with joy when she appeared.

I tried to keep my mind away from these. I concentrated instead on the mop noodle on the floor in the hall. I focused on it, contemplated its texture, inhaled its saturated grime as Sonia continued to push at me.

"And some days I just cannot take it. Cannot see how people can shop for holidays. And sometimes I feel like I'm only one who is thinking of that day. Afraid to bring it up. I am afraid people will say: *Stop talking of this!*"

That's exactly what I wanted to say. I let her finish in silence and was relieved ten minutes later when she packed up her stuff and left. I locked the door behind her. She had squeezed my body into a rock. She brought the city into my apartment and packed its misery into every pore. I took a shower with the hottest water I could stand. When I stepped out of the tub, down to the floor, my body was bright red. Too soft, too tender. I had scorched the outer layer of my skin, scrubbed off all the dead cells and let them drain away. Before I finished drying, there was another knock on the door. Again I was terrified, now naked and vulnerable. I wrapped the towel around my waist and tiptoed to the peephole. There was my sister in her urban costume: a shawl of muted tones elegantly wrapped around her shoulders; a red FDNY baseball cap perched unevenly atop her head.

"I see your shadow in the hole," she informed me. "Let me in. There are roaches out here." I took a breath, turned the locks, and opened the door. As I peered past her into the flickering darkness of the hallway, Beth gave me a kiss on both cheeks, another of her new metropolitan habits, and pushed inside. I shut the door. She asked, "Are all three locks necessary?"

"Well, I don't have a doorman like you do."

"Put on your clothes, Andy. I'm taking you shopping."

"Taking me shopping?"

"Mom said if I can get you outside, I can use her credit card to charge outfits for both of us."

I ignored the first, more potent, part of her sentence and said, "I don't need an outfit, Beth."

"At least shoes. You can never have enough shoes."

"Yes, I can."

"Do you only wear towels now? Come on! I only have a couple hours free."

"I can't go shopping," I told her, and she slowly shook her head.

"Andy, we gave you space. When we really could have used your help."

"I'm sorry."

"It's agoraphobia, right? That's what you have?"

"I don't *have* anything. I just prefer not to be outside." Here was another opportunity, but I just said, "I don't interact well with others. Leaving my apartment turned out to be the first mistake of my daily routine, so . . . I changed my routine." Beth didn't look satisfied. "So what? It's not a crime. There are places, very cold places, like Canada, where people stay inside during the winters. No one stages an intervention for them. They go to work and they come straight home. Well, I work out of my home, so I just stay home. Big deal."

"This isn't Canada and it's not winter."

"I don't need to go outside. That's all I'm saying."

"Food?"

"They deliver."

"The bank?"

"Direct deposit."

"What about cash?"

"I call a restaurant, I give them my credit card, they make cash for a fee and send it with a delivery boy."

"What about sex?"

"What about it?"

"Do you have people over?"

"Absolutely not."

"So then you take matters into your own hand?" Beth smiled slyly in the manner of one of her heroines on *Sex and the City*, her favorite television show—hence the sex talk, the shopping, the shawl, the never having enough shoes. I didn't answer. Beth rolled her eyes and waved me away. While my mother was disappointed that I was gay, Beth was disappointed that I wasn't gay enough. Since arriving in August, she'd been on the lookout for a gay sidekick, and resented that her brother was never available.

"So everything you need is here in your apartment?" I nodded. "How about an exercise machine? You're getting pudgy." She reached out to poke my stomach, and I jumped backward, surprising us both.

Beth recovered. "If you're not going to take advantage of what the city has to offer, you might as well go rent a cabin in the middle of the woods. Cheaper."

"True, and I'd probably have fewer guests." I told her it was hard to retreat from society when people kept popping by.

"So why are you retreating from society?" she asked. She sat down, unwrapping herself, pulling off her cap and placing her things on the sofa.

"I'm not the first. I'm following a long tradition."

"Like the Unabomber?"

"It's not crazy."

"I didn't say it was. Who are the people in this tradition?" I wanted to step into my office and retrieve my notes, but knew my argument would be more effective without them.

"Well, for one, there's Gulliver."

"Who?"

"Lemuel Gulliver. Timon of Athens. Alceste. The Underground Man. The Invisible Man. Raskolnikov . . ."

"Are those real people?"

"They're in books, but they're . . ."

"What about *real* people?"

"I'm trying to show there's literary precedent."

"Literary precedent? What does that mean? Because it happened in a book? That's like saying, um, saying . . ." I watched as Beth squinted at the ceiling in search of an example. "Like I'm going to go to Wizard School."

There was another knock on the door. I was thrilled. Anything to rescue me from this line of interrogation. I approached the door for the fourth time that morning and looked through the peephole: dark, curly hair, a trimmed beard and mustache, glasses, and a head set forward on his neck, his body hunched beneath a book bag. It was Sonia's friend, Rod Hamilton. The tour guide. He waved at my eye, and I was forced to admit him. I shut the door behind him but turned only one lock, to indicate that this would be a brief visit.

Beth, taking in the new arrival and the fact that I was wearing only a towel, said, "Oh, I'm sorry, boys. I should be going."

"No, Beth." I glared at her and shook my head. I could see that she was again let down. What was the point in his being gay, she seemed to wonder. "Rod, this is my sister, Beth; Beth, this is Rod

Hamilton, a friend of Sonia's." I stressed this last phrase for Rod's benefit. I never socialized with Rod without Sonia. The first time we were alone was when he came to my place shortly after the attack in August.

They shook hands, and he dropped three books on the coffee table. "I brought these by. I thought you might like them."

"Ooo," Beth said, leaning forward. "I've been looking for a new book."

Rod baffled me. I never considered him a friend of mine, and because of the scholarship fallout, I deeply resented his existence. If Rod hadn't been so negative that night and just accepted the shitty award Brad was offering, then I wouldn't have been obliged to propose the Andy Green Academic Scholarships. Since Rod first showed up at my door in August, I tried my best to make him pay, but the ruder I was, the more he visited, and now he was taking an unoffered seat while I glanced at the covers of the books in Beth's hands.

I asked, "Why would I like these?"

"Might cheer you up." Each book chronicled a different disaster in New York history. I stared at Rod and waited for the explanation. He reasoned that each was a testament to our resilience. We had faced other insurmountable traumas, but soon forgot that they ever happened. He mentioned a bomb blast on Wall Street in 1920, which killed thirty-eight, and asked me if I knew of the *Slocum*, an excursion boat that burned in the East River and killed over a thousand, mainly women and children. I didn't. He asked me how much I knew of the Civil War Draft Riots. I told him I wasn't an expert. He hoped that we learned from our disasters and lived with the lesson, not the tragedy. The *Slocum*, for example: live with the improved safety standards, but not with the images of children washing up on shore. "It's best for us all. If we keep moving forward. In history and in our own personal lives."

"Absolutely," Beth affirmed. "See, Andy? There. We should keep moving forward."

I ignored her and kept my gaze on Rod. All of what he said was trite, but there was something in the way he said it: slowly, as if we were two of his tourists, and with great precision, as if he was trying to say something more.

Beth said, "I doubt September eleventh will be forgotten."

"In one sense, it already is. I was with a tour group yesterday, and I had to walk them past all the T-shirts, hats, photographs, tchotchkes being sold. 9/11: WE WILL NEVER FORGET. Mass-produced sentiment. Hallmark's first great tragedy. A mother and daughter in my group posed for a picture. In front of Ground Zero! The daughter pushed her hair over her ear and the two smiled. They were standing with charred buildings in the background and smiling and posing like they were at Niagara Falls. Smoke was rising from the demolition and the smell was so strong you could taste it."

I told Rod that it was extremely disturbing, and by that I meant that he shouldn't talk anymore.

"They also bought a bunch of hats. Why are all the tourists wearing NYPD and FDNY shirts and hats? Isn't this offensive?" I noticed Beth reaching behind her to cover her cap with her shawl. "People are buying them for their families and friends. People too scared to come to New York are wearing shirts of people who died for New York. It's for a good cause, they say. So just give the money. You're not a cop or a fireman. You have no right to wear their clothes."

Beth said, "Well, they're our heroes."

"No, they're not."

"They're not?"

"We're not treating them as heroes. We're just throwing five bucks on a table and wearing their hats. A hero is someone we emulate. We hold them up and imitate them, follow them, take inspiration in their acts and perform heroic acts of our own. Like Aeneas carrying his father out of burning Troy or like Jean Valjean . . ."

"Who and who?" Beth asked.

"Literary precedent," I said, a little too loudly.

Rod continued, "We should at least live our lives in a way that would honor them and earn their respect. Instead we say, 'Oh, I love the police and firemen, they're so brave. Let me buy a hat.'"

"For the people back at home afraid to come to New York," Beth said.

"Afraid to leave their town, afraid to leave their house. People talk pejoratively of Osama bin Laden hiding in his caves, but where are they? Too scared to come out of their living rooms, burrowed just as deep and with far less reason."

Beth again looked at me and said, "He's got you in a nutshell."

"Well, Rod, it's a good thing you give tours then. It's your job to make sure people won't forget the history."

He leaned forward. "I don't let people forget my *version* of history."

"Oh, right. Remember the lessons, forget the sorrow."

He looked into my eyes and said, "We need to move on. I've always believed that. We all have something we wish would be forgotten."

"I have multiple things," Beth said.

Rod did not take his eyes off me, and I stared back at him.

Everything he said seemed so heavy with meaning. What was wrong with him? I always felt I was missing something, a legend to navigate the conversation. Perhaps he was high. Powder, pills? Did he shoot up? Had I ever seen him in short sleeves? I nodded to break off the glaring contest, and Rod stood, danced into his backpack. To my surprise and pleasure, Beth also stood to leave, wrapping herself in her shawl, her FDNY hat stuffed behind a couch pillow.

"So no shopping?" Beth asked me.

"Not today."

Rod asked Beth where she was planning to go, and she began listing some stores that were not at all near each other. I reached through them to undo the lock and opened the door.

Rod turned to me and took my hand in the kind of handshake where the knuckles and thumb point upward, where the elbow bends and the grip is brought up to the sternum: "So we're cool then?"

So we're cool then? Cool? The light in the hall was pulsating.

Without thinking, I said, "Yeah, we're cool." With that, I freed my hand and shut the door on them both.

Their voices receded down the hallway and staircase.

"My mother and I are staying on the Upper West Side."

"Oh, the Upper West Side. Bloemendaal, the Valley of Flowers."

"Oh, my God! You must know everything . . ."

Why was I letting myself be provoked by these emissaries from the wrong side of the door? This was my home; I was master. I picked up Rod's books, with their bombings and fires and drownings and lynchings and riots and mourning which I was supposed to apply, like assigned homework, to the terror that was now called Ground Zero, and dumped them into the garbage can in the kitchen. I pushed the lid off, lifted the bag, twisting it and knotting it up in its own neck. Why should I explain myself to these people? I wasn't hurting anyone. I opened my door and dropped the bag of trash on the doormat, grimy from the dirt these visitors had wiped from their shoes.

MY BOSS CALLED THE first week in December, her voice full of concern but with a reserve that hinted there were others in her office, witnessing and perhaps advising her through my termination. When I told her that both Peter and I were recovering but that I still wasn't ready just yet to work in an office environment, she began a statement which she was obviously reading. While everyone understood the physical and emotional trauma associated with the attack, they'd hoped for a speedier recovery and return. It was important that her employees spend the better part of their working hours in the office. I interrupted her when she mentioned "face time" to tell her that my current productivity far exceeded my past performance, because I wasn't wasting any valuable time looking at people's faces.

She reminded me that my job involved much more than the

drafting of multiple choice tests. "Of which, frankly, we have far too many."

"You can never have too many," I countered, and I must have been on speaker phone, because at this point I heard the others in her office gasp.

My boss said kindly, if not fearfully, "You sent enough questions for us to administer a different test to every individual student in the country for the next two years." I didn't argue. I was too nervous. This was the work that had kept my hands and mind busy for almost four months, and they were shutting down production. "We're worried about you."

How would I fill my days without work? I couldn't sleep in any later than I already did or take any more naps. As it was, I watched television for only an hour a day, which was enough now that scrolling headlines on the bottom of the screen left no grief untold. If a bus overturned in Mozambique, killing four, I heard about it. For most of the day, I left the television draped with a blanket. I couldn't read a newspaper for more than five minutes, because every story seemed linked somehow to skyscrapers, rebuilding, airlines, rescue, sickness, death, unemployment, and Ground Zero. Other reading material was difficult to get through, because everything seemed either too irrelevant or too timely. I tried to read the Koran at one point, but I had to keep putting it down with the same mild astonishment I felt when I read the Bible—adults were taking these books literally. I tried to learn other languages but always gave up as soon as I had to conjugate verbs. How much easier would it be to learn a foreign language if people didn't move around or do anything? Any hobby I tried to pick up was usually exhausted within a couple of days, but my mind would drift outside the door whenever I was idle. What would I do without my job?

"Andy? Andy?" I heard my former employer ask.

It was difficult for me to get the words out. "Are you going to stop paying me?" There was a silence on the other end of the line while words were mouthed and fingers presumably held up.

She gave the offer: "We can pay you until the end of the year and then we'll help arrange for unemployment benefits. You should call today and see what you need to do to avoid a lapse between checks."

"That's great advice," I said. I thanked them and then hung up, an unemployed recluse who, though poorer, could still sustain my solitude for several more months. I didn't call the Department of Labor that day. Instead, I continued designing multiple choice tests. Without the paycheck, I was now free to enter another realm, more abstract and hypothetical. I began keeping journals—various legal pads with different headings strewn throughout my apartment—and spent a substantial amount of time pursuing the white whale of the multiple-choice waters: the spelling test. This is exceedingly tricky, because the test taker can see the word. In this puzzle, you cannot write: "How do you spell the vegetable that is orange and popular with rabbits?" You are also prevented from using different font types or other optical illusions. The closest I came to harpooning the leviathan was by concealing the word in the middle, overwhelming the test taker with redundancy, and playing against an old spelling mnemonic (in this case, *i* before *e*, except after *c*). *How do you spell "neither"? (A) niether, (B) neither, (C) niether, (D) niether, or (E) A, C, and D.* Was I losing my mind? No more than anybody solving a crossword puzzle or working on a word search, I told myself. Or playing solitaire.

Two friends from work, probably sent by our nervous supervisor, came by to see how I was, but fell victim to my new visitor policy: no one was permitted to stop by without calling first. I gave the mailman and all the delivery people a password; if someone knocked on my door without uttering it, I completely ignored the door. I initiated this after Ruby began assaulting me with her fellow volunteer grief counselors who no doubt saw me as a rewarding opportunity. From all reports, the number of missionaries on Manhattan had exploded after September eleventh, all churches knowing that the best time for conversion is in childhood or in moments of great distress. My mother's colleagues probably thought there were things I would say to them that I wouldn't say to her. I ignored them; eventually they walked away. The only visitors admitted in December were my mother and sister and, of course, Sonia, who never met a closed door she didn't try to crack in half.

● ● ●

SONIA'S LAST VISIT TOOK place shortly after I was fired. She came without the massage table, which I vowed never to roll onto again. We sat at the kitchen table. She was there to ask a favor, but began with chatter, raging a bit against a recent fling and claiming to be through with love forever. She spoke passionately against romance and the sacrifice that came with it. I asked her how she would sing cabaret if she felt such contempt for love, but she told me to leave that to her. Which brought us to her favor. She had a Christmas Eve gig. I assumed she wanted me to e-mail her usual suspects, but no, it was an out-of-town job in Wheeling, West Virginia.

"Really?"

"It is only one song in variety show."

"How did you land that?"

"And there are words of mouth. This woman calls. An aficionado. She calls all over America. It is mainly those singers . . . those singers who sing through their nose . . . but I am paid and I am traveled and I say yes." Sonia elaborated by pointing out that there were many people afraid to come to New York, so they were now hiring New York's talent to come to them. "And you are not the only one hiding."

I asked, "So what are you going to sing?"

" 'Love for Sale.' "

I didn't laugh, which I later considered troubling, because in my earlier state of mind I would have at least smiled on hearing that during a Christmas Eve concert in West Virginia, between fiddlers and yodelers, Sonia was going to croon the weary lament of an urban prostitute.

"And so this is my favor of you."

"Of me?"

"I want you to escort me."

"Oh, Sonia . . ."

"I want you to drive me. I am very bad driver and besides this I am desiring company into the heartland." Sonia was sitting across from me so peacefully. Her hands were folded on the table, waiting for my reply. I forgot to breathe. I felt sweat break out on my forehead.

"I can't drive you," I said with a suddenly parched mouth. I stood up and poured myself a glass of water.

"And why?"

"Sonia, you know why. For obvious reasons. You have other friends."

"And it's Christmas and they have plans. Or they don't drive."

"What about your sponsor who's helping you with your green card application?"

"I ask too much already."

"Can't you fly?"

"Fly?!" she screamed, shocked at the suggestion. "And you are wanting for me to do hand-to-hand battle with terrorists?" I didn't answer. I drank my water. Sonia tried to express how important this was to her confidence, explaining that this was the first gig since breaking it off with Brad and she needed to know if she remembered how to perform in front of an audience. She started talking about her grandfather again, and I remembered our afternoon in Central Park when we sat side by side at Turtle Pond, conjoined in misery, supporting each other through jokes.

"I want to help you, Sonia. Really, but. Could I do anything on the computer?"

"Drive me to Wheeling."

"Publicity?"

"Drive me to Wheeling."

"I could e-mail the theater and see if anyone from New York is driving down there." I moved toward my office, but Sonia slowly shook her head.

"Drive me to Wheeling."

"I could look up train rates, bus rates, and schedules. I really, really want to help, but I can't. I just can't do that."

"But that is what I need."

"I'm sorry," I said with genuine remorse, which she met with a look of genuine contempt. I avoided her eyes until she finally stood up.

"I cannot count on you. And then this is over."

"What's over?"

"This. You and me. I give all to you, you give nothing to me. I am ennobling you to coming here and giving you news and massage."

"You mean *enabling*."

"I mean what I mean." She took my hand, shook it, threw it down, and passed out of the kitchen and through the living room. I heard her open my door without any confusion over the three locks. I entered the living room to see her standing in the doorway. "And I will see you outside. Never again here. Never again here." She closed the door, and I heard her slowly descend the staircase. She hadn't stormed out; she hadn't slammed the door, which meant that very possibly she meant it this time. I almost called after her to wait, but she would have just shouted up the stairs, "Drive me to Wheeling." So instead I sat down with a legal pad and tried feverishly to occupy myself with other problems. *Which best describes the color red? (A) maroon, (B) crimson, (C) magenta, (D) scarlet, (E) brick red.* (Answer: *D* or *B* . . . maybe *E*.)

● ● ●

THE FINAL TRIAL OF the year took place on Christmas morning when, after taking a deep breath, I pulled open the door on my mother and sister who stood there bearing gifts and holiday cheer, which I tried to top: "Welcome! Merry Christmas!" I shouted to them, through them, into the hallway, down the stairs, and out the front door. Beth looked at me sideways, but Ruby returned the sentiment as they entered and I closed the door behind them. This time I was ready for them with presents—the first two seasons of *Sex and the City* on DVD for Beth, three books on card tricks for Peter, and a new winter coat complete with hat and gloves for Ruby—ordered online and delivered two days earlier, wrapped with elaborate bows and sitting in a pile on the coffee table, next to the plate of breakfast muffins and three mugs to be filled with either eggnog or hot chocolate. All of it was defiant proof that I was functioning quite nicely and didn't need their grief counselors or a shopping spree in SoHo. I hung up their coats in the closet near the door as Beth arranged the gifts on the floor and Ruby went to the kitchen to wash her hands in the sink.

From the floor, Beth asked, "How's your rejection of society going?"

"Fine, thank you," I answered, gesturing toward the gifts and the muffins and the mugs, as if to say, *See.*

"It smells like feet in here. So why don't you open this one first?" She handed me what turned out to be a box of sandalwood incense sticks. I thanked her and she suggested I set a few of them ablaze.

"I don't have any holders," I said and was promptly given my next three gifts. Beth set out my holders and, using a lighter, started filling my rooms with smoke. Ruby reentered and began filling the mugs with hot chocolate. Months of nursing Peter and volunteering in the recovery had made them an efficient team, but this was not abiding by my new policy: "Mom, Beth, why don't I take care of the drinks and smells?"

"All done," Beth said.

"Me too," said Ruby.

"You're my guests, so just sit and let's . . . be merry." Ruby sat on the couch, I sat beside her to serve the muffins, and Beth nestled back into her spot on the floor. We ate and periodically opened the presents that Beth took it upon herself to hand us. I led the discussion so as to keep it focused on the muffins, the temperature of the hot chocolate, the quality of the gift wrapping. I was successful until I opened up my final gift from my mother: *Portraits of Grief,* an oversized hardcover book published by the *New York Times,* which was the compilation of photographs and obituaries they had been running for months in a special section dedicated to the individuals who died in Lower Manhattan on September eleventh. I didn't know what to say. Was this a coffee table book? Did people leave obituaries out for guests to peruse? My mother's only explanation was "Each night I read a few of them before bed."

"Thank you," I said and set to clearing the dishes.

"Let me do them," Ruby said and took them from me. She withdrew into the kitchen to do the dishes and dry the sink. I sat down and stared at the cover of the book.

Beth said, "It's taking its toll, Andy. Everything is taking its toll on her." Ruby did look the worse for wear. Her hair was still without gray, and sensibly trimmed, but her eyes were puffy, she'd lost weight, and her forehead was developing creases only fishermen had. Recently, as I closed my door behind her, I felt like Peter must have felt closing the door to the magic vanishing box, except that my door closed on the world, so when I reopened it, instead of a lovely assistant in sequins stepping over the threshold with a smile and a wave, the fatigued wounded fell forward, aged and scarred. Every time my mother came in from outside, she looked more battered.

"I think we should try to get her back to Maryland," Beth proposed.

"I agree completely. I've been thinking that for months. Why are the three of you still here?"

"Well, Peter's doctors . . ."

"Oh, come on."

"We have a routine that works and I'm not ready to go yet."

"Mom won't leave, Beth, unless you go back with her. You should all go back."

"Why do you want us out so badly?"

When I didn't answer, Beth stared up at the ceiling. I wanted to tell her that I longed for them to leave because I wasn't safe to be around. Look what I did to her fiancé. I didn't want my family in New York because I didn't want anything else to happen to them. It wasn't just for my safety that I locked myself inside this apartment. It was for the safety of others. It was a philanthropic gesture and maybe the greatest gift I'd ever given.

"Unemployment!?" Ruby's voice sounded from the kitchen. Suddenly she was standing in the doorway, holding a letter.

I asked, "Why are you rummaging through my mail?"

Ruby brushed that aside. "You lost your job?" I didn't answer. "There's no reason you should be on unemployment. You have resources. You're educated; you're healthy. Are you looking for a job?"

"Mom, let's not spoil Christmas."

"Are you sending out résumés, Andrew? Are you going for interviews?"

"Sure. Yes." Ruby and Beth looked at each other. "I am!"

"Put on your coat," my mother instructed. "We're going for a walk right now."

"What?"

"You are leaving this apartment right now."

"No, I'm not."

"Beth, get his jacket."

Beth, sitting on the sofa, legs crossed and hands folded in her lap, said simply, "This is my one morning off."

"Andrew, get your coat."

"You can't tell me what to do anymore. I'm almost thirty years old."

"Well, act like it!" she cried. Beth and I both shrunk from her. "There are people out there who have it so much worse than you do. Did you know that?"

"This isn't about anyone else. It's *my* life."

"Well, it's hit bottom." She looked at the letter again. "*Andy* Green?! This is made out to *Andy* Green." She gaped at me in pure disbelief. "You're almost thirty. No one ever took Andy Green seriously and no one ever will."

"Jesus."

"Don't!" my mother warned me against the blasphemy.

"Do we have to have the same conversation over and over and over?"

I could see her hands trembling, but I was unsteady as well in the face of this intervention: "I'm begging you to please leave me alone. This is my life."

Beth, from absolutely nowhere, said, "Andrew Green is a prestigious name. Well, it is. Andrew Green was the treasurer of Central Park and he led the drive to turn the boroughs into the city of New York." Mystified, Ruby and I just stared at her. "You know, like Brooklyn, Manhattan, Queens . . ."

I turned back toward my mother, and any pity I might have been feeling a few minutes earlier vanished. Again and again she barged into my rooms, nagging and berating me, accusing me and drying my sink; now here she was, threatening to drag me out of my apartment in an attempt to get me to change my name and control my life.

I blurted out, "This city is my home. Not yours!"

"What do you mean by that?"

"I mean . . . I came here ten years ago to put three hundred miles between you and me. You make me nervous and you always have."

Ruby's eyes spontaneously filled with tears. Neither Beth nor I had ever seen her cry. She started to chew her lower lip, and I took an apologetic step toward her. She quickly threw the letter on the floor, grabbed her purse, her coat, and went to the door, leaving her gifts behind. I didn't move. She turned locks and pulled at the knob, turned more locks and pulled at the knob, and finally found the right combination that freed her from the apartment and sent her out with a slam.

Beth looked at me, "That was very good, Andy. Thank you."

"I'm sorry, but she makes me feel like a child."

"Andy, you're an adult now. You don't have to feel like anything you don't want to. It's in your head."

Beth found her coat and pulled it from the hanger. "I'll go after her." Sarcastically, she added, "You stay here."

"I will."

She looked into my eyes and said, "We can't really count on you, can we, Andy?" She left, closing the door behind her. I wish I could say that I flung the door open and shouted that she was wrong and that I was ready to come outside and be a reliable brother, son, friend, and citizen, suddenly strong enough to walk straight to the Upper West Side and pitch in with Peter before renting a car and driving to Wheeling, West Virginia, where I would find Sonia and drive her back to the city where I would donate blood and find a job and raise money for scholarships, but I didn't do anything but turn the locks on my door.

WHAT FOLLOWED WAS A dark winter, two missing, irretrievable months. There is little to share from my waking hours, but there was a recurring dream I should have paid more attention to. A part of my brain was trying to tell me something.

I am sitting at a school desk in space, high above the earth, close to the moon, in a large examination room without walls or floor. There are rows of test takers stretching toward every planet; winged teaching assistants glide up and down the aisles. I have to answer only one question on this exam. My fate will be decided by my response to this one last multiple choice question. There is no time limit; I sit pondering for hours. When morning arrives, I settle on an answer and approach the table at the front of the room with my final answer.

"Well?" the ultimate proctor patiently asks.

I reply, "The answer is C."

"Are you certain?"

"Yes. Absolutely."

"I'm sorry, that's incorrect. The answer is *None of the above.*"

None of the above?!

"That wasn't an option!" I object. "That's not even down here."

"No." He chuckles. "It's not. It rarely is."

● ● ●

"HELLO, I'M CALLING FOR Andy Green," a voice greeted my answering machine on March fifth. "My name is Drew Sprouse, and I'm calling from the Sheraton Manhattan on Seventh Avenue. I'm embarrassed to say there's a package here for you that's been sitting in our hotel for several months. It was left here on August tenth by a Brad Willet. There was a call put out that day, but I don't see a followup note. Our number here at the hotel . . ."

I couldn't hear anything else. I was scrambling to locate the phone, underneath or behind all of the garbage, legal pads, loose notes, magazines, dirty clothes, throw pillows, and towels. I found the phone on top of the refrigerator and pressed the TALK button just before he disconnected.

"I'm here. I'm Andy Green."

"I can barely hear you," he said. I hadn't spoken much that winter.

"I'm here! I'm Andy Green!"

"My name is Drew Sprouse . . ."

"I heard that. Why did it take you seven months to call?"

"I apologize, but we've been serving as the temporary offices for Lehman Brothers who were displaced on 9/11. We're only now re-opening as a hotel."

"This still doesn't make sense. A friend of mine stopped by your hotel back in August and there was no package."

"I'm holding it in my hand."

"Really?"

"Are you sure he went to the right Sheraton?" he asked, and my head began to throb.

"What do you mean, the right Sheraton?" I thought there was only one.

"This is the Sheraton Manhattan. The other property is the Sheraton New York."

"Which is yours?"

"Manhattan."

"Where are you?"

"Seventh Avenue between Fifty-first and Fifty-second."

"That's the one."

"Yes, but Sheraton New York is on Seventh Avenue also. Between Fifty-second and Fifty-third."

"What?" I had never noticed. "The one I'm thinking of is on the east side of Seventh near the Hilton."

"That's the Sheraton New York."

That's where I sent Peter. "Where's the other one?"

"On the west side one block south."

"Which is yours?" I asked again.

"That one. Manhattan, the one on the west side."

"You've got to be kidding me. There are two Sheratons with the same name one block away from each other . . ."

"No, no, no. One is Manhattan and one is New York."

"That's the same name!"

"They're different properties. If you stayed at the Sheratons you'd . . ."

"I live here! I don't stay in hotels."

"Mr. Green, I am very sorry for the confusion, but the package is still here if you care to pick it up. I hope it wasn't timely."

"Could you please describe it?"

"It's a ten-by-thirteen envelope."

"Could you open it?"

"It's marked *Personal.* It feels like there are papers inside."

"That's all? Papers?"

"Feels like it. I'm on until ten tonight. Can you come by?"

"No." Then I shocked myself. "Tomorrow morning. I will be by tomorrow morning." This must have sounded like an overly dramatic declaration, because Drew Sprouse laughed nervously. He told me he was going to leave it behind the desk with an extra-large Post-it note. I hung up the phone.

A package I formerly dismissed as irrelevant in the scheme of my past year suddenly took on overwhelming significance. I wondered why. Was it because the package had sat in the hotel for seven long months? If so, that had nothing to do with its contents and everything to do with my ignorance. Or was it because the package was left there on the tenth of August, the same day Peter and I were attacked? Was that just a coincidence? Maybe the violence of the tenth had a reason and the package could explain it. At the very least, the package might provide a reason why Brad disappeared from my life and, if Sonia was right, from New York City.

Was it that easy though? Could I just leave? Could I simply put on my coat, slip into shoes, tie the laces, find my keys, and go? No. It was late, and it was beginning to feel too much like August all over again for me to venture out into the dark side streets lined with pear trees and swarming with strangers.

I was sitting on the arm of my couch, taking in my cluttered apartment with its stacks and piles, all of which was now suspect. I picked up one of the notepads and flipped it open. My barely legible scrawl filled the pages, ran up the margins. On one page was a critique of a documentary on the Mormons I had seen during the Olympics. *Not only do they believe in a literal Garden of Eden but they believe it was in Missouri. How are these people not institutionalized? Tabernacles full of crazies. They say they're committed; they should be.* I flipped through the rest of the notepad—there were lists of my favorite foods ranked on a scale from one to ten, a betting game I was playing with myself about which delivery person would show up with my lunch, bleak financial calculations, sexual fantasies with which I must have been doing something, pages filled with ways terrorists could bring New York to its knees and on which I'd written CLASSIFIED, an occasional abstract multiple choice, a sketch of my kitchen table, a couple of rough drafts of nasty letters I'd sent off to restaurants, a television network, and a congressman from Oklahoma. I grabbed every legal pad I could find and dumped them in the bottom of my front closet. The pile rose over two feet high. I threw a blanket over this tower of lunacy and shut the closet.

I walked into my bathroom and looked in the mirror, consulting a harried freak who stared back at me. My beard was so old and unkempt I couldn't find my jawline. My hair was long in the back and the bangs were uneven, cut with the same scissors I used to clip out news articles and magazine photos. I decided to shave. I stripped, dropping my clothes as I moved through the apartment. I found a *Time Out* magazine, fingered the staples open and carpeted the bathroom floor with the pages. I started cutting. The soles of my feet were sticking to the glossy magazine pages, and I remembered my sandals from August and how they stuck to the city's hot tar as I walked with Peter toward the Sheraton. If I had sent him to the right Sheraton that afternoon, we never would have been walking along Fifty-first Street that night. We would not have been attacked. I filled my palm with shaving cream, a giant melting marshmallow, and then smeared it over my neck, face, and crown. I reached for the razor and thought about the past year as I scraped the metal over my skin, deliberately against the grain on my throat, carelessly over the bumps on the back of my head.

I recalled a spring weekend a decade earlier, when I was still up at college. It was daylight savings time, and I'd forgotten to set my clock forward. I was too busy studying to notice that there wasn't a crowd at dinner or that the stores had closed earlier than usual. I thought I was early for my quiz the next morning as I crossed an empty campus. I was looking forward to going over my notes one last time and was stunned to see my classmates turning in their blue books and gathering up their bags when I arrived. I took my seat at the seminar table and pulled out my notes. The teacher made a joke that I was better late than never. I laughed at the joke, but I didn't get it. She told me I could reschedule and then left. Students from the next class walked into the room, and the more of them that entered, the less I felt like I belonged. I ran into a friend on the way out who told me what time it was, and I felt that I was behind the clock for the rest of the day. It was amazing what one hour's confusion did to me.

This, my life now, was so much worse. I was more than two hundred days behind.

I put the razor back in the medicine cabinet and took a look at myself in the mirror. Above my shoulders, I was wet and shiny. My neck, cheek, and the top of my head were streaked with blood, which reminded me of Peter and of August. I splashed my head and face with a painful aftershave and dabbed my head with a wad of toilet paper before sticking Band-Aids over the cuts. Wounded upon leaving the world, wounded upon returning.

For the first time since September, I entered my bedroom and gently tugged at the hem of one of the blinds. The vinyl loudly flapped into its roll, and I took a startled step backward as my existence suddenly expanded by miles. There was a sky again, though currently dark. The streets were lit by lamps and headlights, neon glowed above storefronts, and incandescence spilled through windows onto sidewalks. Not much had changed on Ninth Avenue, but there were more American flags than I remembered, and the Afghani restaurant across the street seemed to stand out now. The people of Hell's Kitchen looked harmless enough, though I made it a point to stay out of sight as I observed them all coming home, going out, meeting friends, reading menus, getting drunk, and planning for tomorrow, when I would be out there among them.

I felt dizzy, but I had no choice: I had to start over.

SOMEWHERE IN THE PALM of Michigan, in the summer of 1982, a teenager named Jack Cort left his house wearing a coat in the middle of a heat wave. He was wearing a coat to better hide the ax which was hung from a loop of fabric, a recent alteration made with a stapler. The trembling in his hands was not due then to the cold but to the amphetamines he had just downed with a full pot of coffee. He opened the door to his green Dodge Duster and slid behind the wheel. This drive would take two hours and, as long as he didn't fall asleep at the wheel, he would arrive by nightfall.

Jack's parents were killed six years earlier. Jack's older brother woke him up in the middle of the night, telling him that the police had just called but insisting that they couldn't be sure until they identified the bodies. Yes, their parents were supposed to be home by eleven, and they weren't; yes, the party at the Kimball house was long over; yes, their parents would have called if they had decided to alter their plans . . . They set out for the hospital. Chad told Jack to keep an eye out for their parents' car, which would probably pass them in the next ten minutes. The twelve-year-old tried to keep an eye out, tried to keep his eyes open, but he was exhausted. Later he wondered if his brother hadn't shaken him awake out of a sleep stage so deep that he would have difficulties keeping awake for the rest of his life.

He was asleep when they arrived at the hospital, and when he woke, he could tell Chad was disappointed in him. Chad, the older brother, the recent high school graduate, was the one who would identify the bodies. He presented identification and was led through a door with metal plating, in which Jack could see himself. He sat on the floor, looked into his own eyes, and felt as if he might nod off. Why was he so tired? He heard his brother's wail through his reflection. He sprang to his feet and looked for a way to run. Chad burst through the door and threw his arms around Jack.

Jack didn't go to the trial. He was afraid to hear a lawyer describe in detail what the defendant's vehicle had done. He didn't want to know how the cars collided or how much alcohol was coursing through the defendant's bloodstream. Chad went to both days of the trial and the one afternoon of the sentencing. Jack forced himself to stay awake until Chad had left for the courthouse. Then he collapsed on the couch and slept through the alarm set to wake him before Chad returned. Each night Chad came through the door with bags from Burger King and shook Jack awake. Friends and neighbors supplied the boys with lasagna, salads, and casseroles, but they only ate Burger King. Even when their relatives took them out for dinner, they filled up first on Whoppers and chicken sandwiches, french fries and Coke. They talked little while they ate. If Chad tried to describe the drunk driver to him, Jack would shake his head before he heard too much. He didn't want to know anything about him.

Jack eventually came out of his stupor and asked what the sentence was. Chad emptied the paper bags, ate a loose fry, and said the man was going to jail for two measly years. Chad had stayed up late the night before, writing a speech for the court, and woke up early to rehearse it. After the judge sentenced the defendant, "a businessman with a drinking problem," to two years, Chad felt he had failed his parents miserably. Jack looked at all the food his brother had brought home and knew they wouldn't be able to eat all of it. After fifteen minutes of trying, Chad told Jack that they were going out for Chinese with relatives, to plan the future.

Chad pulled on his parka and went quietly outside. Jack watched through the glass door as his brother began chopping wood. The thuds were furious but repetitive, soothing, and Jack let his eyelids droop as he reclined in the chair near the door. Chad split and stacked the wood against the house. Jack wanted to help, but the sounds were so hypnotic. He pulled a soft blanket up to his chest, folded his hands on his stomach, and let himself sleep until shaken awake by his sweaty brother. They left to stuff Chinese food into their bloated stomachs.

Four uncles, two from each side of the family, were sitting at a long table beneath a gilded lion, sipping tea and beer when the boys entered the restaurant. The men had already ordered the dinner for everyone. Jack sat down quietly at the foot of the table, willing to pick at anything that arrived. Chad, on the other hand, called a waiter over and inquired about the specials. He chose a sesame beef and then poured himself a glass of water. Before anyone could say any-thing, Chad let his relatives know that he was not leaving for college in January. He had already deferred the first semester because of the trial, and now he would defer the second. He planned on serving as guardian for Jack as he finished tying up the loose ends and manag-ing his parents' estate. He was adamant. Jack looked at his brother and noticed his eyes slowly taking in each of the uncles, letting them know that the only acceptable response was a nod of consent.

Chad deferred his second year, because Jack didn't want to change middle schools. Then Chad deferred another year and an-other and another, until 1982, when Jack graduated high school and Chad decided to give up the idea of college for himself. His life was chosen for him. He was an auto mechanic, and he had a cheerful girlfriend who taught kindergarten. "You're the college boy, Jacko." Which was true. Jack was graduating near the top of his class and had been accepted to the University of Chicago. Seventh and eighth grade had been excruciating for him, but he soared through high school. When he brought home his first quarter's report card and showed his guardian the 4.0, he was rewarded with a pizza party at the newest fast food franchise. With that initiation and the support his brother gave him at his soccer and baseball games, there was no stopping him. Jack's teachers knew his story, gave him all they could offer, and Jack's friends thought Chad was the baddest parent in town—what other parent's initials held the five high-score positions on the PacMan game at Pizza Hut?

By the spring of his senior year, however, Jack found himself once again utterly exhausted. He nodded off several times during his graduation ceremony, waking from a dream that explained the re-turn of his narcolepsy. He was now the age his brother had been the

year their parents died, and those events came back in all their start-
ling detail. That night, still wearing his cap and gown, a little drunk,
thanks to his brother and the guys at the garage, Jack took the un-
necessary precaution of locking his bedroom door. Under the bright
flood of the desk lamp, he flipped through a phone book in search of
a name. There it was. *Sam Dubin*. There was the phone number and
there was the address. He found the road in the atlas. Measuring
with his finger, it looked to be about a two-hour drive. He saw, too,
the road where his parents and Sam Dubin had collided, almost
halfway between their two homes. He fell asleep on the floor and
dreamt of vengeance.

A graduating senior who saw every event as an epic rite of passage, Jack decided that he couldn't leave for Chicago without for-
mally appealing the court's decision. He chose a night in July and
planned, between naps, how to commit the murder. While stocking
shelves as the assistant manager of the nearby drugstore, Jack tried to
settle on the murder weapon. A gun? No. Although it was Michigan,
where acquiring a gun was only slightly less convenient than buying
gum, Jack didn't want to leave behind any paperwork or person who
could help trace the weapon to him. Nor did he trust himself with a
gun. The same for a knife. He thought of the hammer or the wrench
from Chad's toolbox, but didn't want anything to be traced back to
Chad, and didn't want to take anything that Chad might miss before
it was returned. He thought nonsensically of a sock full of rocks or
nails, but pictured it ripping and the contents scattering across linoleum. He thought of how his parents had been killed, and wished he
could murder Mr. Dubin with a windshield. Or a tire iron. Or a car
antenna. As he drove home one afternoon, Jack passed a liquor store
and thought of knocking Dubin dead with a bottle of Jack Daniels.

If the bottle broke, he could stab him. Though what if the glass cut his own hand? At home, pacing the backyard, his eyes settled on the perfect weapon: the ax. Unlike the tools in Chad's box, this ax belonged to Jack now. Chopping wood was his chore. Chad wouldn't notice the absence of the ax. Especially not during the summer. With that decision made, Jack took off his shirt and took a nap on the lawn.

He woke up, thinking about the narcolepsy. If, whenever he thought of his parents or their killer, he felt an irresistible urge to sleep, what would happen when he met their killer face-to-face? On the three different nights he drove to Sam Dubin's house for reconnaissance, Jack became so groggy that he was hardly able to keep his eyes open on the trip back. He blasted the radio and sang at the top of his lungs until his throat was sore. CUZ THIS IS THRILLER!! THRILL THE NIGHT! With a hoarse voice, he began casually questioning the pharmacist at the drugstore where he worked, and three days before the big night, he stole four pink tablets. Having been told that two "were more than enough," Jack swallowed all four tablets with five cups of the strongest coffee he'd ever brewed.

He was still trembling when he reached the road that led to Sam Dubin's house. Jack clicked off his headlights and slowed to a stop. He turned off the engine. Sam Dubin lived in the woods, on a barely paved road that circled a pond as it approached and then passed his driveway. The layout afforded Jack the opportunity to park without being heard and then observe the house through the trees. At night, there was no way that someone in the lit house could look down the driveway and across the pond to spot a dark vehicle with its lights off.

He smoked a few cigarettes in hopes that they would calm his nerves. Jack had picked up the habit in January, when he turned eighteen. For Jack's birthday, Chad surprised him with the car, which he bought used and then fixed up. In the inaugural photograph, he posed on the hood of the car and, to look just a little tougher, lit one of his brother's cigarettes. He liked the photo so much, he picked up the habit full-time. Jack reached across and opened the glove compartment where that photo was now jammed between road maps. He looked closely at the face and then looked at himself in the mirror. Lit only by the glow of the cigarette, the face was tougher, more manly. It was the face of a man who was about to avenge his family. He put out the cigarette and placed the picture on the dashboard.

Jack peered toward the house and its front door. He had already observed through binoculars that there were small signs in the yard, advertising an alarm system, which was why he chose not to break in late at night and surprise Sam Dubin in bed. He was also unsure which of the upstairs rooms was the bedroom, and didn't want Dubin, who had a home-turf advantage, to surprise him. He wanted to meet the man face-to-face and then dispatch the drunk devil to hell.

He knew very little about Sam. He knew, of course, that Sam had served two years in jail. Before that, he had worked as the vice president of a local bank and was a visible member of that community. He was somewhere in his late forties or early fifties. He was feeble-looking and almost bald. He had no family, no wife or kids. Nobody had testified on behalf of his character. He didn't like dirty bars, loud music, or playing darts, and preferred the bar at the hotel in town. It was respectable, and he was able to do business there. He swore that he didn't normally get so inebriated. He liked to drink but usually knew his limit. He had forgotten to eat dinner on the night in question, and the time got away from him. He wanted the court and the family of the victims to know that he was deeply, deeply sorry. That's all Jack knew, all he ever wanted to read, and all anyone ever told him over the years.

So, how do you get a lonely, bony-shouldered fifty-year-old banker to open his front door? A knock should do it. As long as you drive up into the driveway and walk all friendly-like up to the door. Don't creep out of the woods on foot. Ring the bell, and maybe even hum a tune, keeping your hands out and empty when he peers through the curtained window. Then you ask directions. Then you seem confused. Then he invites you in and shows you a map. You're just a nice kid who keeps his hair cut shorter than most in Michigan these days, and has just sucked a cherry LifeSaver to disguise his cigarette breath. What if a guest is sitting in the living room? There's no guest; there's no other car. Just the one that's been in the drive-way the last two Wednesdays. What if he's on the phone? You don't want to do the job and then hear a voice calling from the earpiece. So *you* ask to use the phone. To call for directions. You ring the bell, hum the tune, smile when the door's opened, ask for directions and to use the phone to call your friend, because your friend's road isn't on any of the maps. After he hangs up and offers you the phone, you tell him you miss your parents and then chop his head open.

Jack had to pee yet again. The coffee. He quietly opened the door and stepped across the road. He opened his jeans, pulled down the front of his briefs, and enjoyed the gushing release. He listened to the caffeinated puddle growing at his feet. This was what he thought about Sam Dubin and the court system in Michigan. He closed his jeans, but as he crossed the road, he felt himself leak into his under-wear. Fuck! He lit the lighter and saw the spot in the blue denim. He could wait for it to dry, but that wasn't what bothered him. Here he was, about to execute a grown man—perform a life-altering act that demanded the closest attention to detail—and he couldn't even remember to shake his dick before zipping his fly. His hands were shaking. He would smoke one more cigarette as he waited. He took long, slow drags and held the lighter's flame near his crotch. "Howdy," he rehearsed. No. He was going to use a Southern accent, but he didn't want to overdo it with phony words. "Hi. I'm not from around here and got completely turned around. I'm looking for a place called Jackson Road, which is where a friend of mine lives. I don't know the town. No, no, I do know the town. It's called . . . Cambridge. Jackson Road in Cambridge."

Jack put out the cigarette and snapped shut the ashtray. He threw a LifeSaver in his mouth, hand-brushed his hair, and turned the key in the ignition. He drove down the road, losing sight of the house, following the bend around the pond and then coming closer to the house than he'd ever been before. It seemed taller. A two-storied box with an A-frame roof that descended farther down the back of the house so that in profile it looked like a redneck with a mullet haircut. *Concentrate. The house is a house.* Most of the house was dark, except a room on the right side of the first floor and the room directly above it. Into the driveway he drove and flashed his headlights into what he assumed was the living room. He turned off the engine and stepped out of the car. He began humming immediately and walked to the front door. There was no bell, so he rapped with the knocker. He would have to hide his hands—they were shaking too much. He listened for the approaching steps. No one was coming. It was late. He started tapping his left foot. He heard movement. This was it. Where was the ax? In the coat. But where was the coat? In the car. He'd taken it off hours ago. It was too hot. The door swung open as the tune caught in Jack's throat.

"Can I help you?" the balding banker asked.

Jack pulled it together to say with an accent straight out of *The Dukes of Hazzard*, "Howdy. I'm not from around these here parts."

"Doesn't sound like it."

"I'm way way lost. I'm looking for Madison Street in Jacksonville."

"Jacksonville? Michigan?"

"Yup, sir. I'm one lost cracker. Could I use a phone and call my friend? If it's long distance, I'll pay."

Sam Dubin smiled and invited Jack inside. Jack thought about going back to the car "for the directions and phone number" but then how would he explain the coat? He would have to stay inside. Sam pointed to the phone and Jack looked around the living room for anything blunt or sharp. There was a fireplace, but no poker. Nothing. Jack smiled. He picked up the phone and was forced to fake a call. He dialed his own phone number. Chad, who was supposed to be out on a date, answered. Jack hung up.

"That's not the number." He smiled and Sam smiled back. "Ooh, let me think here," he said with the accent. Jack thought maybe he should stop talking. His accent would betray him. He dialed six digits of his home number and then faked a seventh. Jack pretended the call had been picked up.

"Hey! Buddy. It's me. I'm lost. Totally lost. Buddy. Yeah. Where am I? Sir?" Sam told him and then offered to get his atlas from his study. He left Jack alone talking on the phone. Not knowing what else to do, Jack kept talking on the empty line, until he realized that Sam might have gone to another phone to pick up on the line. He hung up and left the living room. He was in a dark hallway with three closed doors. At the end of the hall, on the left, came light from around a corner. That door he found open. He could hear Sam opening cabinets in search of the atlas. Or a gun? Jack had to move. He walked into the room and saw Sam crouched next to a desk. Sam looked up and smiled. He didn't suspect anything.

"It's not too bad. We're not too far off. I just need to get back on the highway." As he talked, he looked around the room. Sam was a bowling fanatic. He had trophies, tiny gold-plated men with bent knees and bowling marbles held behind them. Eternal upswings. There were decorative silver bowling pins lined up on a shelf flanked by two genuine bowling balls. Those looked heavy, lethal. Also cumbersome.

"Wow, you like to bowl."

"Just a bit. Do you need something to eat? You're shaking like a leaf." Jack had to move, his mind was racing on those fucking pills. He reached for a trophy, slid two fingers under the bowling arm and two fingers under the lead arm.

"That's one of my first . . ."

"You killed my parents, you drunk fuck!" and Jack swung the trophy above him in an arc that came down on the top of Sam's forehead as he rose to stand and reminisce. Jack heard the crack. The base of the trophy was made of polished white stone and the blunt edge made a dent in Sam's skull. Jack saw his eyes roll upward, and Sam slumped against the wall between his desk and the bookcase. His hand clutched the atlas. Jack looked closer. Was he breathing? He raised the statue and bludgeoned the head once, twice, three times. The fourth and fifth time Jack shut his eyes. He stopped when he felt the warm blood spray his own face. The smell hit him instantly, and he lunged for the other side of the room, where he threw up the Whopper, coffee, and fries. Jack looked at the floor. He couldn't believe it. Could the police track him down through his vomit? He needed to clean it up. Fingerprints! He was going to have to wipe off the phone, the trophy. He looked at the trophy he still held. The hated name, *Sam Dubin*, smeared in blood.

Pull it together. Make it look like a robbery. He stood up. He didn't want to put the bloody trophy down, so he held it between his knees as he pulled the latex gloves from his pocket and covered his hands. He carried the trophy in his right hand and, with his left, opened drawers and scattered their contents. He would have to pocket what-ever money or valuables he found, to make it look like a real robbery. There was no money, no safe in the study. He ran out into the hall-way and climbed the stairs to the bedroom. He found Sam's wallet on the dresser. He pulled the cash out and pocketed it. He tossed the wallet into the middle of the beige carpet. Then he began to empty more drawers. He came across a blue rubber rectangular case. Hold-ing it between his legs, he unzipped it with his left hand. Cash. Lots of it. Son of a bitch banker. He zipped it up and jammed it into the back of his jeans.

Jack examined the room. The mess looked credible. He spotted a pack of cigarettes on the bedstand and chose to light up. One quick smoke. He would flush the cigarette later, so they wouldn't be able to trace his saliva. Very shrewd, he thought, before remembering the vomit in the study. He sat on the bed. He still had so much to do. He took quick puffs of the cigarette, hated the brand, coughed twice, and caught his reflection in the mirror hanging on the closet. He froze. Someone else was sitting on the bed holding a trophy and smoking. Chad was bound to notice, just as Jack had noticed Chad's metamorphosis in the Chinese restaurant six years earlier. While he stared at himself, at his pasty complexion, his puckered mouth and squinting eyes, at his trembling hands and crooked posture, he heard the front door open downstairs.

Jack froze. Was it Sam? Was he still alive? Impossible. Who could it be?

"Dad?" a voice called. "Whose car's outside?"

Jack ran out of the bedroom and stole down another staircase that should have led to the back of the house. He entered the kitchen just as the young man did. They looked at each other in shock. The young man wore a shirt and tie. His armpits were damp. He spoke first.

"Who the hell are you?" he said with hostility laced with fear. Jack reacted and swung the bloody trophy across the stranger's open jaw. The young man stumbled back into the kitchen counter, and Jack swiveled, a backhand, and with the corner of the trophy base put a hole in his head. The man fell hard on the linoleum, twitched, and then lay still. The blood ran across the floor.

Dad?! Sam Dubin didn't have any children. That was one of the few things Jack knew. Jack looked at the trophy again. *Sam Dubin.* With his thumb, he wiped the blood off the gold plate and saw something else. *1978.* In 1978, Sam Dubin was serving his sentence. He was already in jail. How could he be winning trophies at bowling while he was in jail? He suddenly recalled something else and dropped the trophy to pull the rubber bag out of his jeans. *PINS!* There was a receipt inside along with the cash. The bag was from a bowling alley, not a bank. Sam Dubin didn't work at a bank. Well, why would he? He wouldn't be hired back at a bank after serving time in jail. Jack ran to the study and frantically scoured the walls and the shelf. Sam had been winning bowling tournaments nonstop since 1973.

Jack tossed the receipt onto the floor to continue the robbery ploy, but he had no idea anymore what he was supposed to do. Jack shoved the bag of money back into his jeans. How long before someone else came through the door? Jack jumped against the wall when he heard an alarm blaring. *What the hell was that?* The sound was coming from inside the house. He ran into the hallway, back into the kitchen, where he slid through the pool of blood but stayed on his feet, and then up the staircase where the sound seemed the loudest. Before he got to the bedroom, he remembered that he was smoking when Sam Dubin's son had entered the house. There was no cigarette in his hand now, but he didn't remember putting the cigarette out. He looked through the doorway to see the bed on fire.

Jack was soon maneuvering his Duster around the parked car of Sam Dubin's son. He sped down the road and around the pond. When he reached the other side, he looked toward the house to see the second floor ablaze. He accelerated. He accelerated and cried. The pills were turning him into somebody else. He couldn't concentrate; his mind jumped from thought to thought but didn't dwell long enough on any one to think it through. He tried to remember what he had left behind. The fire might be a blessing, might disguise the murders. The fire, if it spread through the entire house, and it certainly would, would burn away his vomit, his fingerprints on the phone, his bloody footprints in the kitchen, the latex gloves which he pulled off and left somewhere in the house. The fire would melt the murder weapon. He had to get rid of the ax. No, he didn't. He never used it. Did anyone see his car speeding away? He'd passed three houses by this point. He'd left his tire tread in the lawn. As he drove, he cried for fear that he'd left too much incriminating evidence. Exhibits A through P. The fire would be treated as an arson to cover up what was meant to look like a robbery. He would never be able to hold out at home. The police would work this out in minutes and come visit the children of the parents Sam Dubin had killed. Stop, stop, stop! This Sam Dubin hadn't killed anyone!! Jack chewed on one of his thumbs as he drove at fifty, sixty, seventy miles per hour . . . he could be pulled over . . . sixty, fifty, forty. He wasn't thinking clearly, though he was wide, wide awake. There was absolutely no connection between this Sam Dubin and the children of the parents that the other Sam Dubin killed. The Sam Dubin Jack had killed had a son, owned a bowling alley, and didn't have bony shoulders. He didn't have bony shoulders!! How did he let this happen? Jack had looked up Sam Dubin's name in a phone book and from that, from that only, he plotted this murder. In what seemed like days after graduating first in his class, he had become a double-murdering arsonist. How could he go home again? Chad was home and would know something was up. There was a change of clothing in the trunk—Jack had enough foresight to expect blood on his clothes—but how was he going to walk nonchalantly into their living room that night? Chad was home; he wasn't staying over at Anne's. He had answered the phone. The phone call! The police would obtain a record of all outgoing calls and he had been stupid enough to call his own home number. He left a tire tread in the lawn, called his own home, and sped away from a fiery house.

Jack pulled off the highway and turned left beneath it. He was not going home. Ever again. He searched for a sign directing him south and he merged into the traffic. Jack would make only one more choice that night and that was to follow the eighteen-wheeler that was rumbling by. He would drive wherever this truck took him, and he immediately began breathing easier once he gave his life over to something else.

AFTER SEVEN MONTHS, I was standing on the sidewalk two floors below my apartment, breathing deeply, acting as if I belonged there. I was dressed for the part. No one was stopping to stare at me, though I felt extremely uncomfortable. My shaved head was itching inside my wool hat, and I was trying to get used to the first pair of shoes I'd worn since August. All circulation felt cut off at the ankles, my feet crushed by the tight binding of the laces. I breathed even more deeply as I took in the impossible, unceasing swirl of color and noise around me. Cascading down Ninth Avenue were cars, buses, trucks, and cyclists, everyone speeding and ignoring their lanes, but there was no accident or even the blare of a horn. A carriage driver trotted his horse east on Fifty-second, and two other men walked north in the street alongside their motorized hot dog stands, indifferent to the oncoming traffic. The pedestrians, too, seemed fearless and respectful of some understood rhythm. Even when they crossed the streets in their various tempos and angles, no one collided. There was no screech of tires, no injured horse or shower of pretzels. How was I supposed to move into this ordered chaos without hurting myself?

TRY JESUS. My eye fell on these words scrawled vertically down the base of the pole marking the bus stop at the curb. Try Jesus? I remembered the bus stop had been designated to take family members of the missing to the pier on the Hudson last fall. A thought occurred to me. I stepped up to the pole and crouched to inspect the graffiti. I didn't recognize the lettering and doubted my mother would deface public property, but I couldn't be sure. "Try Jesus." Try Jesus? It sounded like an ad for something to spread on a cracker. I stood back up and asked myself what I was doing. I was not going to blend in by squatting on a sidewalk mumbling to myself over vandalism at a bus stop.

There was someone watching me. A man in a green raincoat, twenty feet off to my left, under the canopy of St. Clare's hospital. My knees almost buckled. I'd forgotten what it felt like to be observed for longer than it took the delivery men to make change. I stared back at him. His face seemed harmless though a little cartoonish: his skin was too white and his cheeks were too red and chubby to be real. His brown hair was thick and feathery, more illustrated than brushed. He turned away and walked into St. Clare's. I assumed he was watching how autistically I was studying the pole, but then I recalled seeing him before. Through the peephole of my door. Two or three times in the past couple of days. He had knocked, but since he gave no password, I didn't respond. Now I was on the sidewalk, wishing I knew what he wanted. I walked over to the entrance to the hospital and peered through the glass doors. There was no sign of him. Nothing to get nervous about, I told myself. He was probably an employee of St. Clare's and had been asking the neighbors to fill out a survey. Finding new sources of fear was not in my best interest. What I needed to do was get to the hotel. I turned my attention back to the pedestrians, selected what appeared to be the middle tempo, the speed used by those running errands, and stepped into the white-water rapid of bobbing faces.

Was the man in the green raincoat significant in some way, or was I so disconnected from the world by this point that everything appeared to be meaningful? As I walked past the establishments that had sustained me for seven months, I was fascinated by all the purposeful activity and the tangible sense that all of it was somehow interdependent. The mail that was dropped into the blue box had everything to do with the delivery rolling down the ramp from the back of the truck, which was directly linked to the cook stepping out of the basement with the giant pan of pasta and glancing at the woman who was photographing the dirty aquarium left on the curb while her boyfriend held her coffee from the café that provided Internet service for the man who stacked the fruit in front of the store into which the mother pushed the stroller carrying the little boy who was clutching the naked Barbie doll minus a head. Everything was in motion and connected.

I reached Seventh Avenue, and there they were—the two ridiculous Sheraton hotels. As I approached the entrance to the one I never knew existed, a cab driver pulled up to the curb beside me, stuck out his hand, and showed two fingers followed by thumb-and-forefinger zero. The doorman pulled a roll of tips out of his coat pocket and counted twenty singles. The cabbie held out a twenty-dollar bill. No words, just nods. The doorman consolidated his tips and the cabbie broke up a bill to make change for later fares. I had never seen this before but realized from the speed with which the trade was made that this curbside banking happened all over Manhattan every day of the week. It wasn't just stockbrokers flashing fingers atop swiveling wrists anymore. Everyone had a sign language.

To my left, the revolving door began to move. One by one, three people popped out of the hotel. Out of practice, I mistimed my jump, and the spinning door caught my right shoulder with a bang. Whimpering, I massaged my arm and stepped more fully into my chamber. A woman opposite, her exit temporarily halted, glared at me. As far as she was concerned, I'd gotten what I deserved. We both leaned into the door and it slowly advanced, bringing me into a hushed, separate time zone, where business associates conferred and tourists examined guide books to plot out their day. A blond woman standing directly in front of me greeted me with an employee's smile. I stuttered that I was there to pick up a package, and she pointed me toward the bell desk. The man there was on the phone, which was a relief: I didn't want to have a discussion. I wrote my name on a pad in front of me. His lip curled slightly at my impatience, but when he saw the name that matched the package left at their hotel for seven months, his sneer vanished and he immediately handed me the yellow envelope.

I thanked him with a nod, ready to go home, then caught myself. Staying outside was the best way for me to catch up to my life; I did not want to make a beeline back to Ninth Avenue. I looked for a seat, but there was too much distraction in the lobby. I pushed into the men's room, where four stalls with strong, tall, clean doors stood securely in place under track lighting. I pushed inside the last stall, locked the door behind me, took off my hat, hung up my coat, and sat on the toilet lid.

The first page in the envelope was a note handwritten on hotel stationery, dated August tenth. "A. This is for your own private records. I wasn't the only one with a secret. For my safety, I'm telling Rod that you have this. For your safety, I recommend meeting him somewhere out in public. (If he wants to talk to you.) I still don't know what you were playing, but I am sorry. You should know I only had good intentions. B."

This remained indecipherable through repeated readings.

Brad had then enclosed a chronological series of news articles from Michigan. One paper followed the disappearance of a local boy in the summer of 1982; the other paper, with the same date but a different typeface, followed a murder investigation. One paper featured several photographs of an honor student named Jack Cort (a young Rod Hamilton); the other eulogized the owner of a local bowling alley and his son, an accountant who lived in Lansing and was visiting town on business. After a week, the stories began to merge and information pertaining to one became vital to the other until both were reporting jointly on a case of mistaken identity and an act of vengeance gone awry, in which the only successful part of the crime had been the getaway. The last article was a feature published in 1992, on the tenth anniversary of the crime. One entire page was allotted for locals to guess the whereabouts of the young man now approaching thirty. A six-year-old claimed that Jack Cort was a werewolf and lived in her backyard. A retired factory worker was sure the boy had committed suicide now and that one day his corpse would pop out of a lake on a fisherman's hook. Not a single person guessed that the boy was giving sightseeing tours in Manhattan.

That was all. I frantically flipped through the pages again, hoping for another note. Sweat dripped onto the paper. I held the sheaf out of the way and wiped my forehead, which was feverish. My stomach and throat were tightening, I could feel the earth rotating. I closed my eyes and tried deeper breaths. The only thing this helped clarify was Rod's visits and why I never understood what he wanted from me. *We need to move on,* he'd said. *We all have something we wish would be forgotten* was a recurring theme. I remembered his last words to me: *So we're cool then?* I was glad I told him yes. He must have thought I was holding my cards close to the vest when I just wanted him to leave. What did Brad think I was "playing"? What did he think I knew? Why was he scared of Rod?

I heard the door to the bathroom open slowly. Too slowly. The photos of a young, murderous honor student made me jittery. I lifted my feet from the floor and gently placed them against my stall door. I held the papers out in front of me. I listened to the steps advance and then stop. I heard breathing where knees should have been. He was on the floor. I sensed his eyes along the tile and then heard joints crack as he stood up. "Damn it!" I heard him exclaim. I slowly tilted my head onto my left shoulder and leaned over. Black cowboy boots. Khaki pants. The hem of a green raincoat. There was an over-powering whiff of Obsession, the boots pivoted, the bathroom door was flung open and he was gone. This was the same man from the hospital. From my hallway. Khakis? Beneath the coat was a pair of khakis. Business casual.

At this point, I had my first full-blown panic attack. I repackaged the papers, stood up, and shoved them into my pants. I turned around several times, keeping my hands against the walls as they closed in on me. I leaned over the toilet and held my head. I couldn't breathe. I was sweating like a pig. Get out of the hotel, I heard myself say. Leave the Sheraton. To go where? I couldn't go home; he knew where I lived. Just get out, get out, move, move, move . . . I took my coat off the hook, bundled up, and left the bathroom. I didn't see the boots in the lobby. Lots of business casual, but no green raincoat. Everyone there seemed innocuous, but I didn't trust anyone. I left the hotel as quickly as I could. My eyes needed to adjust to the bright, angled winter light after spending a morning reading newsprint in a dim bathroom, but I couldn't stand still. If someone was following me, I had to keep moving and dissolve into the swarming crowds. I squinted and tried to blend into the activity of midtown. I took detours through breezeways and I maneuvered through buildings with multiple doors. When I assured myself that no one was following me, I went underground and bought myself a MetroCard.

● ● ●

I HOPED I WAS on the right train. I couldn't ask anyone; I was overstimulated by the morning and all the faces on the claustrophobic, speeding 2 train. I stared at the map, trying to remember Sonia's stop, but she lived somewhere in the middle of a spaghetti tangle of subway routes that were marked in dark gray, blue, red, orange, brown, two different shades of green and, most confusingly, three lines of the exact same color yellow. Talk about codes. Trains sped in all directions, connecting at points, running parallel, overlapping and passing one another; some carried on straight, others made sharp turns or curving swirls. This was a new map with all sorts of station closures, ferry lines, and service changes. The 1 was now going to Brooklyn. Where was the 3? What happened to the D? There was also a new line—the W! How could they have added trains after the eleventh? Deep breaths, deep breaths. I noticed that in this section of the map, the black dots representing the local stops on the 2 line were half hidden

beneath the green of the 4 and 5, proof that even the graphic designers were overwhelmed by this area. A woman asked me if I needed
help, but my voice was buried so deep inside me, she couldn't hear a
word I said, so she smiled and returned to her paper. It was the name
for one of these half-hidden dots that I recognized as Sonia's stop, and
I came out of the station at Eastern Parkway with a headache.

At the sight of the museum, I remembered how carsick I was the
last time I was here. The air felt good as I crossed to the sidewalk
and walked past the long row of apartment buildings facing the
Botanical Garden. I looked forward to hearing Sonia's shock when I
announced myself and asked for her help. I couldn't wait to be sitting safely inside and planned to ask if she knew anything about
Rod and his summer after high school. I stepped into her building's
glass foyer, pressed the button for her apartment, heard the antiquated mechanical drone, and waited. Only then did it occur to me
that it was the middle of the day—I'd been living a timeless existence for months—and Sonia was likely to be "hunting rent" in
Manhattan, so I was doubly excited to hear static crackle from the
speaker.

"Hello?"

"Sonia, it's Andy. I'm out. I'm out of my apartment."

There was a pause. "Good. Thank you."

"Sonia?" After a prolonged wait, I buzzed again. Nothing. I
buzzed once more.

"Hello?"

"It's still Andy. Buzz me in." Silence. "I need to talk with you.
Something very, very important has come up." More silence. "Sonia,
come on."

"Yes, someday, okay?"

"Are you all right?" She didn't sound like herself.

"Okay. You go now. Thank you. Good-bye."

In my mind flashed the image of Sonia with her wrists taped together, a gun pressed to her temple, and a man in business casual, reeking of cologne, standing behind her. I felt the urge to turn and run, but the last time I'd done that, I left Peter alone defenseless on a dark street. I couldn't run away again. This was the moment I would redeem myself. I pushed at the front door, but unlike the one in my building, this one was securely locked. I had to wait. Her apartment faced Manhattan, so I couldn't see her window from the street. I returned to the foyer to stay warm and wait it out. I tried to connect the news articles from Michigan to the man in the coat to Sonia to Brad's mysterious secret, and the longer I waited, the more elaborate the connections became.

I saw the elevator open in the lobby. A woman with a schnauzer was heading toward me. I struck a nonthreatening pose—hands on hips, legs slightly open, a cheery smile, and pretended to talk to someone upstairs. Just as the woman opened the door, I faked a laugh and spoke to no one: "No, I don't want to come up. Just hurry, I don't want to be late. We'll get a quick lunch and then . . ." by which point the woman and dog were out of earshot, and the toe of my right shoe had caught the door before it closed. I was pleased with myself. There was hope for me.

I took the elevator to the eighth floor. I scrutinized Sonia's door. A painted-over mezuzah on the doorjamb gave an idea of the apartment's history, but there was nothing to indicate what was happening at the moment. I stepped up, took a breath, and knocked. Three sharp raps. I hadn't been a knocker for months and found it just as nerve-wracking on this side of the door. Was it possible Sonia was just in the middle of a sexual romp, or were bullets about to splinter the wood? I stepped to the side. I heard slow, creaking steps approach the door. I prepared to run. I stared at the peephole and saw the light disappear, the abstract outline of an eye and then the resumption of light. I waited for Sonia to turn the knob. No movement.

"Sonia! Sonia, are you all right?" No response. "I just saw you look through. I know you're in there. What's going on? Do you need help? Sonia?" Nothing. Nothing at all.

Another tactic. I cursed at her through the door and told her I was going home. I pushed the elevator button, ignored the inevitable eye at the peephole, cursed one more time, boarded the elevator, disembarked on the fifth floor and stealthily climbed the three floors to find a seat on the staircase. A stakeout. I would wait.

I looked left through the window on the landing between the seventh and eighth floors. It was the view I had seen many times from Sonia's window, but something was wrong with the picture. Everything in the world seemed different, and my brain couldn't process it. I was surprised to feel rage and wondered what should receive the brunt of my wrath—the spinning planet or the soggy cauliflower spoiling at the top of my spine? With time to kill, I stared out the window and resolved to solve at least this one puzzle of the day. The sun changed position before I was finally able to recognize that the last time I'd seen this view, there had been two giant silver towers on the left of it. I leaned forward, half expecting to see them come into frame. This was my first view of the altered skyline, and I did what I assumed millions had done: I turned away and looked somewhere else.

After two hours, I heard the locks of Sonia's door turn. I hunched down in the stairwell and waited. A strange woman emerged, locked the door, and passed out of sight. When I heard the elevator doors open and close, I hobbled over to the apartment and knocked again. No one approached the door; no one peeked through the hole. There was no sound. The woman hadn't stolen anything—her bag was too small—and she had a key, which she had used conscientiously to lock the door. I tumbled down the stairs and exited the building, panting, unused to exercise. I was like a calf raised for veal taken out of my box and set on a track to race greyhounds. I saw the woman ahead of me clipping along the sidewalk toward the subway.

It wasn't until we were both on the platform for Manhattan-bound trains that I was able to get a better look at her, concealing myself behind a group of teenagers in oversized jackets. She had strong Slavic features—a short, upturned nose, high cheekbones with supple jowls, and slightly slanted eyes that were a piercing green. She was reading a Russian-language newspaper. I wondered if she was a relative or a new roommate. She didn't look dangerous, but again, I trusted no one. When the train pulled to a stop, I entered the same car through a different door and sat on the same side as she did. She continued to read the paper, and I tried to read her. She exited on the Upper West Side, at Seventy-second and Broadway, and made her way toward the Hudson, against a wind tunnel of frigid air. She turned up West End Avenue with its bulky prewar apartment buildings, walked north, and made a left. I refused to believe it until I turned the corner myself and saw her nod at the doorman and enter the building that housed my aunt's apartment.

I fell against a neighboring edifice, hoping it would hold me. I felt like a bottle of seltzer was shaken and opened inside my skull. I could not follow her inside. I hadn't seen my family since Christmas, and I hadn't seen Peter since the neuro-ICU. After a few minutes, on unsteady legs, my swollen feet pinched in their shoes, I made my way past the front door and across Riverside Drive. I took a seat on a low wall and faced the building. I shoved my frozen hands in my pockets and sat there tormented. I saw my sister emerge. She stood in front, posing for her nonexistent paparazzi before tying up her coat and pulling up her hood with a graceful gesture. She turned east, crossed her arms, and moved with the elements. I was inclined to follow her, but I couldn't move. I remained at my post. A few minutes later, my mother, visibly hunched now, exited and walked up the street in her old coat, without the scarf and hat I bought her.

I looked up through the tree branches at the building lit by the white winter sun and located the windows that belonged to my aunt. I hoped to see the pudgy Russian face, to confirm the connection I'd made in my mind. I saw nothing except for a curtain being jerked on the floor above by a cat or a toddler. My mind tried to puzzle it all out. Maybe the two men in business casual were working with the man in the green raincoat who was working with the Russian woman? Were Rod and Peter somehow involved? Where were Brad and Sonia? Was my family in any danger? They didn't seem to be, but I still wished they'd leave, for their own safety. The sun was sinking behind me, and a line of shadow crept up the exterior of the apartment building. Lamps clicked on, floor by floor, until the sky was deep blue. I could hear squirrels or rats scurrying in the park. I looked back periodically, to make sure that no one was there, but for the most part, I kept my eyes trained on the building, dedicated to my task. Somehow I'd gone from protecting myself to wanting to protect everyone else in my life.

My mother returned with groceries from Fairway, and the front door opened for her. I stood up, fairly certain that I would soon see the mysterious Russian. Surprise, surprise. We were moving once again. The streets were filled with shadows. I wanted to go home, but I urged myself on: *Redeem yourself, you have the advantage.* I predicted each of her turns on her way to the subway at Seventy-second. I suspected she was returning to Brooklyn, which meant I had forty-five minutes or so to strike up a conversation. I chose to approach her on the platform. In a stroke of genius, I pulled off my hat: my shaved head was my disguise.

"Hey! Brooklyn, right?" She regarded me with suspicion. "You live in Brooklyn. My name's Dan. Dan Blado." I kept smiling as if we once shared a chat over eggs in a diner. She looked at me but couldn't place me. She might have recognized me from a photo in my aunt's apartment, or through the peephole this afternoon, but she couldn't make the connection underground at Seventy-second Street. I held out my hand and she took it, her eyes glancing at the Band-Aids just above my forehead.

She gave me her name: "I am named Sonia Obolensky."

I would have fallen onto the track if we had been on the edge of the platform; she saw my face give way. She tried to pull her hand out of my grip, but I held it tightly.

"I have a friend named Sonia Obolensky. She lives in Brooklyn too."

"No. I am only one." She pried herself free. She recognized me now.

"Where's Sonia?"

"I am Sonia." She began walking down the platform. I followed.

"No, you're not. I know Sonia very well, and you're not Sonia."

"Yes, please."

"You don't talk like Sonia. Talk, say something else. Let me hear your accent."

Under the rumble of an incoming train, she said either "please" or "police."

"Go ahead. Call for the police." As I was saying this, I noticed her fat fist coming straight toward my face. I tilted my chin up, which saved my nose, but exposed my neck which is where her knuckles sunk. Punched in the throat, I crumpled in shock. Some people glanced at me, looked like they might help, but the train was in the station, so they had to move into boarding position. I had completely lost control over that conversation and remained on my knees, fretfully fingering my windpipe, as Sonia's impostor elbowed her way onto the train. She peered at me nervously through the window as the train slid away.

My hand pressed to my neck, I crawled over to a bench and took a seat. I didn't know what to do next. I didn't know where Rod lived, I didn't know where Sonia was, and I didn't want to visit my family. I couldn't go to the police, because even though I considered myself in the midst of some elaborate criminal network, what could I possibly tell them? A man in a green raincoat followed me into a bathroom? I must have been mumbling to myself as I rubbed my throat, because people were making quick peeks my way, and probably trying to determine whether the crazy man on the bench with his head covered in Band-Aids was dangerous or not. So much for blending in. I pulled my hat down over my head as a downtown local entered the station. I stepped on board and tried to pass myself off as a mere commuter.

●　●　●

THE SKY WAS BLACK when I came out of the subway. The wind was stronger and colder. I realized that my headache and jitters were now coming from hunger, so I started looking for dinner. I picked the Thai restaurant owned by a woman through whose delivery staff I had been cashing my checks since September. I wanted some familiar faces who would recognize me and perhaps congratulate me on the phenomenal accomplishment of leaving the security of my home. The owner/hostess gave a quick bow as I entered, but didn't smile. She may have seen my arrival as a direct threat to the steep five percent transaction fee she had been charging me for half a year. Ravenous, I slurped the spicy soup, swallowed the dumplings whole, burped a number of times, and devoured two servings of shrimp pad thai. Everything tasted better served on china. The last time I'd eaten at a restaurant was with Peter. Which got me to thinking. . . . By the time the owner/hostess offered a sherbet with pineapple "on the house," I had decided to visit the scene of the attack. Before returning home in defeat, I could at least face the cage, reclaim the dark street and the pear tree.

There was no trace of blood on Fifty-first. The puddles had long been washed away, the stains covered with more recent grime, and the pear tree was leafless now but still spreading out its naked branches against the sky. It was what I'd expected. No plaque or a shrine with photographs and deflated red balloons. I was the only one who considered the place a symbol of the world's contention. I stepped into the street and leaned down toward the asphalt to see if I could find indentations left by my knees. Nothing, though I did notice something on the curb. In an incompetent attempt to parallel park, someone had backed into the cage that protected the tree. Two of the poles were bent and pulled out of the shallow soil. The corner pole now tugged east, cutting into the bark of the trunk. A knot in the pear tree was shredded wood. Part of the bar disappeared into the tree itself. I quickly looked away.

Then there he was, standing on the corner: the man with the cartoon face. I saw his green raincoat quickly withdraw behind the yellow wall of the Mexican restaurant. I was rooted where I stood beside the mutilated tree. I heard Peter's head ringing against the cage. Was there really someone on the corner or was I hallucinating? Just like the last time, my cowardly legs took me east. I sensed that the stranger was following me, so I was relieved to reach Eighth Avenue, which was better lit and more populated. I moved north again, just as I had in August, and then, at the next corner, realized that I wanted to go home. I could hear the locks turning. Halfway down Fifty-second, I envisioned him following me inside, and I started to panic again. He knew where I lived. I crossed Ninth and headed toward Tenth, which was darker, more desolate and dangerous.

Who was this man? What did he want? He had knocked on my door but hadn't approached me since then. In the morning, at the TRY JESUS, he stepped out of my sight as he'd done just now. Whoever he was, he didn't want to confront me; he wanted to observe me. After losing me at the hotel, he probably returned to stake out the streets near my building until he found me swallowing noodles and peanut sauce. How long had he been watching me? At Tenth, I turned, looked over my shoulder. No one. I was tired and cold and too nervous to walk anymore. I planned to turn at the next corner and aim for home. This was crazy, I told myself, but felt the potential for disaster in every doorway I passed. I was back on Fifty-first Street, now one block west of the pear tree—closer to the river, farther from the theaters and the restaurants. My eyes were on the sidewalk, and

I took one square at a time. I vowed to go to sleep early, and to wake up refreshed, saner, more lucid, more hopeful, less fearful . . .

Then there he was again. Beside me. Sitting on a stoop, four steps up, his hands together, his artificial face alight with a toothy grin.

"Andy Green." He knew my name. His head shook from side to side. "I had a feeling you'd come this way." He stood up, his feet firmly planted on the second step, so that he loomed above me. "Allow me to introduce myself." This was too much. I kicked at the side of his knee as hard as I could. He bent over, balanced on only one leg. His face was now directly in front of mine. I struck out with the back of my hand, very weakly, I thought, my arm filled with helium, but my knuckles caught the side of his mouth. He collapsed back to a seated position.

I shuffled backward into the street, panting wildly, and shouted, "Who are you?"

His face darkened and he barked back, "I was about to tell you!" He rubbed his face, touching it gingerly as if the color would smear and the animator would have to be called in. "I don't have dental coverage, jackass." When he was assured he was intact, he began again, "Like I was about to say, my name is Reed D'Carloff."

The name seemed familiar but didn't register. Was it a name from Michigan? Did he know Brad?

"Am I supposed to know what that means?" I asked, still in the street, behind a fender of a parked car.

"Your sister might have mentioned me."

My sister? What does she have to do with this?

"We used to be colleagues in Waldorf."

My memory was still foggy.

"I was her manager at a restaurant in the mall there."

This was Beth's ex-"boyfriend"? The man who got into fisticuffs with my sister while she was dressed up as Petey Pepperoni? I leaned against the car.

"We were lovers for a time . . ."

"Please. I know all about it."

He bristled at this: "What did she tell you?"

"I'll ask the questions." He narrowed his eyes, clenched his jaw, and then winced with pain, bringing his hand up to where I'd hit him. "Who are you working for?"

"What?"

"Who sent you?"

"No one sent me."

"Then what do you know about the Russian?"

"The Russian?"

"The Russian woman posing as my friend Sonia."

"I don't know what you're talking about. A Russian!"

"What about the two men last summer?"

"What two men?"

"The two men who jumped us at that pear tree?"

"The pear tree?" he sputtered. "Are you fucking around with me? Who's us?"

"Peter. Beth's fiancé."

"That dork magician?"

"That's right."

"I know that Beth came up here because something happened to him, but I didn't know what."

"You're telling me that you don't know anything about last August or anything about the Russian woman who just attacked me in the subway?"

Reed dropped his hand and both arms now hung at his sides: "No. I don't."

I stepped back onto the sidewalk. "What about the Sheraton Manhattan?"

"No!"

"You were there this morning. You followed me into the bathroom."

"You were still in there?"

"Why are you following me?" I shouted. I heard the voice rush up and down the street and Reed looked up toward the windows. I repeated myself, more calmly this time. "Why are you following me?"

He looked long and hard at me before admitting, "Because I need to see Beth and I don't know where she is."

I couldn't believe it. This had nothing to do with me. I turned and walked up the street toward Ninth. He followed a few yards behind me, explaining that my number was listed, but that I never answered the phone. He'd knocked on my door, but I didn't answer even though he heard me inside. I told him, "You almost gave me a heart attack. I'm not in very good shape." I needed a drink.

"Where are you going?" Reed asked as I stepped up toward the door of a small bar near the corner. Pointing to a rainbow flag above the door, he said, "I can't go in there."

"Good," I said. I pushed into the room of brick walls and a tin ceiling painted white. The bar was on the left; there were chairs and ledges for drinks on the right and a small lounge one step up in the back. I squeezed through the men, ordered a beer, and took the one seat left at the far corner of the bar. I could make out Reed on the other side of the glass door peeking in after me. He was nothing like I expected him to be. I always pictured him with a braided ponytail and severe acne. I drank my beer in this sanctuary while he mustered the courage to enter. With his shoulders thrust back and a hint of a swagger, he opened the door and moved into the crowd, taking care not to meet anyone's eyes.

Reaching me, he shouted over the music, "I need to see Beth."

I was still at a loss: "Did you think I'd lead you to her?"

"Or she'd come to you."

"Why didn't you just ask me instead of playing James Bond?"

"Would you have helped me? You looked through the door and didn't open up."

"I didn't know who you were."

"I thought you were some kind of mental patient. You didn't come outside for *three days!*" The man next to me left his stool, freeing up the seat for Reed. "Listen: it's urgent that I see your sister."

"Write a note then," I told him. "I'll give it to her."

"This is personal."

"I won't read it."

"I'm not much of a writer."

"Then give me a number where she can reach you."

"She wouldn't call me."

He wasn't being cooperative. I pulled my hat off and asked, "How do I know you're not going to stalk my sister . . ."

"I'm not a stalker!" He seemed very offended. "Why's your head covered in Band-Aids?" I slipped my hat back on without answering. "Where's your sister?"

"I'm not telling you!"

He grabbed my arm and said, "Don't make me beg."

"You already are." I stared at his hand until he removed it.

"Would it change matters if I told you that my wife recently died?" He put his head in his hands and looked as if he was going to cry for a second, but then, suddenly, as if this moment of his vulnerability was my fault, he furiously whispered, "Beth's been here since August! I've been waiting for her to come back to Maryland. I didn't think she would stay in New York this long."

"I didn't either."

"Then I was driving by her house and I saw the FOR SALE sign."

The entire room seemed to tilt at a forty-five-degree angle before crashing loudly back into place: "What did you say?"

"The FOR SALE sign."

Some of my beer came back up. I told Reed I had to go. I needed to make some phone calls.

"Are you going to call Beth?" He pulled a cell phone out of his pocket. "Use this."

"So you'll have her number?" I stood up. "I'm going home."

"Fine. Let's go back to your place."

"Forget it!" I almost shouted. He looked around at the men now watching us. They must have thought this was a very bad date. He turned back to me and kept talking, but I couldn't hear anything. My head was spinning; my stomach was in my throat. Reed was holding on to my arm again. The date got worse. I vomited beer, shrimp, spicy soup, dumplings, and noodles with peanut sauce into Reed's lap, onto his coat and boots. I could hear again. Reed was moaning, and bar stools were skidding on the floor. The bartender took a glance at Reed's lap and bent behind the bar where he began to retch.

Someone was trying to help Reed when he shouted, "Don't touch me!" Reed was as still as a statue. He said quietly, "This is my only coat."

"I have to get home," I said and wiped my chin with my hand.

He looked at me in disbelief. "You can't leave me here!" Reed was desperate but frozen in place. A noodle flopped from his knee onto his boot. "Meet me later." I shook my head. "Tomorrow morning then. After this, you have to meet me."

I had to get out of the bar. "Tomorrow."

"Breakfast. At the diner across the street from you." He shouted, "Promise me!"

"Fine," I said, moving toward the door. A wide passage quickly opened for me, the men pressing up against the bar or the wall.

Reed gave the crowd another wrong impression by shouting, "Don't forget me! Promise me!" Unfortunately, I forgot about him as soon as the cold air hit my face. My mother and sister were selling their house in Maryland and apparently had no intention of ever leaving New York. I needed to call them, tell them that it wasn't safe for them to stay here, and that they needed to pack and get out of the city as fast as they could.

MY AUNT HAD MOVED out of the city six years ago, but she refused to give up her rent-stabilized two-bedroom, returning for lengthy stays only when she needed to prove the apartment was her primary residence. In case there was an emergency and the superintendent or landlord had to enter, she wanted the place to look as if she'd just stepped away for groceries. There was nothing my neat-freak of a mother could do about the clutter. There weren't enough shelves for the books, so the overflow was stacked in piles on the floor; magazines from 1995 were spread out on the coffee table; there were various bric-a-brac from Africa and Asia via Harlem and Chinatown; thick area rugs covered large portions of the parquet floor; framed photographs hung on one wall near the kitchen, and posters from museum shows from the seventies and eighties consumed the rest. It was a very quiet place, dim for most of the day, lighting up in the late afternoon, and smelling of used paperbacks and kettles of peppermint tea.

When I knocked the next morning on my fact-finding mission, my mother was the one who opened the door. Neither of us said anything for a few moments, shocked as we were by the sight of the other. Her face was too thin, her cheekbones protruded, her eyes were sunk, red, and rheumy, and the tiniest of purple veins were now spun like webs in patches on her temples and jaw. She was holding her Bible with a finger keeping her place. She, in turn, couldn't take her eyes off my head. The Band-Aids were peeled off, but there were scabs amid patches of stubble.

"What did you do to your head?"

"I shaved it."

"I see that." She leaned toward me to inspect each side of my scalp. "I'm glad to see you. I hope this isn't just a phase."

"I called you last night."

"I was going to call you back after lunch. I was alone with Peter all of last night."

"It was important."

"Your message sounded like . . ." She rubbed her forehead. "Like I didn't have the energy for it."

"Then tell me now. Who's the Russian girl who was here yesterday?"

Concerned, she took her hand from her head and placed it on my shoulder. "Sonia?"

"No, not Sonia. The woman who was here yesterday."

"Sonia Obolensky?"

"That was not Sonia Obolensky. My friend, Sonia, is the one I told you to call for help with Peter, the one you gossiped with."

"Right. That's Sonia Obolensky."

"What does your Sonia Obolensky look like?" My mother described the woman I'd followed from Brooklyn and not my friend of three years.

"Does Sonia start most of her sentences with *And*?"

"Not that I've noticed. She doesn't talk that much."

"Well, that's definitely not Sonia. Is your Sonia coming today?"

"No."

"Is Beth here?"

"We're expecting her. She was away last night, but she told me she'd be back by lunch. Let me take your coat."

While she was hanging my coat in the hall closet, I blurted out: "Are you selling the house?"

She heard the question but ignored it. "Andrew, I have a friend over. Come in and meet her." It was only a few steps into my aunt's living room, where a thin, sullen woman sat with a Bible in her lap. She was in an armchair, resting her head against the pillow made by her hair, which was pinned up and held in place with a pencil. Her eyes were closed. She opened them when we were both standing in front of her. "This is Catherine Reynolds." I smiled weakly, and she did the same. "Catherine lost her husband on September eleventh." I looked at my mother. That was a terrible way to introduce someone. I told Catherine I was sorry. Ruby then said, "This is the son I was telling you about." Catherine told me she was sorry. My mother invited me to sit down with them. I didn't move. She told me, if I preferred, I could visit with Peter, who should be waking up from his nap any minute. I sat down. "Catherine has been sorting through her husband's papers. Please, go on."

My presence didn't faze Catherine in the least. The past weekend she had given herself the task of going through another part of his desk. She discovered pictures of herself that her husband had taken without her knowledge. There was a picture of her hanging clothes on a line in the backyard, a few of her at a family picnic, several of her sleeping. She couldn't figure out why he would have these photographs. My mother, a professional widow coming up on her thirty-year anniversary, suggested he was stockpiling images of her in case she ever left the world prematurely. My mother and this woman must have grown close for her to say something that morbid and get away with it.

Catherine shook her head ever so slightly and said, "He probably thought they were beautiful and never showed me, because he knew I would call them ugly. I would have. I did that all the time. We were watching a sunset in Montauk once, and I told him the sunsets in California were so much more beautiful. Why did I have to compare? If someone thinks something is beautiful . . . why would I take that away?" She paused. "I never thought I was very pretty, but Richard thought I was." She vigorously rubbed the bridge of her nose with a fingertip. "I also found some magazines in his drawer. Women with enormous breasts." I felt completely trapped. I didn't move a muscle. To my relief, she didn't dwell on the pornography and moved to her husband's handwriting. She felt she'd taken it for granted. The sharp downward strokes and the curves that rose above them. His *R*. She wanted to incorporate his *R* into her alphabet. She drew it for us, and we both commented on how nice a letter it was. She said she felt him whenever she copied his name. Now there were tears.

My mother leaned over, touched Catherine's knee, and said, "Cry . . . cry." Not "Let it out." Just "Cry . . . cry." I felt my usual confusion. When Beth and I were in elementary school and our only dog was hit by a car, our mother told us to cry even though we had already been hysterical for thirty minutes. There was no end, no objective in it. When the grief-stricken at funerals shared stories of their loved ones, she pounced on anyone about to smile with a fond memory and reminded them, "Yes, but now he's gone." The memory would be lost and tears would well. "Cry . . . cry," like an incantation. When Catherine stopped crying, she looked as if she was simply waiting for the replenishment of her tear ducts. In the interval, the two of them continued their devotional. My mother, to show she would never give up, that the door was always open to me, asked if I wanted to read a passage. I told her I didn't have my glasses.

As they read, I observed my aunt's living room, noticing the encroachments made by my mother and sister. I could see evidence of Beth in the entertainment magazines stacked on the coffee table, in the DVDs I'd given her for Christmas beside a television equipped with only a VCR, and in the *Times* crossword puzzle with twenty blocks filled in and bold lines scratched furiously through the rest. My mother's presence was more difficult to locate. I assumed she was staying in my aunt's bedroom, which was the largest and could easily accommodate her belongings, but there was bound to be some overflow since August.

Then I spotted a familiar religious figurine on top of one of the bookcases. My mother, besides nailing crosses on walls throughout our house, collected various Christ-related arts and crafts. The kitschiest was a series in the dining room of seven statuettes depicting Jesus and his apostles as bearded little children doing good deeds, like rescuing cats from trees. A kind of *Peanuts* for the New Testament. The most disturbing, however, at least to me, was the variety of statues she kept in her bedroom depicting the Pietà—not just Michelangelo's but a wide array of presentations. She had brought a figurine from this collection, a foot-high replica, all the way from Maryland. I couldn't take my eyes off the heavily draped Mary with the beaten, dead, almost naked Christ sprawled across her lap. The lifeless body reminded me of Peter's twisted torso lying on the sidewalk as the paramedics worked on him.

Beth appeared in the doorway to the foyer, her mouth falling open when she saw me. She then grinned broadly. I touched my mother's shoulder and nodded to Catherine, who waved to Beth, and quickly followed my sister into the kitchen.

Beth said, "I like what you've done with your hair." She dropped the overnight bag slung over her shoulder to the floor next to a closet and emptied the grocery bag she'd carried inside. "Peter's going to be so excited to see you." A tightening in my stomach, a weakness in the knees. "So what finally got you out of that stinkhole?"

"A puzzle to solve," I said. "A gross misunderstanding I've set out to correct."

Beth smiled as if that made all the sense in the world to her. She patted my hand, turned around, and opened the refrigerator.

"Who's the Russian who was here yesterday?"

"Your friend. Why?"

"It's not my friend, and I don't know where the real Sonia is. I called her last night, no answer." I waited in vain for her reply. "Aren't you concerned that you're employing an impostor?"

"Mm. That's a lot to take in," she said without bothering to take it in.

"Where were you?" I asked.

"When?"

"You spent the night away?"

"I had the night off. Mom took care of everything."

"Where did you go?"

"A hotel."

I stared at her and she smiled a Mona Lisa. She arranged food on the counter, gripped a knife, and pulled a few strands of hair over her left ear. For the sake of the gesture.

"With someone?" I asked.

She set the knife on the counter and looked into my eyes. "I won't discuss my love affairs."

"Love affairs?" I asked. "Aren't you engaged?"

"Andy, I'm going to let you in on a secret." She blew hair out of her eyes. Again, needlessly. "I don't think it's working out with Peter. He's not the same man." She picked the knife up again and resumed her work.

"Do you have a boyfriend?" I asked incredulously.

Beth considered the question, scrunched up one side of her face, lifted her free hand and tilted it back and forth. "We'll see."

"That's kind of incredible to me."

"Andy, I love you and I'm glad you're out of your apartment, but don't come here if you're just going to make me gloomy." She pointed toward the living room. "You saw that in there, right? Well, when I'm not dealing with Peter, I'm dealing with her. I'm still on a high from last night so I want to ride it out for as long as possible. Got it? Great."

I looked down at the counter and noticed Beth's lunch. Everything she did was charged with a misapplied elegance. She seemed in such control of the kitchen that you would think she was preparing tea-smoked duck with a soy-ginger glaze rather than a plate of corn chips, cheese, and chili from a can. She placed the nachos in the microwave, pressed START with a flourish, and turned back to face me.

She asked, "So are *you* dating anyone?"

"No."

"Are you looking?"

"No."

"Do you have a new job?"

"No."

"Are you looking?"

"No."

"Are you seeing a therapist?"

"No, and I'm not looking."

"That's sad."

This was rich, after all I had done to protect her from Reed D'Carloff. "Beth, I've been spending most of my time running from a friend of yours."

"Wow." She humored me as if I were a four-year-old talking about pirates.

"I'm serious. It turned out to be someone trying to track you down."

"Hm."

Most people would register some fear in such a situation. Not Beth. The microwave beeped and Beth pulled out the nachos, the cheese melted, the chili steamy.

"Hmm. Who do I know in New York? Missy Potter?"

"Don't guess. I'll just tell you. Reed D'Carloff."

"Reed D'Carloff?" she repeated as if she smelled a gas leak. "Why would he be here?" I wanted to say, *Why are you?* Beth scooped sour cream on top of the nachos and placed the plate between us.

I wasn't hungry for nachos at eleven in the morning. She used a fork and knife. As a lady would.

I continued, "He wants to see you, but he doesn't think you'd call him if I gave you his number."

"He's right. He's a pig. Disgusting control freak."

"He's persistent. He says it's urgent."

"It's not. He just wants to get back with me. Did you tell him to screw off?"

"Actually, I threw up on him last night."

"Good for you!"

"He's not going away. He wants to see you."

"Well, I don't want to see him."

"So what do I tell him?"

"Nothing. Don't tell him anything."

"I have to tell him something. He'll keep following me. I had to take two cabs, the subway, and then walk all around Riverside Park today to make sure he wasn't behind me."

"Don't you think you're being a little paranoid?"

"No, I'm not."

"Maybe a little girly?"

"It's for your sake! This guy is unhinged. Tell me what to say to him so that he'll leave me alone and go home."

She wiped her hands. She turned from her lunch and began arranging more dishes, noisily, with anger.

"Okay. You tell that sleazy prick that our business is over. Since we parted, I have gotten older, and since we both know he likes younger girls, I'm no longer suitable for him. Tell him that. Better yet. I'll write it down." She jotted the words on a sheet of paper near the phone and signed it with an exclamation point. "This should do it. If not, just ignore him. That's what he really can't stand. Throwing up on him was perfect."

"It wasn't deliberate."

Beth laughed. "Let him talk and then say: *Are you still here?* He loves to talk. You wouldn't believe his staff meetings. We were serving pizza to nine-year-olds and he'd have us sit there every shift preparing for war. He thought he was giving the State of the Union. Yawn and roll your eyes. That'll piss him off."

"He has a strange face, don't you think?"

"How so?"

"Like a cartoon. Animated. Flat, white with red cheeks."

"His eyes are different."

"I didn't notice."

"Different colors."

"What attracted you to him?"

"He was the manager. I was impressed with his power, I guess."

"A manager at a family pizza arcade?" I asked.

"Yep."

"I'll relay the message."

"I appreciate it." Beth smiled and actually began humming to herself. She was thrilled to have three men in the city—a fiancé, a lover, and a stalker. *C'est l'amour.*

I stopped her song. "Now to what really intrigues me. Reed had some real estate news."

"Did he?"

"Mom is selling our house?"

"Yes."

"Why?"

"You should ask her."

"Usually when people sell their homes they have another place to move into. So where are you all going?" With a nacho in her mouth, Beth pointed to the floor, gestured to the walls.

"Why would you move here?"

She spoke with her mouth full: "Hey! No drama. I'm still on my high." She swallowed. "New York has eight million people in it, so it's not technically *your city*."

"That's not what I meant." I looked down again and saw her hands at work on a new meal. "What's that? What is that?" She was arranging a tray of mashed potatoes, creamed carrots, and pistachio pudding.

"Peter's food."

"He's not eating solids?"

"Not today. Chewing gives him a headache sometimes. Come on. Let's go. He's going to be thrilled to see you. He's making a strong comeback. A week ago the doctor took him off this one medication he probably should never have been on in the first place and it's like he's waking from a nightmare. He's better every single day." She picked up the tray. I faltered. I would have fled in the other direction but for my mother in the living room. I would never be prepared to encounter Peter. Beth stepped into the hall and backed into the door that opened into his bedroom. "Peter, look who's come to see you."

From inside, a gruff voice shouted, "Bob! Bob Cratchit!!"

Beth looked back at me and whispered, "It's going to be one of those." She disappeared into the room. I took a moment to plaster a smile on my face before following inside.

Peter looked considerably better than he'd looked in the neuro-ICU. Obviously. He wasn't hooked up to any machines or plastic bags. His hair, longer and disheveled from sleep, concealed the scars on his scalp. The abrasions on his face had diminished, and only if you looked closely could you imagine how bad the cuts had been. His nose, however, had been broken, and his left eye socket was noticeably smaller and much rounder than his right. He was wearing a yellow T-shirt and baggy gray shorts and lying in a full-size bed. The comforter, blanket, and top sheet had been kicked off to the floor, where there were at least three decks of playing cards. The steam heater was rattling and the room was extremely stuffy. My nose recognized a few fetid strains familiar from my apartment, and I saw a box of my sister's favorite brand of incense sticks on the dresser next to an oversized ceramic clown head. This was the room that my aunt had decorated as a nursery during the brief spell when she was considering adoption, so the room in which Peter was recovering was adorned with clown lamps, curtains, and figurines.

Peter looked at me with his small, round eye. He couldn't quite place me.

Beth set the tray on the bedside table and gently scolded him, "You should only play with three cards at a time. Let's sit up now." I was happy to see that he was able to sit up without much help. Beth positioned the pillows behind him and then the tray over his lap. "Do you have to use the restroom before you eat?"

He shook his head irritably and asked with a slight slur, "Who's that?"

"That's Andy. My brother. Remember?"

"Hi, Peter," I mumbled.

"BOB!"

"Hi, Bob." I walked to the other side of the bed so as not to crowd

Beth, but she explained Peter's hearing was much better in the right ear. I walked back around.

"I remember you," Peter said. "You were there."

"Yes," I spoke loudly. "That was a rough night, but we did have fun at dinner."

"He's not six," Beth felt she needed to point out.

"Remember all the great tricks you showed me?"

At that he reached for some cards on the table, but Beth snagged him by the wrist. "You can barely hold a spoon, Bob. Let's work up to the cards, okay?"

"He can't use a spoon?"

"He can. It's just not worth the cleanup. You have to be in the mood."

"Where were you?" he asked.

I said, "I've been downtown for some time."

"Not you," he said to me and rolled his head to Beth who had deliberately maneuvered to the side of his bad ear. "You! Where were you?" Beth slipped some mashed potatoes into his open mouth. He sucked and swallowed, then asked again, "Where were you?"

"Peter," Beth said pragmatically. "You're not going to remember if I tell you, so let's not quarrel."

"Where were you?"

"He has on-and-off memory," she explained.

"Where were you?"

"I just told you."

Peter thought about this and then said, "No, you didn't."

"I was passing out your flyers. There are many people excited for your comeback." Peter again reached for the cards, and she again caught his wrist. "Later. Let's eat first." Beth looked over at me and asked how I was doing. I wasn't throwing up, so I nodded that I was fine. "Could you do me a huge favor? Could you feed him and let me finish my lunch?"

"Feed him?"

"Have some of my food," Peter bellowed to her.

"I don't like your food, Bob. Please, Andy?" I didn't answer, but without transition she was out of the room and I had a spoon in my hand.

"Do you want me to feed you?" I asked him.

"I want to eat," he answered.

"Well, I want you to eat." Peter picked up the deck of cards he'd wanted since we entered the room and started to shuffle with both hands. If he could do this, I thought, why couldn't he use a spoon? "Where should I sit?" He patted the bed beside him. I sat down in an awkward position, keeping my shoes from touching the sheet but turned enough to reach the tray and bring food to his mouth. I began feeding him as he shuffled. His mouth clamped down on the spoon, and we suddenly met an impasse. I didn't want to pull the spoon upward and wipe the food against his upper lip—he was an adult, and I wouldn't treat him like a baby—but he didn't want to use his tongue or pull his own head back, so the food remained on the spoon and the spoon in his mouth, and his small, round eye looked at me and blinked twice. I twisted the spoon in Peter's mouth and pressed downward as I cleanly withdrew it. That felt less condescending somehow. As strange as my technique might look, Peter went with it for a few more spoonfuls, and then he burst out laughing and spat the potatoes over his shirt.

From the kitchen, Beth called out, "He laughs sometimes for no reason. Ignore it." She appeared, pinching a chip with sour cream. "Unless you made a joke."

"No."

"I didn't think so. I think it's a nervous laughter. It's probably because of all the fucking clowns," she added and then put the nacho in her mouth and walked out of sight. I held a spoonful of carrots up to his mouth. He appraised it and then took the bite. I twisted and withdrew.

"I'm sorry, Peter."

"What?"

I spoke up, "I'm so sorry this happened to you." I wiped his shirt with a napkin. I wanted to tell him it wasn't my fault. I didn't run this city. I was just as defenseless as everyone else.

"Peter, do you remember . . . ?"

"Baaaaawwwwwb."

"Bob. Do you remember how I sent you to the Sheraton?" He didn't respond; I tried to jog his memory. "The Sheraton New York? The hotel near the Hilton? Where you were staying? For a package that they said they didn't have?"

He looked at me closely and asked suspiciously, "Who are you?"

"I'm Beth's brother."

"My fiancée."

"That's right. You and I had dinner in August the night we were jumped."

"You only look a little bad," he said. I let it slide.

"We were on our way to a hotel to pick up a package that wasn't there. I sent you to the wrong hotel earlier that day and you wanted to go back. Remember? I should have put you in a cab after dinner; none of this would have happened then." He burst out laughing again and sifted through his cards for one in particular. "You don't think it's funny, do you? I ran away. I didn't protect you. I was the host, you were my guest, and I ran away. I came back, you don't know this, but I did come back and I was going to kill them. It was too late though. They were already gone. I did come back. I am back."

Peter leaned forward over his tray and tried to eat the mashed potatoes by lapping them up with his tongue.

"I'm sorry," I said. "For everything."

His only reply, one I interpreted as a gesture of forgiveness, was to hold out his deck and say, "Pick a card, any card."

Gladly, I thought. I was willing to sit through any magic trick Peter wanted to show me. I pinched what I thought was a random card in the middle of the deck.

"Not that one!" he shouted.

"I'm sorry," I repeated and tried again.

● ● ●

BACK IN MIDTOWN I found Reed D'Carloff outside, leaning against the plate-glass window of the Renaissance diner. He was holding open his green, vomit-stained raincoat, trying to block the view of the patrons behind him.

"Oh, now he shows up!" he shouted at me.

"I thought we'd meet inside."

"So did I," he said with a freakish smile. In the afternoon light, I could have reproduced a lifelike portrait of him with construction paper and three crayons. "Five hours ago." The threesome in the booth behind Reed were making gestures to a waiter about the man in the filthy coat who was pressed up against their eating space. "Apparently, a full breakfast, a piece of pie, and an order of fries isn't enough for this place. There's also a limit on coffee refills."

"They probably had to cut you off."

"What does that mean?" he snapped.

"Well, you're very hyper," I said, noticing the waiter coming toward us.

The door opened: "Friend, why don't you just go?"

Reed redirected his hostility toward the waiter. "I need to be here, I told you."

"Please go."

"It's a public sidewalk."

"It's a private window." Like a petulant, powerless schoolboy, Reed leaned forward, keeping an inch of air between himself and the glass. The waiter told him he was nuts.

"You just lost a customer, jerk."

"I'm calling the police." The waiter turned.

"Aww, go back to Egypt."

"Try Greece, asshole." The door closed.

"Why don't we go somewhere else?" I suggested and stepped out of the sightline of the people inside the restaurant. Reed wiggled his lower jaw and spat on the window. I started walking away from him.

He was beside me, gesturing toward the other pedestrians. "I sat there for four hours watching all these people with the same terrified look on their faces. They know another plane is going to crash here. More anthrax, bombs on buses. This city is just a big countdown clock. I want to get out of here, but you, you, you . . ." He jabbed my shoulder with his fingertip, ". . . are keeping me here."

"You're free to go," I told him. "I have other things to worry about."

"Like the Russian woman?"

"Among other things."

"I saw you get in that cab this morning. They brought me my

orange juice and I looked out that window and saw you get in a cab. I couldn't believe it. I thought this jackass throws up on me . . ."

"I'm sorry for that."

". . . then leaves me alone in a gay bar. They all thought you were breaking up with me."

"You shouldn't have been yelling *Don't forget me.*"

"You did forget me!"

"I didn't know what time you wanted to meet."

"I said the morning! You went to see your sister already?"

"She's not interested."

"In what?" he asked in a high-pitched squeal.

"A relationship."

He halted, grabbed my arm, and spun me around. He was apoplectic. "Is that what you told her? Damn it!" he screamed at the sky. "I only want to talk to her! That's all. What exactly did she say?"

I took Beth's note out of my pocket and held it out. He snatched it and quickly read her message. His cheeks reddened even more, and he tore the paper into pieces. He was trembling. I could almost hear him boiling, his face a painted teapot, his hair the lid clattering with steam.

"So that's that then?" I said, moving to cross Ninth, holding my hands out as if urging an animal to stay put. He was mumbling to himself and cursing my sister in graphic detail. I was still waiting for the WALK sign, watching the signal for the traffic.

"What does she want from me?" he asked. The green turned to yellow.

"Nothing."

"I'm through talking to you." The yellow turned to red. WALK.

I took him at his word and crossed the street. He followed me. "Wait."

I stopped on the opposite corner. "What?"

"What did she tell you about me?"

"Nothing."

"Where's your sister?"

"What don't you understand about this? I'm never going to tell you."

"Then I'll keep following you."

"Why?"

"I don't have a choice."

"Then follow me over to the police precinct." I started to move north.

"Sure. Wherever." He was clearly unstable, but I couldn't tell how dangerous he was. I stopped walking, because he was pressing me into oncoming pedestrian traffic. He had another strategy: "Hear me out."

"Oh, my God."

"Hear me out," he said, "and if I can't convince you to help me, then I'll walk away and you'll never hear from me again." He must have been working on this speech all morning, scrawling notes on napkins. He apologized for being angry—he wasn't an angry person. It was the fault of the waiter who didn't know how to treat customers with the respect they deserved. We all deserved respect. Had I ever lost a job? he asked me. He'd lost three. One because of my sister, one because of affirmative action, and one because of downsizing. At that last one, they had to ask him what he did. They didn't know why he worked there. When he told them what he did, they actually laughed. Really? they said. They couldn't believe it. This is exactly why we're restructuring, they said. Sorry we wasted a year of your life, they should have said. His wife left him, because she didn't like being seen with him. I hate my life, she said. You're just depressed, he said. Because I'm married to you, she said. Then she died. Karma maybe. He had a difficult life, he wasn't going to lie to me, but it's when the house comes crumbling down that you really show who you are. He was ready to start a new life. Could I help him?

Reed must have thought he was a masterful elocutionist, from the way he kept raising his eyebrows as he hit each point, but listening to him was the equivalent of watching the last amount of bathwater swirl down the drain. I could only think of one way to make him leave. I pulled a pen from my coat.

"Do you have a piece of paper?" I asked.

"Why?"

"I want you out of my life." He found a napkin in one of his pockets. I pointed the pen at him and said, "I'm going to call to warn her that you're on the way."

"Thank you." He was convinced that his speech had influenced me.

"Then I'll never see you again, right?"

"Of course not."

I wrote down Beth's name and an address—623 East 68th Street—which was not, of course, where Beth was staying. It was the address for the Ricardos in *I Love Lucy*, a fictitious address that, if followed, would dump Reed D'Carloff in the middle of the East River, where he belonged.

TWO DAYS LATER, **I** was in a small park in Tribeca, a trendy, shabby-chic enclave of multimillion-dollar lofts wedged between heavy tunnel traffic on the north and catastrophic tragedy on the south. I was sitting on a bench, marveling at how low the airplanes were allowed to fly over Manhattan. I watched several planes until they passed out of sight. In my mind, at least two of them were bound to collide with a skyscraper uptown, but no one else seemed alarmed, so I took my cue from them and feigned indifference as I waited for Sonia to arrive. She had left a message on my answering machine while I was feeding Peter his creamy lunch. Her voice was full of her usual energy but her message was oblique and unhelpful. She hadn't bothered to explain the Russian or her own whereabouts; she simply instructed me to meet her in this park in Tribeca on Saturday morning. She didn't sound like she was being held against her will. On the contrary, she sounded like she was the brains behind the operation, ending with a directive: "And do not call Brooklyn. Do not speak of this thing to anyone."

I heard my name and turned to see Sonia walking toward me. She was wearing a red-and-white athletic suit that made her look like a gymnast. When she raised her arms to wave, I expected her to vault over one of the parked cars.

She shouted, "Welcome back outside! I am thinking this is a good thing!" We embraced and she whispered in my ear, "And here I am not Sonia."

"Who are you?"

"Debbie Lubag."

"Sonia . . ."

"Debbie."

"I have a lot of questions."

"And I think I am helping. But inside let's talk. Come, come." I opened my mouth and she covered it with her hand. "Follow me this way." I obeyed. Furtively, my eyes scanned the park for any sign of a green raincoat, but I hadn't seen Reed since I sent him on his goose chase.

"I cannot believe all these liars." Sonia was holding a copy of the *Daily News*, which had uncovered another corporate scandal. "And how do they think they get away? So much money. Everyone is liar. At Ground Zero, all these people here sell products for cause. And it is not for cause. Raise money for relief donations. And it is not for relief donations. All those people who went to Ground Zero, as soon as it happens and stole! Art and watches from Ground Zero! And those people who say they lose children want money. They lie, they are caught. Two people in Georgia—Georgia, America—they claim this life insurance, and this is thousands and thousands of dollars, and they are both alive. And they are nowhere near Ground Zero. Ever. And do you know someone stole a truck that is pushing dirt? NYPD dirt pusher. It is worth very much. Thousands of dollars. Gone. How do they think they will be free?" Disgusted, she pitched the paper into a garbage can. "And those judges at Olympics. There is much, much corruption in that skating. Much, much corruption. Now remember: Debbie."

We entered one of the older buildings, an old factory or ware-house, a couple of blocks south of Canal Street, which was now full of luxury lofts. The lobby was a long corridor decorated with potted ferns, glass floor tile, freshly painted lime-green walls with pink Art Nouveau sconces, and an obligatory American flag. On my walks, I'd noticed the city was full of American flags as well as flawed security systems. Sonia took keys out of the pocket of her jacket. I opened my mouth again; this time, she silenced me with a look.

"And I think new color is better. I hated old color." I didn't bother asking her what she was talking about. She was speaking for someone else's benefit. We took the elevator in which I was also forbidden to speak to Debbie. On the fourth floor, we stepped out and I followed Sonia through a door into a loft ten times the size of my place. There were floor-to-ceiling windows down the entire length of the living room, and even though there was a substantial amount of furniture—all polished wood and pillows—there was an even more substantial amount of open floor space.

"There is kitchen and bedroom too. And bathroom is through that glass. Do you see this glass wall? The shower. There are slides, there are slides in shower with four . . . *kak skazat* . . . where water comes?"

"Spigots."

"Yes."

"Sonia . . ."

"Debbie."

Unable to wait any longer, I ripped off my hat and asked, "Why am I calling you Debbie?"

"And who did that to you?"

"I shaved my head. Don't change the subject."

She stepped down from her clogs and walked to the nearest sofa where she sat, pulled her legs underneath her, very much at home, and looked at me.

"And life, you know this, costs money. First, my living situation. Debbie Lubag is crazy rich woman I clean for. I clean this apartment. I was assistant to her for time. One month only. And after September eleventh, she left New York. She is broken. She wants me to clean apartment still. Calls me, tells me she's crazy, tells me to keep cleaning apartment, but she won't know when she is returning. She will never return I think. She lives in other home. In Florida. So I say, Fine, good. I clean apartment. And then I think. I can live here. No rent. And since Christmas I am here."

"So you've assumed her identity?"

"What?"

"You are now Debbie Lubag?"

"Yes. In way. Only when I'm here."

"The only Lubag I ever knew was Filipino."

"And the world is small place. People move. I am Russian Lubag."

"So who is Sonia Obolensky?"

"There are two of us now. This is only among us. A cousin of mine comes to America in March. Last year. I don't even know this. Nothing. And she stays too long. She stays too long in America and INS wants her. And she leaves Chicago, and comes to me. October tenth. And I let her stay with me. Then I think of brilliant thing. I make very little money, I struggle, I cannot sing when I want to. There are not hours in day for me to do my dream. BUT! But if there are two Sonias, then there are two incomes. I give her some jobs I have in past. Cleaning, coat check at place in Brooklyn. And she tells everyone she is Sonia Obolensky."

"You don't look anything alike."

"Enough! We are both Russian girls, and we do different jobs. And once, maybe twice, someone knows me and tells her she is fatter. And this does not matter."

"Have you ever gone to help with Peter?"

"No. I talk to your mother on phone but then other Sonia goes to her face. We make sure we are never together. I live here now and am Debbie Lubag. This helps. And until I become famous and then maybe she speaks English better and she is Debbie Lubag."

"Oh, you definitely have this worked out. You have an identical twin who looks nothing like you, and you're squatting in a loft whose owner is going to come home."

"Fine! I keep my belongings in my bag and if I hear the door I jump up and dust. I jump up and clean toilet. And I say 'Welcome back! I am just dusting, I am just cleaning your toilet.' And here is where it gets complex."

"Sonia, I have something very important to talk about. The reason I left my apartment."

"Wait, wait. I must tell this crisis. I have dream. You know this. And I have money now for my dream. Do not think other Sonia is that great of worker. She is not. She is lazy." Sonia stood, crossed to a desk in a corner. She opened the drawer, pulled out a check, and displayed it for me. It was a check for fifteen thousand dollars made out to Debbie Lubag. From the Red Cross. "And I would have money left over for my release party."

"What are you thinking?" I worried aloud.

"This check is for me."

"No, it's not. It's for Debbie Lubag."

"And she is crazy and won't know it arrives. I sign her name and then my own and that's that. She does not know I cash it. The copy goes back to Red Cross."

"Debbie . . ."

"Listen. I come home three weeks ago and people are in lobby getting checks. Red Cross is going to all Tribeca buildings and giving checks. They ask no questions. You sign paper that you get it, done. At first, I walk by but people call me back. They know me Debbie, call me Debbie. No one is showing IDs. Some are angry and say they don't want checks. They don't need checks. And the Red Cross says: 'Take it! Take donations!' One rips up check. But most are taking checks. For suffering. I wait until all are gone and then say 'Debbie Lubag.' I think if they say, 'You are not Debbie,' I say, 'I am her cleaner. She is out of town.' If they don't give it, fine, I go upstairs. But they don't ask, they give me check. They ask me questions and I tell how I suffer. How sad it still is. Which is true. Not a lie. I tell them I was volunteer at Ground Zero. I tell them I massaged dogs at Ground Zero and still feel fur in my hands. Which is true. I did this with my teacher. They give me check."

"You haven't cashed it yet."

She held it with both hands in front of her, reading it over.

"I will. I am trying to think how they would know. How can I be caught? I can't. I know this. I can't."

"So why haven't you cashed it?"

"Do not judge me. Do not start."

"Because you know it's not right."

"What is the harm? All those rich people in lobby take money. Only one man said no to them. I am tired of being bohemian. I hate it! To be poor artist means you work twice. You work at job to make money and you work to be artist. Work, work. I thank God I have two of me now. One Sonia to work . . ."

"One to cash a check illegally."

"Do not judge me!"

"Doesn't the fake Sonia have her own bills? She eats quite a bit, that's apparent."

"And seventy-five percent of earnings come to me. Yes, seventy-five. Do not judge me. I will repair later. When I sell my CD."

"Give me the check, Sonia."

"Call me Debbie," she said and pocketed the check. "Now no more talk. Come to this bathroom and look at this shower."

"There's something I need to talk about, Sonia. The reason I left my apartment."

"Oh, you said something about this."

"Brad is running from someone. Do you have any idea why?"

"No. I do not know this."

"Are you sure you're not keeping something from me?"

"I am sure."

"I think you were right when you said Brad left the city."

Sonia groaned, "Let him go, let him go. It is over between you. There are other fish in Chelsea."

"Sonia, please! It's more than that. Something very serious made him leave the city. Last summer, he left a package for me at a hotel in midtown. I never picked it up. This past week I got a call from the hotel about it. That's what got me outside. It was important information about your friend, Rod." I watched Sonia's face, but she registered nothing other than confusion and slight boredom. "Did you know that twenty years ago Rod Hamilton murdered two men and burned their house down around them?"

Sonia looked out a window and tried to remember if she had known this. It was as if I had asked her if she knew Rod's middle name.

"No. I do not think I ever know this."

"That he killed two people and burned them?"

"No."

I waited. "Aren't you disturbed by this?"

She shrugged. "We are not that close to him and me. We never talk about this."

"I know him less than you, but I'm extremely disturbed by it."

"And why? There is so much more death now. You said he did this twenty years ago. We all did things twenty years ago."

"We did not all murder someone twenty years ago."

"You judge, you judge. He did not murder anyone since that day, did he?"

"I don't know, maybe. Maybe Brad. What did you and Brad talk about that last time you met?"

"Oh, and I cannot do this again. I tell you! I tell you over and over. We did not talk about you! We did not talk about Rod! We sit at this bar, I cry and tell him that I cannot take his money because Porfiry and I don't want handout. Stupid! Stupid! I'll take handout every day now."

"That's all?"

"Yes. Then he runs out."

"Yes, but he *ran* out. He ran out! I think you're missing a part of your story."

"No, I am not."

"Why would he run?"

"He is embarrassed. And we are friends. He loves giving money away. You know he does this. He loves it, and I tell him no. I tell him I do not want his money. This hurts his soul so he leaves. Now I do not do this. I do not hurt Red Cross when they want to give me money. I say, 'Thank you, Red Cross. Thank you very much.'"

"You just ranted outside about all the liars and cheaters . . ."

"This is different!" she shouted but didn't elaborate. After a few moments, I asked if I could have Rod Hamilton's phone number. She climbed off the couch and dug deep inside her bag. Through the wall of windows I watched another plane narrowly miss five or six towers. Sonia shoved a piece of paper into my hand.

"And I will say two things, Judger. The first thing is I told you all about Brad. No more! And about Rod, I don't know these things, but I like him. And what he does twenty years ago is milk! Milk! Now, come. Look in shower with me. There are slides in this. You will laugh and die."

I didn't laugh, and I didn't die. On the other side of the glass wall was a shower larger than my living room. Because of its size, there was no curtain or door. There were four spigots spaced four feet apart from each other and three four-foot-high slick slate sliding boards in those empty spaces. A bath could be drawn; the base board could be raised from the floor to create a pool four feet deep. There were eight floor lamps bordering the glass wall that, illuminated, would produce a show for anyone in the living room. What Sonia found funny, and what she assumed I would, was that a woman who tastefully decorated her living room would have a shower more suitable for a water park, but I was still out of touch with what was and wasn't normal, so I alternately regarded everything as normal and preposterous. On my walks, I had tried to take my cue from others, but New Yorkers were ignoring what I considered the most outrageous behavior, signage, architecture, conversations. I walked by battalions of anemic young men and women covered in pimples, wearing Scientology uniforms, cheap white shirts tucked into navy blue pants or skirts, clip-clopping back to headquarters as if they were preparing to invade Presbyteria, and nobody paid them any mind or acted as if they were in the least peculiar. I walked by an adult girlie club where a doorman stood dressed in a long maroon coat with gold epaulettes as if he worked at the Four Seasons or the Ritz. Nobody else thought it weird. I supposed the shower Sonia showed me was strange and out of place, but why not have slides in your bathroom?

I could tell Sonia was disappointed by my solemnity, but I was disappointed by her confession. I wasn't, at the time, much bothered about the Red Cross check or that she was harboring and perhaps abusing an illegal alien. I was disturbed because her secrets had nothing to do with Rod or Brad or Peter's attack. Sonia couldn't tell me anything I needed to know. Nor could the violent Russian or my man with the cartoon face, who I assumed were part of my larger story. My larger story! This was my biggest problem: I had no idea what my larger story was. On August eleventh, I walked off the set while my life was still being filmed, and since the costs were too high and the logistics too complicated to simply shut down production, everyone else from Ruby to Sonia, even Peter, continued filming, so when I returned to the various locations, I discovered that I'd relinquished every right to star in my own picture, that it was a different picture anyway and I had obviously misread the script.

• • •

ROD HAMILTON REFUSED TO say anything incriminating over the phone, and I refused to meet him anywhere but out in public, as Brad's seven-month-old note recommended. On Monday afternoon, I wound my way east through Central Park, gripping a steak knife in my coat pocket in case he chose to relive his youth. Certain that the tour guide expected me to descend one of the terrace staircases to meet him at the fountain, I deliberately approached the Bethesda angel from behind, along the lake, and past the Bow Bridge. When I turned the bend, I saw Rod sitting on a bench on the very same path, just ten yards away, watching the fountain through the trees. He sat with his legs out, his hands in the pockets of his coat, a black wool hat pulled down to his glasses. I watched him waiting for me and tried in vain to reconcile him with the boy I had read about. I felt my heart pumping—the man in the green raincoat had turned out to be an ex-restaurant manager, and the Russian was Sonia's cousin, but this person in front of me had, in fact, committed a heinous crime and was still hiding from the consequences.

"I thought you said the fountain." He didn't hear me. "I thought you said the fountain." My voice was too deep inside my body. I approached and shouted, "I thought you said the fountain!" He spun his head toward me and sat up.

"I wasn't, I wasn't sure you'd be alone," he explained. I sat on the next bench and we appraised each other. I asked if he had a weapon hidden in his coat. He told me he wasn't a sniper; I asked him to prove it. He stood, opened his coat, emptied his pockets, and I found myself wishing for one of those beeping metal-detecting wands used all over New York now. He sat down. Neither of us spoke. I didn't know how to begin, afraid I would ask the wrong questions.

To break the silence, he pointed to the fountain. "Do you know the story behind the angel?"

"I'm not here for a tour!" I cut him off. I couldn't afford to lose control so early and trail behind an irrelevant lecture on sculpture or urban angelology.

"I love this city," he said simply. We sat in silence for a bit longer. The day was cold but not so frosty as to keep visitors out of the park. Three teenagers were crossing the terrace and heading up our path. "There are too many people. Let's find somewhere more secluded." I didn't budge; I didn't want seclusion. "It's too open here," he pleaded, and gestured toward the woods on the other side of the lake.

"You want me to follow you into the Ramble? Where I could be ambushed?"

"Andy, who do you think I am?"

"No. Clue." I then lied, "I left the information about you with a neighbor. If I don't come home today, she sends it to the police."

"You're safe. I promise. I'm not a violent person."

"Fine." As we walked toward the Bow Bridge and the hills of trees and outcroppings of rock on the other side, he answered a few of my questions without my having to ask.

"I thought you knew, Andy. Since August, I thought you knew. Brad showed up at my building and told me he knew about Michigan. Then he said that he left copies of the clippings for you."

"Why?"

"The same reason as you did—to protect himself. Also I think because he wanted revenge. He thought I was the one who told you about his job."

"What about his job? He didn't have a job."

Rod peered at me. "You don't know?"

"Know what?"

"Where he got his money?"

"His family was in cardboard," I mumbled.

"I can't believe this. He was convinced you knew and thought I told you. I almost moved in August. I always thought I'd leave the city or even country if anything came out, but I didn't want to leave New York. I don't want to run again. I went to your apartment to see what you wanted from me. I should have been more explicit, but I just asked if you wanted to talk about it. *It*." He looked at me with an expression of irritation and anguish. "What did you think *it* was, Andy? You told me you didn't want to talk about it. *Least of all to you*, is what you said. Why not me?"

I could not remember. It was right after Peter and I were attacked, right after I locked myself away. Did I think he came by to chat about the attack? I considered Rod one of the least significant people in my life; I couldn't transcribe every conversation I had with him. What did I think he was talking about? It must have been about the attack. I wondered why, of all people, he showed up to counsel me. I blamed him for refusing Brad's offer for an award at dinner that night. He was the reason I initiated the scholarship program and turned the summer into what it was, which included the assault on Fifty-first Street. This is what I probably meant, but I couldn't recall the exact conversation, which Rod remembered in such detail.

Rod shook his head. "For months. I thought you and I were mired in this game. I kept coming by, kept touching base, because not knowing . . . was excruciating. That last visit. You said we were cool."

"No. You said we were cool. I didn't know what you were talking about! I just wanted you to get out. I never knew why you were there."

"I thought it was understood. Sometimes Beth says something that makes me think you told her . . ."

This floored me. "Excuse me. What?"

"What?"

"Are you talking about my sister, Beth?"

"Yes." We both stood on the muddy path staring at each other, stalled yet again, in complete befuddlement.

"Why would you be talking about my sister?"

"We met at your apartment. The last time I was there. I helped her to find some shops. We had fun. She's funny."

"Are you dating my sister?" I didn't wait for an answer. "You are."

"I thought you knew."

"Again: wrong! Beth doesn't talk about her 'love affairs.' Beth doesn't know that you're a killer, does she?"

"I'm not a killer. I killed someone . . . two people . . ."

I shook my head, and we stood there trying to work out what we both now knew. Near a stream, Rod led me off the path to a small clearing between a fallen tree and a large boulder of schist, a conference room in the woods. I spotted three condom wrappers on the ground. This is where people came for seclusion—a history of copulation since the Civil War could be readily imagined—the unfastening of belts, of buttons, snaps, zippers, and the dropping of jerseys,

bonnets, feathers, bowlers, Levi's, and leathers. This was too intimate. He took a seat on a ledge of the rock. I leaned against the
tree.

"You have to tell my sister. Or I will."

"We all have things we wish would be forgotten." Rod pulled off
his hat, scratched his sweaty head. He replaced the hat, leaned forward with his elbows on his knees and said, "Brad and I made this
pact and he broke it."

I whispered, "I can't follow any of this. Please. Start from the beginning."

"There's nothing I can say to justify it. When I was eighteen, I saw
a man's name in a phone book. The name was so vile to me I couldn't
conceive of there being another Sam Dubin. This Sam Dubin was
THE Sam Dubin. People confuse names. It happens. A hundred
years ago it happened with your name. Andrew Green was the Father
of New York, the Great Consolidator, the comptroller of this park. He
was in his eighties, shot on his doorstep by a man who had issue with
another, much younger man with a similar-sounding name."

"Please," I begged him. "I don't want a tour."

"I'm just saying assumptions are made. Based on information we
think is accurate. When we're not in the right state of mind. We
think we know something we don't and then we fully commit to it."

● ● ●

JACK CORT FOLLOWED THE eighteen-wheeler to New York City
in 1982 and immediately found several under-the-table jobs to work,
mainly as a waiter and bartender. After ten years, he emerged from
dark pubs and restaurants with a new name, facial hair, eyeglasses,
a new laugh, a new accent, a new Social Security number, and a new

story, which he used to begin soliciting work as a guide to the city. There were precautions. He avoided groups from Michigan, and though difficult, he was able to keep the photos to a minimum, often turning to acknowledge an unasked question just as the camera flashed. Over time, he feared less and less the moment in which someone knocked on the door with a warrant to drag him away.

One night, however, after too much wine, he declined an award because he was afraid that the benefactor would probe too far into his life. He should have smiled, nodded, acted grateful, and then later slipped free. Instead he rejected the honor flat out and insulted a man who viewed ingratitude as a personal affront. When he went to bed that night, he knew that aspirin couldn't prevent the next morning's headache, so he changed into sweats and ran up and down the hill in front of his building for an hour in the dark. He sweated the alcohol out of his system and guzzled a liter of water.

He knew he could not ignore Brad Willet. Brad Willet was determined and wealthy, which meant he would begin research without Rod's cooperation. Rod didn't know what he would find. Rod had covered his tracks and diverted attention, claimed he'd grown up in Florida, but Brad's foundation would doubtlessly have a crack team of researchers. Rod resented and feared the Internet and its search capabilities, but sitting and sweating merlot on a grimy curb, he reminded himself that the door swung both ways. He went upstairs and turned on his computer. He felt encouraged when his search engine couldn't locate a Web site for the foundation whose founder was such a proponent of publicity. Then he began pondering the wealthy man's resistance to discussing his fortune or his family.

On Monday and Tuesday, Rod followed Brad Willet from his apartment in Chelsea to the World Trade Center, where Brad, dressed in corporate attire, ascended one of the express elevator tubes. Rod stationed himself in the lobby. He watched the elevators. Brad took lunch at twelve and left at five on both days. He purposefully and confidently walked to a deli on Church for lunch and to the IRT in the evening. Brad was not visiting the World Trade Center; he was there as part of a routine.

On Wednesday morning, Rod dressed in a suit. As he knotted the tie, he yawned. He had slept well, so he wasn't sure why he was so groggy. He lay on the bed for one quick power nap. Three hours later, he woke up and ran in his slightly wrinkled suit to the subway. In forty-five minutes, he was standing in the atrium, holding a large coffee, with his eye on the elevator bank. He hadn't seen Brad enter the building that morning, so his wait was infused with doubt and anxiety. When noon passed, he began to fear that he had wasted a day and that Brad was closer to uncovering what Rod wanted burned and buried. He also began to fear that Brad could come in late, run into Rod, and ask him why he was standing in the lobby staring at elevators. Rod moved into a corner and felt too conspicuous. He moved slowly around the elevators. At twelve-thirty, a crowd, including Brad Willet, spilled out of an elevator. Rod saw that he was talking with a short, pregnant woman with fastidiously curled hair. They parted, and Rod chose to approach the one with whom Brad seemed so familiar.

"Do you know if Jack Cort's on the sixtieth floor today?" Rod asked innocently enough, though he realized with terror that in his bluff he had just used his real name for the first time in nineteen years. He kept his smile.

"I don't know. I don't work on the sixtieth."

"No?" He feigned surprise. "You look familiar." She told him the floor where she—and, presumably, Brad—did work. He thanked her, let her make her way to lunch, and then he passed through security for a meeting with Brad Willet. The elevator rose and his ears popped as he yawned for the fortieth time that hour. He told himself to keep calm, his nerves were prone to mutiny. The doors opened. While the atmosphere was very professional, the office did not provide any clue to its function or position in the world of commerce. The name was unfamiliar; the logo was generically important. Rod walked directly to the receptionist and told her he was early but that he had an appointment with Brad Willet, a friend from college and cochair for the upcoming class reunion. He held his breath, but was rewarded:

"Mr. Willet just left for lunch, but you're welcome to wait."

Rod thanked her and sat down. He coughed a few times, establishing a later ploy, and then said, "I always thought Brad would end up a musician. He loved the guitar."

"Really? I didn't know he played."

"Oh, yeah. Loved music. I never thought he'd be in an office. I don't even know what he does here." There was not the slightest pause. The receptionist told him, and everything made complete sense. Rod needed to remain composed, because this was the moment when an unexpected son would pull into the driveway. He coughed again. "Do you know how long he'll be? I think I'm coming down with that flu. My whole office had it. Violent and nasty this year." The receptionist forced a sympathetic smile. "Knocks you out, keeps you in bed for three days." He could see her distress. "I'm going to fight it. I refuse to let it . . . (cough, cough, groan) . . . I refuse to let it get me." He breathed, sighed, and moaned for only fifteen seconds before she asked if he would prefer to wait in Mr. Willet's office.

Rod pretended to deliberate and then said, "Sure. That's fine." She pointed him to the office almost directly behind her. Glass windows, a door, and a view of the Brooklyn Bridge. He sat in one of the two chairs in front of Brad's desk. Beyond glancing at pages that were up-turned on the desktop, Rod did not snoop, did not open file cabinets or surreptitiously click through the documents on Brad's computer.

When Brad Willet entered his office, he regarded Rod Hamilton as one would an uncaged tiger. Rod smiled. Brad hesitated at the door, looked around, and closed it softly behind him. Both wondered what the other thought, knew, and wanted. Each waited for the other to speak. Brad sat at his desk and joined his hands.

"I couldn't find your foundation," Rod finally said.

"I couldn't find your high school," Brad replied.

"Stop looking." Rod leaned forward. "Let everything stay between us." Brad looked at his computer. Rod saw that the screen saver was an eternal series of curtains rising, parting, rising, parting, constantly anticipating a nonexistent performance, opening and lifting onto other curtains that would separate and rise on even more curtains. "You're in charge of the company's corporate sponsorship and all the money distributed to nonprofit organizations." Brad looked composed, but a whimpering sound escaped him. "It must be nice to set up a foundation, make out checks to yourself and then bask in the glory of being a philanthropist. You love to be thanked and it's not enough being thanked as a representative of a company. You want them to think it's all coming from you. I'm sure it's illegal. This company donates for the public relations and you're taking all the credit."

"We donate to many organizations."

"How much of it has gone to your fake foundation? Over the years I assume six figures? Seven?" Brad tried a pathetic laugh as a last-ditch effort to brush the matter aside. Rod would have none of it. "Is your boss back from lunch? Is there a board meeting? I'll walk through that door right now and cry it out, I swear to God. I'm telling you. I'm telling you I will spread the news in a heartbeat. I will post it at the receptionist desk. I'll use the intercom."

"Please."

"Who knows about this?" Brad shook his head. "Nobody knows except for me?" Brad nodded. "Then we're even. Your secret is safe."

"How can I trust you?" Brad asked.

"You know I'm not from Florida. That's enough. Nothing leaves this room, I promise you, but if you dig any deeper, I will spread this like a virus." There was a long silence, and the gilded drapery gave way to blue folds, which opened on red velvet, which parted for green silks. "Well?"

"There won't be an awards ceremony. As far as I know, you grew up in Tampa."

"Or a small town nearby. Deal." With that, Rod stood, shook Brad's wet hand, and walked out of the office. At the receptionist's desk, he picked up a card with three office phone numbers and a general e-mail address. He lifted it up as a wave to Brad and coughed one last time for the receptionist before he boarded the elevator down.

That was it.

That was all.

Until, months later, on the humid, stinking afternoon of August tenth. Rod came home after a long, air-conditioned lunch. His shirt was sticking to his back after only a block's walk. He turned the key in the front door of his building and pushed into the warmth of the lobby. A man in shorts and a T-shirt, in a baseball cap and sunglasses, sat off to the left. Rod acknowledged him and crossed to the staircase.

Two words. The man behind him said two words, and it was as if all of Rod's pores throbbed open at once and he was even sweatier, more dehydrated, light-headed, sleepy.

"Jack Cort?" Rod turned and shook his head. He couldn't speak. The man held a large yellow envelope and was now standing. Rod looked at his face but didn't recognize him. "You grew up in Michigan, not Florida." Rod looked closer. He had grown a goatee, his blue eyes were covered by dark sunglasses, but it was Brad Willet. "You left Michigan when you were eighteen. It's all in here." Walking over to Rod, Brad reached into the envelope and pulled out a photograph, a snapshot of himself standing next to a man in front of a garage. Rod recognized his brother's smile, sweated some more at the sight of his gray hair. Brad pointed to his own baseball cap: CORT'S. "I didn't tell him I knew you. I just told him we had the same name and I bought his hat. He owns that garage."

Rod slowly led Brad up the stairs toward his apartment, muttering *why* on every landing.

When Rod opened the door, Brad whispered, "Just so it's understood: I left an envelope for Andy, so I'm not the only one who knows who you are."

"What do you think I'm going to do?"

"I don't know, but I don't trust you."

Inside, four fans circulated warm air throughout the rooms. The two men sat on opposite ends of a sofa, cautiously facing each other at forty-five-degree angles. Brad, still wearing his hat and sunglasses, placed the envelope between them and let Rod skim through the contents, copies of articles regarding his disappearance, the murders, and arson.

"I thought we had a pact," Rod said.

"So did I."

"Well?"

"You broke it." Brad said.

"I didn't."

"You told Andy and Sonia."

"I haven't seen either of them for months."

"That's a lie."

Rod insisted. "It's not a lie." Brad stared at Rod for a full minute. Because of the sunglasses, Rod couldn't see his eyes. "I didn't tell anyone anything. I don't care how you made your money." The sunglasses were giving away nothing. "Why do you think I told them?"

"I won't say."

"Did they tell you I told them?"

"No."

"Ask them."

"I haven't seen either of them since I left New York."

"You left New York?"

"I couldn't trust anyone, and I'm not going to jail."

"Then why are you back here?"

Brad took off his sunglasses and stood up. "Why am I back? Because I want you to know that I know your secret." He sat down. "I need to start a completely new life and I want your help."

● ● ●

"ARE YOU ALL RIGHT?" Rod asked me.

"I don't understand what's going on here." I was having difficulty breathing. How could I not know Brad had a full-time job? I felt like one of those wives who discovers her husband is married to three other people.

"Brad was very nervous. Something spooked him in June. He cut off all ties, cashed out his foundation, and left the city. He came back to ask me about Social Security cards, driver's licenses, new identities."

"Where did he go?"

"I don't know. We talked for an hour and he asked for some water. When I was in the kitchen, I heard the door open and close. I haven't heard from him since."

"I've got to walk," I said. "Why did Brad think I knew?"

Rod shrugged his shoulders.

"Why were Peter and I attacked that night? That's the same day Brad was with you!"

"I don't think that has anything to do with Brad, do you?"

"I don't know!" I began to exit Rod's little conference room in the woods. "What about my sister?"

"What about her?"

"I don't want Beth to get entangled with you . . ."

"I'm not the person you . . ."

"According to the law, you are. Turn yourself in, tell a judge that you're a different person . . ."

"Let me break it off with her . . . in a way that won't seem strange. I'm trying to keep this contained, you see." Rod was on his knees, his hands clasped together, and I was feeling trapped in the middle of all that rock.

"Fine," I said.

"Am I safe with you?"

"Fine." I just wanted to get out. I left and headed south, not looking behind me, since I was too busy revisiting every exchange I'd ever had with Brad. All of them needed to be revised in view of the fact that Brad Willet was a con artist who committed crime to capitalize cabaret.

I was coming to fully appreciate how much of my life happened behind my back: decisions were made, plots hatched, schemes dreamt, passions indulged, and judgments cast, all when I was out of the room; worse, most were made, hatched, dreamt, indulged, and cast in rooms, or caves, in which I've never stepped foot. Terrorists, CEOs, employers, politicians, my family, friends, and lovers were all talking of me, some conceptualizing me as a vague notion, part of a larger group, and some actually targeting me by name. Lost in such thought, I plodded down the hill toward the bridge and, despite my epiphany, I wasn't looking behind me, so I didn't see Rod stepping out and moving up the hill in the opposite direction, and I didn't see Reed D'Carloff slide down the schist and follow him from a distance.

AFTER I PIECED TOGETHER what Beth and Rod later told me, and what the news reported, Reed's story must have gone something like this.

Having just heard the stranger from Michigan say that he was going to break it off with Beth, Reed followed Rod up the hill on a winding, scenic route through Central Park that ended an hour later at Fifty-ninth Street. With finely honed techniques of urban tracking, he kept the perfect distance between himself and his quarry as they dodged traffic, block by block, down Seventh Avenue. He was convinced that Rod would lead him to Beth. At Forty-ninth and Eighth, however, he discovered that he wasn't the only one who was following Rod Hamilton through midtown Manhattan. He was joined by a middle school group of over forty students, teachers, and parents from Reno, Nevada, and this is how Reed D'Carloff found himself on a four-day tour of New York City. Fortunately, the tourists moved slowly and in a herd, so it was always easy for Reed to follow them. The tourists also tended to visit crowded locales, where it was easy for Reed to blend into the background, and there was always a taxi to keep up with their occasional bus tour.

Reed disliked New York at first, for all the usual reasons. He thought it dirty, loud, and intimidating. On every street corner, there was insurmountable competition and endless opportunity for failure. The threat of humiliation loomed even at delis—the servers barked at you in their accents from who-knows-what-country and no matter how fast you ordered, you weren't ordering fast enough. Reed felt inadequate, which was not why he had come to the city or how he wanted to live. Homeless people picking through the trash seemed more self-assured than Reed did. New York reminded him hourly of the chasm separating who he wanted to be and who he, sadly, was.

Each passing day, however, instilled a dose of confidence. After the first week, Reed was able to spin safely through a revolving door without a break in his stride, in the subway he was able to swipe his MetroCard without a glance at the monitor, and he was able to move through the streets—at least in midtown—without feeling lost. One afternoon, someone asked him for directions and, just before he explained he was from out of town, he realized that he knew exactly where they wanted to go as well as the fastest route to reach it. There was something empowering about giving directions, about knowing the geography and storefronts of the Big Apple. He could only imagine what it must be like to guide a group up those avenues and to know boundless trivia about the streets. Reed began to admire Rod. Twice he found himself stepping in front of one of the students in the back so that he could hear better.

Reed's favorite site was the Brooklyn Bridge, and he was spell-bound as Rod spoke of it. When built, the suspension bridge rose high above the five-story skyline and demonstrated that New York was not limited to outward expansion: Manhattan could explore the up. The bridge leaped over the East River and never disturbed the maritime traffic below. The bridge was spectacular. Not only did it function in connecting two major cities at the time, but the stone towers and steel cables were an artistic masterpiece. (Reed fully agreed with Rod.) The designers had utilized twenty different quarries to achieve slightly different coloration and texture so that the enormous bridge would not look like an overwhelming monstrosity to residents peering up from their windows or passengers looking up from their boats. Such an attention to detail for one of the largest structures on the planet. Reed thought about the thousands of men who built the bridge. To lay even one stone or hoist one cable as part of a team must have provided them satisfaction for the rest of their lives. Reed had never worked on a construction crew; he couldn't really conceptualize how a project of this size would develop—he just pictured men stacking stone and threading cable like string through the eye of a needle, pushing a dream upward and then tying it together. How inspiring just to gaze on this bridge, to be a member of a species that possessed the ingenuity, craft, and technique to visualize, design, and build something so majestic!

He listened intently as Rod spoke of the obstacles and the history of the construction. The only man able to build a bridge like this was hired and then promptly died of lockjaw, which left the massive responsibility to his son. Imagine having so many people trusting you with so much capital and actually believing you could meet their faith. When he then heard that the son was struck with the bends and was confined to a house in Brooklyn, Reed was perfectly awed that someone under so much pressure, metaphorical and actual, could complete such a task. He dismissed the story of Emily, his wife, who carried his instructions to the river and oversaw work at the bridge. Emily, the first female lawyer in the United States, reminded Reed too much of Hillary Clinton. Picturing himself working along the river—cutting stone for some reason (why, even in his fantasy, did he assign himself a prisoner's task?)—he felt emasculated by Emily Roebling, and he conveniently excised her role. He preferred the idea that Roebling, the son with the bends, shouted instructions from his window, and the men, listening very carefully, copied them down and set themselves to their work.

Later that evening, Reed envied the tourists, not because they were on their way to *Mamma Mia*, a musical made up entirely of ABBA songs, but because they had an hour to rest before dinner. Reed was as exhausted, but had to follow his indefatigable tour guide as he ran his errands. Reed felt his arches collapsing, the soles of his feet burning. Pink the night before, they were bound to be red or purple now. This was the city that never sat down. Rod was tireless and led Reed on a circuitous route that entailed stops at a drugstore, a post-office, a bookstore, and a florist. It wasn't until they reached a Mexican restaurant that Reed's mind registered the significance of the flowers.

Sitting in the window of the Mexican restaurant was Beth Green, her chin in her palm and an obscene orange flower stuck in her hair. Reed stepped out of sight. Keeping his eye on Rod and not expecting anyone to see him, he had almost walked right up to the window, which would have been disastrous. After all this time searching for her, the last thing he wanted to do was to give her the upper hand. Again. If there was anything he truly wanted to do in

New York, it was to slap that upper hand out of the sky. He crossed the street and watched the window from the corner. Rod gave Beth the flowers and they kissed. They were only a few blocks from Andy's apartment, and Reed wondered if she had been living nearby the entire time, sitting in windows that he had passed.

Reed couldn't move off the corner. He always planned to race straight up to Beth and demand to know what she intended to do. He wanted to make her cry. She had ruined a part of his life; how much more did she want to sabotage? For some reason, though, he could not stride into this restaurant, throw the chips to the floor, and splash her face with a margarita. He watched as Rod and Beth leaned in and laughed. They toasted each other and smiled. Beth said something they both thought very funny. He could tell that this woman, engaged to be married and having an affair, was not thinking about him at all.

Reed wanted to be someone others thought about. At least on occasion. At his high school reunion, most of his classmates who had left Charles County seemed shocked when they shook his hand. They had completely forgotten that Reed D'Carloff ever existed, let alone sat beside them in class. Each of them surreptitiously glanced at his name badge and then made a quick visit to the table with the yearbook. He knew that as they dipped carrot sticks and cherry tomatoes in ranch dressing, they were sharing their surprise with one another about how the mind operated, how memory filed what was significant and discarded what was irrelevant. That is how he would be remembered by his classmates—as their first collective memory lapse.

Beth should have remembered him! They'd worked together, had sex, fought in a mall until security separated them, and lost their jobs because of each other. The more Reed watched Beth look at

Rod, the more he felt unseen. He drifted into his own mind with its recollections and resentments. Earlier that day he had studied a bridge sculpted in the air and had yearned for that kind of satisfaction. That legacy. Now he stood above an overflowing trash can as the world went on, oblivious of his existence. How many in Maryland missed him, how many in New York cared if he was still here or had ever noticed he'd arrived? There was a flash in his mind of a manager at Petey Pepperoni sorting through a desk drawer and coming across Reed's name on an outdated health inspection form. Then there was a flash of the manager throwing the form and his signature away. There were more flashes of his diminishing legacy, of people living their lives without him and not feeling any worse for it. Being forgotten was remarkably easy. Maybe Reed thought of me and realized that I had not glanced behind me even once on that last walk in Central Park. Suddenly, there was no one in the window of the Mexican restaurant. They were gone. Reed had lost Beth and Rod. Impossible! He ran across the street and into the restaurant. He was furious and wanted to crack open one of the hanging piñatas. He had one objective, and he had let it walk out the door.

There were those who built bridges to span rivers and those who merely commuted across.

• • •

IT WAS THE FOURTH day on the Reno group's itinerary, and Reed changed his strategy. He decided to confront Rod at the first opportunity. This presented itself on Lower Broadway. Rod was sending the group alone onto the observation platform above Ground Zero. Rod's face was grim as he spoke to the eighth-graders before letting them go. Reed heard only snatches: "This is not Disneyland . . .

remember: you don't know who you're standing next to . . ." Soon Reno, Nevada, was walking up the ramp and Rod was alone, leaning against a Greek column.

Just as he pulled a book out of his bag, Reed walked up to him and spoke: "Sam Dubin sends his regards." Rod blanched.

"Excuse me?"

"I know all about Sam Dubin and your past."

"Okay."

"I want you to pass on a message to Beth Green." Rod looked surprised to hear another familiar name. "Tell her that she needs to meet Reed D'Carloff tomorrow at four o'clock in front of Carnegie Hall. Tell her if she doesn't, then Reed D'Carloff will call Michigan and ruin her boyfriend's life. Now don't get your panties in a knot either. I don't want to report you, I don't really care. I think you're a very good tour guide. My business is with Beth."

"Who are you?"

"Reed D'Carloff!" He said it twice already!

"Beth doesn't . . ."

"Beth doesn't know you're a killer? Is that what you're about to say? I don't care how Beth gets to Carnegie Hall, just make sure she does." Reed heard himself and realized he had inadvertently referenced a joke. He pressed on, in case Rod felt compelled to laugh. "Carnegie Hall tomorrow at four. Alone. We need to talk. Make it happen."

An annoying girl from the tour was standing beside them. She must have walked to the end of the ramp, turned the corner, and come straight back. Or Reno had expelled her.

"Why aren't you with the group?" Rod snapped.

"I'm done."

"You're not supposed to be on your own."

"I'm with you." Rod looked at Reed who just smiled. Reed was in control now. The girl said, "I think that was so sad. When I get home to Nevada, I'm going to cry, cry, cry. Where are we going next?"

"Go back to your group!" Rod shouted. The girl merely blinked and walked to the end of the building. "How do you know about Sam?"

"Never mind that. Beth needs to be in front of Carnegie Hall at four o'clock. That gives you time to persuade her. You're good with words. If she's not there, you're going to jail." Reed walked away, savoring the sensation of putting someone else in his place.

● ● ●

STANDING BENEATH THE AWNING on Fifty-seventh Street, a few minutes after four, Reed wondered two things: Would the high-alert issued that morning by the federal government prevent Beth from showing up, and was Carnegie Hall a terrorist target? He fidgeted. He planned to meet with Beth and then catch the first train—he would not fly on a high-alert day. Where was she? He wanted to get out of this city. The sooner the better. All day long, on this day of extra vigilance, he couldn't help but compose a mental list of all the different ways to attack New York, and as the day wore on, he felt increasingly nervous. Of course, Washington wasn't a low-level target, either, and the radiation from a nuclear blast could contaminate southern Maryland. He considered moving, a fresh start, but first he had to learn what Beth wanted. It was ten minutes after four by this point, but he was used to Beth being fashionably late. She loved to make an entrance.

So he waited there at Carnegie Hall and tried not to think of bombs in the passing trucks, poisoned water supplies, exploding tunnels, collapsing bridges, squadrons of crop dusters spraying the city with smallpox, mailboxes full of anthrax, anti-aircraft missiles, radiation bombs, or that stun device that anyone could make from cheap purchases at Home Depot, which would neutralize all electricity and computer technology in a mile radius at the press of a button.

A taxi stopped in front of the Russian Tea Room next door, and the door opened. Of course, Beth would take a taxi, and of course she would take her time paying, a leg extended from the car. She stepped out and stood up, bored and sophisticated, a thick knitted shawl around her body. She ran her fingers back and forth through her hair. When her eyes alighted on Reed, her face gave an infinitesimal squeeze of contempt.

"Are we here for a concert?" she asked snidely. Reed hailed another cab. "Leaving so soon?"

"We both are. Get in."

"Why?"

"I want to make sure we're not being followed."

"No one's following us. Rod wanted to, but I told him that I was pretty sure I could handle you." The way she landed the *you* was insulting, but Reed could not show that he was riled.

"Get in." She shook her head but complied. He slammed the door behind him and said to the driver, "Driver, I need you to make sure that no one is following us." Beth dropped her shoulders and rolled her eyes.

The driver said, "I do not understand you. Where you go now?"

"Just drive. Straight. I'll tell you when to turn."

"I must get car back. Must be close, okay?"

"Please. Someone is following us."

"What do you mean—when you say follow?"

"We're going to go to Central Park . . ."

"Good."

"But we can't go direct."

"Fast we go now."

"No! Take a longer way."

"I do not understand you. I must be over soon."

Beth was no help. She sat and looked out the window with her arms crossed in complete disdain.

"Just drive." The cab pulled away from the curb.

Beth asked, "Are you taking me on a carriage ride in the park?" Reed didn't answer. He was busy keeping the driver from making a left, which would take them straight to the park. He told the driver to take the next uptown avenue. The driver said that this was two avenues away and was *not rational, not rational,* when Sixth was open to traffic. The driver would not leave the left lane; he would not turn off his blinker.

Beth said, "Can we just get this over with!"

The driver took that as his cue and turned up Sixth.

Reed demanded: "Eighty-sixth Street! Eighty-sixth."

"West Side. I take you West Side." And before Reed could respond, the driver had hooked his cab to the left on Fifty-ninth.

"Perfect," Reed said, but in truth he wanted to enter the park from the east. He wasn't sure he knew how to get where he wanted from the West Side. If he seemed lost, he thought, he could just tell Beth that he was deliberately taking a winding path. "How is your fiancé? Does he know about your boyfriend?" Beth folded her arms tighter and gave Reed a cursory glance. "My wife passed away."

"No, she didn't. She left you. Jamie told me that the last time I talked to her."

"She left me and *then* she passed away. It's still traumatic."

"Get pity somewhere else. This store's closed."

Reed clenched his fists. "I can't expect a whore to understand love." He wanted to snap Beth's middle finger off when she held it in front of his nose. A black woman had done that the summer before as she passed him in her red cabriolet on 210, and he pressed the accelerator through the floor. He was going to run her into the trees or into oncoming traffic, crush her fingers and break her head, but his vision blurred and he had to pull off the road. This time the cab pulled over and he stepped out into a cold wind. Beth remained inside.

"Come on," he told her.

"You actually want me to pay for this?" Reed had forgotten to pay, but now he had to move forward or admit his lapse.

"Pay the man and let's go. I'll reimburse you." Reed began walking into the park. He could use the head start to figure out the way. There was no one he could ask—the sky was gray, the park was empty. He walked and looked behind him only at the turns to make sure Beth was there. She walked behind him, arms crossed in her shawl, taking in the scenery. She was muttering that he had better pay her back. He ignored her and was so proud when they arrived at the Great Lawn below the stone castle. Like the tour guide, Reed chose Central Park to meet with his adversary, but he chose a wide-open field where nobody could eavesdrop. Unfortunately, a green rubber fence surrounded the lawn. Reed could not see a gate or entry point anywhere, so, though many years had passed since he'd climbed a fence, he pressed the links down, swung one leg over, jumped to the tips of his toes as the fence rose into his crotch, and awkwardly hopped his other leg over, catching his heel before stumbling, but keeping on his feet. He offered his hand to Beth, who was not there. He turned to find her somehow already inside the fence and leading the way toward the center of the lawn. Reed quickly moved in front of her to regain control. Thirty yards into the lawn, he swiveled and sat among the empty softball fields. He gestured to a spot near him, and she sat six feet away. They faced the castle above the pond at the lawn's southern end. From the castle, they might have looked as if they were early audience members who had picked their seats for a concert.

Reed waited for her to speak first. He patted the grass on either side of him. He rearranged his seated position, leaning back onto his hands with his legs straight, and then sitting straight with his knees up, his ankles crossed, and his hands in his lap. He waited. What was she thinking, what did she want, what was she going to say? When she said nothing, Reed felt angrier. She was waiting for him to talk, to explain himself, but he did not want to negotiate with someone wrinkling her nose at him. He ripped at some grass, tossed it aside, and noticed how the castle seemed to grow out of the rock at its base. He hadn't been able to follow Rod's group too closely in the park and didn't know what Rod had told them about the castle. They had stood for a long time, listening to him and then taking pictures before climbing up to the castle and chatting some more. He yearned now for that kind of nonchalance—for conversations without consequence, words that merely gave context to the pictures you'd develop thousands of miles away.

Reed vowed not to apologize for what Beth had seen.

"They're my family or they're daughters of close friends," he began. "There was nothing sexual about it." Beth was silent, and he couldn't bring himself to look at her face. "I was taking video once at a picnic and my niece was showing off. She was four. There was nothing dirty. She was a four-year-old and I was her uncle. That's it. So what?" Reed had to barrel through this and then he would be able to look up past Beth's knees. He spoke to the castle and the pond in the distance. "Everybody saw those tapes; everybody laughed. My mom and all her sisters, my cousins, brothers, friends were all at the party. Then there was this section of my niece—running around the yard in her skirt, no shirt. Her mother said she was going to be a nudist one day. We all laughed. Another time, she ran around and I chased her. We played hide-and-seek and then watched the video. Then we played Simon Says. We made a tape of that." Reed watched how the flag ripped in the wind on top of the castle's turret. "I didn't show anyone, because I knew that others would see something dirty in it even though it was completely innocent. That's why I started using the basement, to keep out the judges."

Reed looked to his left and saw Beth staring at him with the very expression of disgust he was trying to wipe away.

"There were not that many others. There were three on the tape you have and two more. That's it. That's all there ever will be, because people put so much into it. A few months ago I was leaving work and this little girl, four years old, she came into the elevator with her father and wrapped her arm around my thigh. The elevator moved and she held on to me. Her father made a joke and pried her loose, but this little girl . . . trusted me. I wanted to pick her up and kiss her head. Women can do that. Mothers can pick up any little girl and kiss her on the lips. My clothes were always on, and I never did anything to those girls except hold them. That's all."

Reed looked at Beth again. She was looking appalled and confused. Now he refused to look away. He wanted to read her eyes.

"That's all I have to say. I don't want the tape back. I want it destroyed. All the others are. So either give it to me so I can burn it or burn it yourself. I don't care, but I can't take these fucked-up mind games you're playing."

Beth looked away, took a very deep breath, and slowly released it. Her eyes were wide and her head was slightly moving from side to side. He waited.

"You just gave me so many new reasons to . . . hate you. Thank you." She looked at him. "I don't know what tape you're talking about."

"Don't," he warned her. "You bitch. You know exactly what tape."

"No, really, Reed."

"The tape was in the *Beaches* box. It was in the *Beaches* box. You borrowed *Beaches* and you never gave it back. You borrowed it the night before you broke it off with me."

"I'll give you the *Beaches* movie back, and you'll see that you're not in it. It's all Bette Midler and no naked little girls in your nasty little basement."

Reed pointed at her. "You're lying. You just gave yourself away. I never mentioned the basement."

"You did mention the basement, you loser."

Reed's neck was hot. He loosened his scarf. Beth had to have seen the tape. That was why she was carrying that sign in the corridor at the mall. "*Watch your children. The manager likes 'em young.* That was your sign. You were waving that around as Petey Pepperoni!"

"I'd just seen you flirting with a high school graduate."

"But 'watch your children'? You were waving that sign in front of a family restaurant. The parents who came there had small children."

"I was mad. You made me dress like a rat while you were dithering around with a teenager."

Reed did not believe this; he had too much evidence. He argued: "I read the note you gave to your brother. About my liking younger girls and you were too old for me."

"I meant eighteen, not four!!"

On the day Beth dressed as a rat and paraded the mall with the libelous sign, Reed had destroyed all but one of the tapes. He had raced home to beat the police or the FBI or whomever he thought Beth was going to send.

"There was only one tape left. It was in the *Beaches* box . . ."

"Bette Midler sings 'Wind Beneath My Wings' in the *Beaches* box."

Reed was shaking with fury. He could not have come all this way and wasted so much time and money to make such a useless confession. Is that what just happened? She stood to go. Did she have a bug on her? He had forgotten about recording equipment. Was she recording him for the authorities? What was beneath that shawl?

"You will not leave until I'm ready for you to leave." He clutched her ankle, held it fast and firm, the muscles in his arms tight and strained. Beth tried to pull away, but he would never let go.

"Get off! Me! Sicko!" She swung her left leg at him and, with her pointed-toe boot, kicked him as hard as she could. He fell back and grabbed his chest with his hands. It felt as if a bullet had shot through a rib. Beth started to run toward the fence. Reed despised her more than he ever had before. Now he wanted to kill this woman. He climbed to his feet and ran after her. He caught her in the midst of her high-heeled run and tackled her from behind. Visitors at the castle might have misinterpreted the scene as a lovers' diversion, but would actually be witnessing a rematch of a fight from the previous year. This time, there would be no mall security to put an end to it, and no oversized mouse mittens. Reed was on top of Beth and choking her, trying to pound her head in the grass, but once Beth caught hold of Reed's ears, he lost his leverage. She tugged at his ears and his body lunged after them. Reed saw her rise above him, her cheeks scratched and wrathful. He tried to stand before she did, but she threw her knee into his face. Reed felt the contact, heard the crack, and smelled his own mangled nose. He saw the blood on Beth's pants before he saw it gushing on his coat. He held his hands to his face. The pain was shocking. He breathed through his mouth, tasted the cold air of the park. Beth ran a few steps away and then turned back.

"There are others. If there is a tape floating around it will come back to get you, and if there is no tape the girls won't forget. They will make sure you pay. Because little girls grow up and look back. Just like the boys and all those priests. You'll go to jail and I hope all the prisoners make you their bitch and then, just like you, try to pretty it up and say you wanted it." Beth turned, effortlessly climbed over the fence, and sailed down the path and into the trees.

Running with Beth was the person Reed wanted to be; supine on the grass with a bloody nose was the person he was. He stood and walked to the perimeter of the lawn, rolled over the fence, such intense pressure in his face, and then walked away in agony. Was it possible that the missing tape was in his dead ex-wife's new home, to be discovered by a sibling sorting through her estate? Or would it turn up at a yard sale? Beth was right—the girls would grow up and even if he swore he would never do it again, there would be consequences. What could he do about it? How do you live your life when other people are in complete control of it? He pressed his coat against his face to stop the flow from his broken nose and tried to plan his next move, which would invariably be foiled.

How did Reed D'Carloff get from the Great Lawn to the moment that would make the next day's news? Maybe Reed sensed what I had: that his life was like the last amount of bathwater swirling down the drain and he must have felt it as he meandered aimlessly through the park. This had to be the end or a completely new beginning. Maybe he found himself standing on the other side of the hill, on the far side of the Glade, in the section of the park dedicated to the children, in front of a bronze statue of Alice on a toadstool in Wonderland surrounded by the Mad Hatter, the Hare, the Cheshire Cat, and, outrageously, a rat who reminded him of Beth and his utter defeat. He might have gazed on the statue of Alice—her legs and bare arms—sensing soft skin instead of cold metal, amazed that of all the statues in the park he was drawn somehow to this one. Like a homing pigeon. He couldn't control himself, and he realized that was far more frightening than his fear of anyone else. So, what could he do? His life was spiraling down the drain, and to fight that pull would require a dramatic lunge against gravity. Then the idea came to him in a flash—where else to make such a lunge? Exiting the park through the Children's Gate, he hailed a taxi on Fifth.

Rod Hamilton had told the group about Steve Brodie, a hero of Lower Manhattan, whose claim to fame, whose tavern and acting career, were the result of a fabled leap from the Brooklyn Bridge. Reed moved toward those arches. There was a chance, he knew well enough, that he wouldn't survive the jump. This Steve Brodie, who became a legend, had no eyewitnesses to the feat that made him one. There was no one to say it was truly possible. As far as anyone knew, Steve Brodie lowered himself into the water and pulled himself out before skipping wet through the streets. The sun had set. Reed got out of his cab and moved toward the elevated walkway. The illuminated bridge rose up in the distance. He had nothing to do with its glorious construction, but felt his fate was linked with the bridge anyway, as if it had been built for the turnaround, or finale, of his life. Splashing into the East River and swimming through the deep waters was just the kind of thing that would invigorate the soul and restore confidence: to spread your arms, look at the birds flying below, smell the air above the harbor, and then propel yourself into the sky. There was no way to back out of it once you bent your knees and pushed off. If you died, what a way to go!—but if you lived, you would exist in a completely new era: life after the Brooklyn Bridge. You could carry that with you; you could hold it close.

Reed's head was light, his nose still trickling blood, as he walked up the approach. Bicyclists speeding down their half of the ramp shouted and cursed at him. He moved on. The windows of the countless office towers and apartment buildings were lit, occupied by people in the midst or at the end of another relentless day. He walked on and was soon in the corridor of steel cables rising vertically and diagonally on either side of him. He moved deeper and deeper into that corridor toward the first enormous pier whose arches were five, six, seven stories tall. He walked beneath and through the southern arch, down the next corridor of metal rope, toward the center of the span.

He reached the point that brought tears to his eyes, where the confluence of stone and steel most inspired him. He would look up, give a prayer to their majesty, and then take the plunge. There was only one problem, he noticed when the tears dried: pulled toward the arches, it was not until he stopped that he realized the pedestrian walkway was raised in the middle of the bridge. In order to jump, he would have to climb up onto one of the beams that ran over three lanes of the vehicular traffic leaving Manhattan. He would have to be careful, walk steadily, keep focused to reach the edge where he could then make his jump. He had to get to the other side, because the fall to the roadway was only a fall of one story, and he was not here to fall into the windshield of a Toyota or under the wheels of a van.

He took a few minutes to assure himself that he could maintain his balance and then stood with his arms out to his sides. Step by step, he advanced across each of the busy lanes. Soon he stood at the edge and gripped a cable, leaning forward against the web of steel. The water was farther away than he thought. Steve Brodie was a liar. Reed also realized that the point where he would make impact was a rather long swim to shore. He could survive the drop and then drown in the current. No matter, no matter! He heard the waters of his life swirling below and knew he had to jump. As he stared down at the floodlit river below, measuring out his swim, he heard voices behind him.

"Hold it, hold it." He turned his bloody face and saw two men in fatigues with their weapons pointed at him. It was a high-alert day, and the Brooklyn Bridge was a terrorist target. This didn't register for Reed. What he saw as he looked into the eyes of these young, frightened men were the two eyewitnesses that Steve Brodie never had.

"Come away!"

"Your hands. Both your hands!"

"Turn around slowly."

"Slowly."

They tightened their aim. They were on very high alert.

Reed shouted his name, which was lost in the whine of the traffic. One hand held the cable and the other made a sudden reach into his coat pocket. Identification. In one move, he pulled his hand out of his pocket and flung his wallet at them.

They pulled their triggers.

11

AFTER **R**OD **CALLED ME** to ask why a man on Lower Broadway knew about Michigan, and Beth called to describe the
conversation in Central Park, and the media began pumping out
their versions of the shooting on the Brooklyn Bridge, I started to
think about Reed D'Carloff and I couldn't stop. I went to my local
police precinct and told them what I knew about Reed and why I
doubted he was a threat to Homeland Security. Shortly thereafter,
the story disappeared completely from the papers, television, and the
Internet, and the national security level dropped a color, which was
extremely empowering for someone like me. For the first time in
months, I was dispensing information that other people needed; I
was able to make the connections—between Rod, Beth, and the
bridge—that no one else was able to see; I was no longer a passive
victim; I was a participant in the world.

That sense of accomplishment and pride might explain the confidence with which I bounced through Tribeca that following Sunday afternoon, on my way to the loft where Sonia was still squatting. Sonia thought I was coming over to help organize publicity for her upcoming gig in early May, but I had another goal. I had decided that if I really wanted to help people, impact their lives, if I wanted to protect them, then I was going to start with Sonia by convincing her to rip up that Red Cross relief check.

The door to the loft was ajar, which allowed me to barge in on Sonia as she frequently barged in on me. "Sonia, where's that relief check?" I didn't see her, so I shouted toward the kitchen, "Where's that Red Cross check?" I opened the drawer of the corner desk but saw nothing. "I need to know right now where you're keeping that check!" I was firm, I was bold, but Sonia heard none of it, because she was wearing headphones. She came in, humming and carrying two mugs of coffee. On the floor, she had set up our workstation, equipped with stacks of postcards, sheets of address labels, notes, magazines, industry listings. She smiled at me and sat down, placing my mug where she expected me to sit. I gestured for her to remove the headphones. She complied.

"Where's the relief check?"

"OH!" She clapped her hands together and pounded her forehead three times. "I do not want to talk about this today."

"It's important," I replied. "I need you to listen to what I have to say."

"And my head is aching." Sonia glared at me as she set to work, removing one of the self-adhesive labels and accidentally licking it. She blamed me. "And now this is ruined! I must do this one with the pen."

"Never mind that right now. Listen, Sonia. I have a strong suspicion that someone already knows that you're in illegal possession of someone else's check."

"How do you know this thing?" I admitted it was just a feeling. She looked at me, considered this, and then said, "I do not have this feeling."

"You never know who's following you, Sonia. I speak from recent personal experience. You must have a sense of this too; otherwise, you would've already cashed the check."

"I will cash this check. But *then* maybe someone follows me. I must be careful."

"That's a scary thought, though, isn't it?" I moved into my second point, encouraged by her attention and lack of profanity. "Once you cash it, Sonia, there's no going back. You're a fugitive living in fear of the numerous agencies of the federal government for the rest of your life, every day, every hour, every minute, until you die."

"I don't think it's this bad." She affixed a few more labels as I paced above her. I had a list of strategies and I was prepared to employ them all.

I muttered, "It's all irrelevant anyway. Those checks have to be cashed within thirty days, and you're past your deadline."

"No, I am not. And is that true?" She moved to stand, to locate the check and confirm its instructions, but she must have detected the delight in my eyes and correctly predicted I would grab the check, rip it to shreds, and end the quandary myself. She remained sitting. "I have time, Andy Green."

I moved on to my next tactic, "What if they send a W-2 or 1099 or some tax form to Debbie? That's where they'll catch you, Sonia. Tax evasion. It's how they caught Al Capone. Think of all those corporations crumbling today because of financial irregularities. Accountants are the law enforcers of our age." She granted this point to me, but said she was trying to find knowledgeable people to help her do it properly.

Then she added, "And I will destroy anything that comes in mail for Debbie Lubag."

"Which is, of course, also a crime."

"Well, nothing's perfect." She shrugged and began to hand-copy the address from the ruined label to a postcard.

"How long do you think you'll be living here? How long do you expect you'll be checking her mailbox?"

"I must take one day by one day, but I will outweasel Debbie Lubag."

"You can't. That's a fact. Crazy people have a way of getting what's theirs. Especially crazy rich people. If there's any trace of a fifteen-thousand-dollar check, Debbie Lubag will track it down and if she finds out that her Russian house cleaner not only stole her check but lived in her apartment while she was in Florida . . ."

"And then I must be crazier than Debbie Lubag. That is my plan."

I had had enough. "Sonia, as your friend and unofficial sponsor in this country, I beg you not to cash that check. Now tell me, please. Where is it?"

"It is not your check. It is mine."

"Your name is not on that check."

"And yours is?" she asked.

"It's Debbie Lubag's check." I stood above her, and she continued her work. I had no idea what else to say, which frustrated me. One of my closest friends sat in front of me, and I didn't know her well enough to dissuade her from committing a felony. As my last resort, I commanded: "Ms. Obolensky. Tear. Up. That. Check!"

A perplexed Sonia looked at me and countered with one of her newer idioms: "Stop busting my balls." I picked up my mug of coffee and sipped the strongest coffee brewed on this side of the Neva. Sonia spoke, "I cannot keep doing this life, Andy Green."

"What do you mean?"

"I am so tired to tell my mother I am succeeding here. I write letters to her about my concerts. I tell her so many people come, I am so popular. And she writes me she is so happy when can I come home and show everyone my success. I can't afford this. I work five million jobs here, she works five million jobs there and we lie about our happiness. I come to this country for my dreams because I do not want to regret my life. This is the golden rule, yes? Follow your dreams and never regret your life. But now I think it is possible you can regret your life *because* you followed your dreams." Sonia took a deep, rattling breath and held it. She chewed her lip, slid a stack of postcards to her right, and blew the breath out. "I want to hold my CD in my hand and say at least I did this thing. And I can send this to my mother and she can listen to it every day. And that is all I want. That one thing. Then I will give massage until I die."

She pulled another stack of cards toward her and very carefully began addressing them, and because she did this without any self-pity, just a quiet determination, I decided to abandon my task for the moment and help Sonia with hers. If I couldn't persuade Sonia to stop saying *And* at the beginning of most of her sentences, how in the world was I going to ask her to give up fifteen thousand dollars that she was convinced was hers? I sat on the floor at my workstation.

In silence, we peeled and adhered until we'd lost our fingerprints and there were fifteen stacks of postcards ready to be sorted and mailed. I did my best not to read any of the addressee names, but my eye did catch both Liza Minnelli and Gore Vidal. I turned over a postcard to read the information with some apprehension that I would find a misprint or omission.

"You're performing for three weeks?"

"Only Thursday to Saturday three weeks."

"That's incredible." I cut her off at the pass: "No, I'm not shocked."

"And no massage for three weeks. Then much much massage. A summertime of sweaty backs. I am going to West Virginia for Fourth of July. But for work."

"Massage?"

"No! I do not tour with massage! A concert!"

"Another one in West Virginia?"

"In Wheeling. Where I sang at Christmas."

"Wow. They love you in Wheeling." We were shuffling cards into stacks by zip code, and a part of me wanted to ask why she didn't sort by zip code on the computer, or why her friend who now kept her contact lists didn't sort by zip code on the computer, but instead I asked what turned out to be a much more critical question: "Why do you think you're so popular in Wheeling, West Virginia?"

"You never question why. If you are loved, you say thank you."

"I suppose, but Wheeling doesn't strike me as a cabaret capital."

"And there are many music lovers. They have symphony, country music. A jamboree." Sonia handed me the theater's newsletter. "This is from Wheeling. I must duplicate this. I am in this article." I found the in-house review of the Christmas concert where Sonia sang

"Love for Sale." She earned a paragraph, which she had highlighted in yellow, that compared her to great cabaret singers as well as to great comics. It sounded familiar, but I froze, and the words blurred when I read that the writer thought Sonia was amusing, was, in fact, "more amusing than mangoes."

I don't know how long I stared at Sonia before she asked me what my problem was.

"Sonia. Who invited you?"

"Where?"

"To the concerts? Who's hiring you for these concerts?"

"Susan Hogan is hiring me. She is the company manager."

"The same woman who invited you for Christmas?"

"Yes."

"Had she ever heard you sing?"

"No. Her friend heard me sing."

"Did you meet her friend?"

She shook her head. "He was not there."

"Yes, he was, and he wrote this."

"And how do you know?" Sonia asked and I stared at her.

"This is Brad's writing. 'More amusing than mangoes.' This is what Brad said about you the first time we met. Brad is in Wheeling." Afraid of being hasty, I tried to think everything through. "I wonder though: Why would Brad have you invited after you declined his help in the first place?"

Sonia treated that as an idiotic question: "Because he wants fantastic show!" Sonia jumped up with her address book and moved toward the phone. I asked her whom she was calling. "Susan Hogan in Wheeling."

I stopped her, "No, no, no!"

Sonia turned to me. "I want his phone number. I want to apologize. I will tell him how I hate Porfiry and I will get money from him."

"If Brad finds out you're looking for him, he'll run again."

"And why will he run?"

I deliberated for a bit, not wanting to share what I knew, but then I told her. I explained everything I'd learned from Rod in Central Park, which was all a surprise to her, but she took it much better than I did.

"Let's go to Wheeling," she proposed. "We'll rent a car, you'll drive. We'll seek him out."

I looked at the newsletter again. Brad was definitely in Wheeling.

"Okay. Yes. When?"

"Right now."

"No, I can't." I was going to the Upper West Side, where Beth was mysteriously hosting a dinner in memory of her former manager, and though I wasn't exactly in mourning for Reed D'Carloff, I could not decline the first invitation since being on the outside. "Tomorrow. First thing tomorrow. I have some place I need to be." I could see in her eyes that she still wanted to call Susan Hogan, and I knew I couldn't turn my back on her for a minute. "Come with me."

"Where?"

"To a dinner party."

"But we need preparation."

I promised her we would have time to prepare on the subway, and then I bribed her successfully with free food. Sonia went off to take a shower in the water park of a bathroom.

"Wear something dark!" I called after her, gazing out the wall of windows on a city that was beginning to make sense again. I was wrong to have left it. I'd learned that the best response to a world conspiring against you is not to isolate yourself but to throw yourself more wholeheartedly into it. I looked forward to the dinner with my family. This was the new Andy Green. I would keep myself very engaged, there would be no surprises, and I would be in complete control.

● ● ●

THE FIRST SURPRISE OF the evening wasn't so bad: the person who opened the door to my aunt's apartment was none other than Peter himself, looking pleasantly alert, dressed for dinner in a bright green polo shirt, light blue jeans, and green socks. His broad smile forced his good eye to squint; his other eye, which I tried to avoid, just stared expressionlessly.

"Andy Green!" he shouted in his loud Southern accent. "Andy Green!" He remembered me—that was good. Since he didn't recognize Sonia, he turned back to me again, shouting, "Andy Green!" He feigned a block, a jab, and an undercut. Neither of us boxers, Sonia and I just stood there. He laughed and welcomed us inside. Then suddenly, without warning, he reached out and pinched my arm and laughed again. I looked at Sonia, who was paying more attention to her surroundings. I think it occurred to her where we were when we entered the building, but her suspicions were confirmed when Sonia 2 entered the foyer.

I needled them both with "Sonia Obolensky, I believe you know Sonia Obolensky." They nodded to each other. Peter smiled as children do when they're not certain if the confusion is in the world or in their heads. The second Sonia, now apparently a housekeeper

as well as a nurse, took the flowers the original Sonia was holding and went off to find a vase. Sonia followed her doppelganger in
order to solidify their identities and define the conventions for the
evening.

"Pick a card, any card," Peter said. Every muscle in my body
tightened. During my last visit, most of his tricks hadn't material-
ized, and he'd begun accusing me of forgetting the card I'd chosen.
I didn't want to repeat that, and, more important, I felt that to pick
one single card this evening would undermine the control I vowed
to defend. As Peter held out his wearisome deck, I politely shook
my head. It wasn't the time or place, I reminded him, and walked
into the apartment. Part of my plan was to keep everyone in the
same room and the secret conversations to a minimum. As I entered
the living room, I saw the two Sonias passing beneath the Pietà
on the bookcase through the small dining room into the kitchen.
I moved to follow but was stopped by the sight of Rod Hamilton
sitting on the couch, holding a bottle of Corona. Judging from his
slack jaw, he was shocked to see me as well.

"What are you doing here?" I asked. Because Peter was directly
behind me, I didn't say anything else.

"I didn't know you were coming . . ." he started.

"That shouldn't matter." Peter was watching us both. "Have
you . . . ?"

"Not yet."

"You'd better."

"I know."

"Or."

"Yes."

"Pick a card!"

Beth came into the living room. Rod tried to take a swig of his beer, but the lime wedge plugged up the neck of the bottle.

"We're all here now," Beth said. "Who's your friend?"

"She's Rod's friend too. Her name is Sonia Obolensky."

Beth said, "Not Peter's nurse . . ."

"I told you Peter's nurse was an impostor. The woman you're re-ferring to is the *genuine* Sonia Obolensky," I said. "The classic." No one understood what I meant—each of them only knew one of the women as Sonia Obolensky—but before I could explain myself, Beth gave me a kiss on the cheek and then pinched my arm hard below the shoulder.

"Ow! Damn it. Why did you do that?"

"You're not wearing green."

"Of course not." Wearing dark brown slacks and a dark gray sweater, I felt I was the only one in the room suitably dressed for this half-baked memorial. Peter laughed out of nowhere.

"Doesn't Peter look great?" Beth asked.

"Fantastic," I admitted.

"I'm done with those blue pills," Peter said.

My mother entered the room in black, as I expected she would. Holding a glass of water, she weakly smiled and crossed the room to embrace me.

"I just met the fabled Sonia," she said. "She's the one who can sing?" I nodded. "Our Sonia could never sing, which was strange, but our Sonia plays the piano. Did you know that?"

"I know she has a history of violence," I said without explaining myself. "Could we all move into the dining room?" That's where the two Sonias were. To justify the move, I said, "I know I'm a guest, but I have something to say to everyone." In the dining room, my

Sonia was pouring two glasses of white wine. At least they had their drink straight. I was sure it was Sonia's idea. If they ate the same food, drank the same drink, and went by the same name, they might fool the INS or anyone else who came sniffing around Riverside Drive.

"I'll have one too," I said. Set up on a credenza opposite the bar and beneath the window was a buffet that looked and smelled of Zabar's or Fairway—salads, cole slaw, sandwiches, pâté, cheese, focaccia with sundried tomato, and even sushi. I knew Beth would be happier with nachos, but she was playing hostess in a Manhattan apartment, and had bought what she thought constituted a cosmopolitan funeral buffet. I happily accepted the proffered glass of wine. All seven of us were now cramped around the set table.

Peter walked to the buffet and said, "Let's eat."

Beth said, "Wait a minute, Peter. Andy has something he wants to say."

I raised my glass and held the room captive. I said nothing at first, as I hadn't expected to deliver a toast. Everyone was watching me. With bated breath, they waited.

Finally, I said, "To Reed D'Carloff. A horrible way to go." Only Peter said *hear-hear* before picking up a plate and digging into the cole slaw. Everyone else continued to stare.

Beth asked, "Why are you toasting him?"

"Isn't that the whole point of this dinner?"

"Of course not."

"I thought that's why we were here."

"No!" Beth whispered in horror. "I wouldn't eat a peanut in his memory. I told you what he was."

"I know. I thought it was weird that you were having a memorial for him, but I wanted to support you through whatever emotional turmoil you were . . ."

"There's no emotional turmoil."

"Then what's the reason we're here?"

"It's St. Patrick's Day," Sonia told me.

I turned to my own guest. "How do *you* know that?"

Sonia pointed at a tray of green cookies in the shape of shamrocks.

Irritated, I pushed on. "Beth, didn't you tell me this was a dinner in memory of Reed?"

"Who's Reed?" Peter asked, now opening and closing sandwiches.

Beth said, "No, I didn't. I said 'come over for dinner on St. Patrick's Day.'"

"Yes, but then you said we were going to have a dinner in memory of Reed."

"I seriously doubt I said that. Or if I did, I wasn't serious. Where's your sense of humor?"

"Good question," I said, noticing that Sonia's pants were dark green. "Well, when did we start having St. Patrick's Day dinners? We're not Irish."

"Peter's part Irish."

"Andy Green!" Peter said again.

"Please stop saying that."

"Let's eat," Peter said.

"Yes, let's eat," I heard myself say.

Beth cocked her head and stared at me as her guests turned toward the credenza and lined up for plates. By the time we had picked through the plates, selected our meal, complimented the hostess, and found our seats—Ruby and Peter at the ends of the table, Sonia and I facing the other three—Beth's look was territorial, trying to make me understand that this was her dinner party, and she hadn't shopped for hours and arranged the buffet and helped clean the cluttered apartment, not to mention nursed Peter through seven months and finally convinced the doctors to take him off the blue pill, for her jackass brother to walk in and start ordering people from room to room and pretend he was the host or man of the household. She would accept the abbreviation of the cocktail hour, mainly because Peter wanted to eat, but she was letting me know that I was not to dictate any more of the timing and was that understood?

This was the point when my mother usually took it upon herself to say grace, which she had exploited over the years as a means of pushing any one of her many agendas. With our eyes closed, she would turn to God with something she wanted to change in our lives, often talking to him about us as if we weren't in the room. *Help Andrew feel that he doesn't need to lock his door every time he's in his room. Should I keep lending money to Beth if she's squandering it on clothes that make her look like a prostitute?* This evening, though, she surprised me by folding her hands in her lap and bowing her head to say a prayer to herself.

Beth suggested, "Mom, why don't we all join hands and say grace?"

Ruby looked at Beth and said, "Oh, thank you. That would be nice."

I placed my hands on the table, palms upward. Sonia took my right one, but there was naturally a conflict on my left, where Ruby's upheld hand was waiting for mine to turn over into her grasp. I pressed the back of my left hand into the table and closed my eyes, waiting for her hand to turn over into mine. I could feel Beth's foot pressing down on top of the toe of my left shoe. I pulled my feet under my chair. Eventually, Ruby and I compromised by making a pretzel out of our thumbs and forefingers.

Since Beth was hosting and had initiated this communal prayer, I expected her to lead us in grace, so I was blindsided by my mother: "Andrew. Why don't you say it?"

Advantage: Ruby Green.

"It would be my pleasure," I said without a pause. "Lord, thank you for providing this bounty and help it nourish our bodies. Amen."

With her eyes still closed, Beth said, "Do you know how long I worked today? Mom, could you?"

"Of course, sweetheart." I didn't adjust the pressure of my fingers at all, keeping everything at an even keel.

"Dear Lord," Ruby began to pray, and I opened my eyes. I wished we were sitting at a larger table. Because everyone was leaning forward, it felt like they were all in my space. I leaned back to take in the room, realizing that I knew secrets about everyone facing me, about Beth, about Rod, about the woman posing as Sonia. I felt another wave of confidence, a sense that I knew everything I needed to know, which was followed by a wave of doubt, because I now understood how feeble that sense of security was. I tuned in briefly to the prayer, hearing Ruby thank God for the recently issued Ohio quarter and to hear her suggest that one "interesting way" to measure our lives in the next several years would be to count how many quarters we lived through. I tuned out just as she began to wonder if anyone at the table would ever make it to Alaska or Hawaii. Sonia's grip on my hand tightened just enough for me to notice but not enough to understand what she was thinking. As I tried to read Sonia's face, I noticed that Peter had his eyes open. He was staring at his plate, not paying any attention to what my mother was saying, and I realized that I knew very little about this man who had changed so much of our lives in the past year. "Finally, Lord," my mother said. "I thank you for the challenges you give us, the obstacles that show us who we are, because it is in adversity that you give us our strength. It is in our greatest times of need that you show us your bounty. Without the difficulties we wouldn't know you and we wouldn't know ourselves. I thank you for Andrew, Lord. In your name, I pray, amen."

"Amen," I said loudest of all. We began to eat. I let the rest of the table do the chatting, knowing that I had some power just by sitting there. Beth, as hostess, asked my Sonia about her Sonia; the real one fashioned an elaborate response that explained nothing except that they were cousins and shared an apartment. Then Sonia handed out some of her postcards for her upcoming gig and went on for a bit about what she was singing and why. Rod showered praise on Sonia's act and was then forced by Sonia to explain how he knew Beth. He told her that he met her while visiting me. He helped her get to know the city and then fell for Ruby and all she was doing for the people downtown. During all this, Peter was concentrating on his food. By the way he used his fork, he no longer looked like a patient; he looked like the man who ate dinner with me the previous August, and something occurred to me. I kept watching Peter, trying to think it through. Rod in the meantime continued to ramble for a few minutes, probably nervous because I was sitting across the table from him. Sonia's double got up abruptly and went to the kitchen. I almost followed her, refusing to trust anyone, but she soon returned with wine. Rod opened the bottle and poured for those of us who wanted it.

"You're awfully quiet, Andy," Beth said.

"I know why Peter and I were attacked in August." The claim had the intended effect. A fork fell on a dish, and a few cards slipped to the floor. I felt a chilling sensation as all attention was given over to me. I pushed away from the table and launched into my opening argument, which I was improvising. "It's all so clear. What do we know of the two assailants? Anyone? What are the only things we know about them? They were men, there were two of them, and they were wearing business casual. They worked in an office." My audience was silent. Beth sat with her arms crossed and an irritated expression on her face. "Which means that someone sent them to attack us."

"How do you get that?" Beth asked.

"Well, think about what they did to us. They jumped us, but there weren't any homophobic slurs and they didn't really do much to me."

"Because you ran away."

"That's true, but they were after Peter, not me. I was just . . ." I paused, searching for the term.

"Crazy," Sonia offered.

"Collateral damage. We've been looking at this all wrong. We weren't attacked because I was gay. We were attacked because Peter had something they wanted. They said, 'Take that.' I thought that meant 'Take that, faggot,' but it didn't mean that. They said 'take that' as in 'I'll take that.' The satchel. The bag he was carrying. They wanted the bag." I swiveled toward Peter. "What was in that bag, Peter?"

"Bob."

"What was in that bag?"

He nervously shuffled his cards; his eyes darted around the room.

"Where are you really from? No one buys that accent."

"Please stop it," Beth said, and the rest of the table seemed to support her.

"Why? Don't you get it? We don't know anything about him."

"*You* don't know anything about him."

"Everyone is harboring secrets." I directed this toward Rod and the Sonias just to keep them on their toes, to keep them from chiming in and disrupting my thoughts now that I was on a roll. "This isn't out of line . . ."

"You're always out of line," Beth said.

"No." This was the duty of the older brother, the man of the household. "I should have checked his credentials a long time ago. That's why you wanted me to have dinner with him, wasn't it? He played magic tricks all night long; he didn't let me ask the proper questions because he had something to hide. Where's his family? He's been in New York since August and there's been no sign of his family. Why are the two of you his caretakers? Where's *his* sister?"

"He's lucky enough to be an only child. His mother is in Texas, she's not healthy, she can't travel, but she calls a couple of times a week."

"Where's his father?"

"He lives in Las Vegas."

"He's a gambler," Peter added.

"Hm. Interesting. How is he involved?"

"Don't drag his father into this," said Beth. "He hasn't seen his father in years."

I leveled my gaze at her and said, "Maybe his father wanted to see him." Peter laughed nervously, which made me think I was onto something. If I could get him to crack . . . "All of this happened because of something that was in your satchel. Tell us what was in the bag, Bob."

"Flyers for my show. My hoops, my cards, my books . . ." His voice trailed off.

"That's what they were—the magic paraphernalia." My mind scrambled to make sense of this. Who would be after his magic bag? His bag of tricks? Of course! The magic syndicate."

"Who?" Beth asked.

"The syndicate. You know. Peter comes to town, tossing flyers around, pushing in on their territory and they wanted Peter stopped. OR maybe you revealed a secret. You told someone how a magic trick worked and they beat you for it."

"Do you have a job yet?" asked my mother. "Andrew, are you job hunting?"

"Not yet. Soon."

"You need to do something with your time. Come with me this week."

"Where?"

"Volunteer with me. If you're not working and making money, then you should be working and helping people. This is your city. This is your community."

"The last time I tried to do something for someone." I saw Karl Johnson leap into the air and heard Angela Cho's *thankyouthankyouthankyou.* "A disaster."

"Then, Andrew, try again."

I felt the eyes on me, all the faces looming into mine.

Ruby said, "You know what it's time for, don't you?" I didn't reply. "You're almost thirty. It's time to get rid of your funny little name."

"Oh, no. Please don't."

"You need to go by Andrew."

"Let's not go through this again."

"Why? I helped send you to a great college, and you're unemployed. I gave you religion, you spit on it. I gave you a name, you changed it."

"She gave you the *Sports Illustrated* Swimsuit Issue and you still went gay," said Beth in what I can only assume was an attempt to lighten the room. Rod, of all people, laughed. Ruby didn't approve of the joke, but was content, since she'd made her point and Beth quickly apologized. The two Sonias were looking at me, knowing I was the butt of a joke without knowing why. Peter was quietly arranging his deck of cards into five separate stacks.

Sonia asked, "And why did you give him that swimming magazine?" Beth looked like she was actually going to reply.

"This is absurd!" I almost shouted. "I can't understand why I'm the one being ridiculed. There's a woman at this table who is an illegal alien posing as Sonia Obolensky. The real Sonia Obolensky is currently squatting in a loft that isn't hers and planning to cash a Red Cross relief check for fifteen thousand dollars, which is also not hers, and I'm sitting here in the midst of a footsie game between my sister and her boyfriend while her fiancé is playing cards . . ." I stopped to take a breath and realized that my point was made.

Peter was staring at Beth, who was scrutinizing her plate. My mother, showing her disappointment, excused herself. Sonia cursed me in Russian, cleared a few dishes, and followed my mother. Mysteriously, Sonia 2 remained at the table as if the affair was her business. I wasn't happy that Sonia and my mother were off in another room. I especially feared their intimacy as the door swung shut, but I opted to stay in the dining room to keep abreast of everything else.

"Is this true?" Peter asked. Beth told him it was. Peter tossed each of us a single playing card that landed facedown in front of us. The gesture was ominous but turned out to be empty. "I knew it all along. We're engaged! She told you that, didn't she, Four-eyes?! Huh?"

Beth shouted, "Rod wiped your ass, Peter. Don't be pompous." From Rod's reaction, it was obvious he had done no such thing, but Peter sat stewing at the end of the table. "The engagement is off and it has been for months."

"I'm getting better!"

"I'm not in love with you."

"How can you say that?"

With what I can swear was a slightly British accent, Beth answered, "With difficulty, Peter. With great difficulty." Peter glared at her but before he could say BOB!, she said, "Bob Cratchit is the worst stage name. *David Copperfield* is a fat book with a huge hero. There's mystery and adventure. I haven't read it, but I'm sure it's . . ."

"Epic," I helped her.

"Thank you. He's an epic character, which makes a great name for a magician . . ."

"Illusionist," Peter corrected her.

". . . but there is nothing in Bob Crachit except a crippled boy and a Christmas goose! It is a stupid name and I won't call you that name again. Ever!" Peter shuffled the deck as if his mind had wandered and he'd forgotten that he was a key participant in this conversation. He looked up and saw us waiting for him. He checked each of our faces for clues. Beth continued, "Peter, I'm here for you, but the engagement is over. The marriage would be a mistake."

"Because I'm not functioning."

"Because I'm not in love."

"Because my eyes are different sizes. Because my face isn't . . ."

"None of that. No, I'm not in love with you . . ." Beth looked around the room for the answer. "Because the magic's gone."

"The magic's gone? Somebody give me a twenty-dollar bill. I'll show you where the magic is."

"Oh, Peter, that is not what I meant."

"Will someone please give me a twenty-dollar bill?!"

Rod handed Sonia 2 a twenty, which she passed to Peter. Beth mumbled something. Peter pulled up his sleeves and folded the twenty several times. He concealed the bill in his fists and held them to his mouth. He blew and fanned out his fingers. The bill had disappeared.

"Who cares?" Beth asked under her breath.

Peter closed his fists again and held them to his mouth. Another blow, and he opened his hands. He held a woman's watch between his right index finger and thumb. Sonia 2 grabbed her left wrist and let out a cry. Peter must have pocketed her watch when she handed him the twenty. Orson Welles once said that men enjoy magic because they like to be fooled; women don't. Sonia 2 was outraged. Peter immediately held it out for her. She snatched it from him. In the meantime, Peter asked us all where the twenty had gone. He asked us if anyone at the table had taken it. When none of us answered him, each of us refusing to participate, he reached over and, from the collar of Sonia 2's turtleneck, withdrew the twenty-dollar bill. She had already endured some hideous duties taking care of Peter, so to have her watch stolen and then to have his hand shoved down her sweater was too much for her to bear.

She sprang after the bill. The dishes and glasses rattled as she slammed against the table. When Peter pulled the twenty out of her reach, she jumped out of her chair and into his. Her left hand grabbed the money, and her right hand slapped his face. Her weight falling against him toppled the chair, and the two of them tipped sideways to the floor, both their heads hitting the credenza where the bottles of alcohol rattled. Beth set her hand against the credenza and steadied it. Rod and I pulled the Russian off Peter. Mortified, she broke free.

"I am quitting!" she said and hurried out of the dining room.

We helped Peter to his feet, and he shook us off.

"It's your fault I'm like this," he snarled at me. He turned to Rod: "Don't touch me again, Four-eyes!" Both of us stepped back. Beth remained in her seat. We heard the front door slam. My mother and Sonia were in the doorway of the kitchen.

There were tears in Peter's eyes. "This is not right. I shouldn't be here." He ran through us and into the living room. Rod began picking up detritus from the floor. Lettuce, a dish, hearts and a diamond. Again we heard the front door. We thought Sonia 2 was back, before we realized Peter had left the apartment.

"Where is he going?" Beth asked. She left the room and again we heard the front door open and close.

"What happened?" my mother asked.

"Why did Sonia leave?" Sonia asked.

The front door opened, and Beth shouted through the living room, "He's not out here. He took the elevator or stairs." She was in the dining room again. "We have to go after him." Rod and Beth rushed out. As I got up to follow the exodus, I noticed my mother touch Sonia's shoulder and meaningfully lead her back into the kitchen. I paused in the living room to decipher that exchange, but then pursued the other four out the front door. The hall was already empty. I pressed the DOWN button and waited. So much for keeping everyone under close observation. This was apparently how the new Andy Green affected others. At the moment, I didn't care about Sonia 2. She wasn't as important as the original, who was probably having a soulful conversation about me with the goddess of grief. Guilt drove me after Peter, but I would have to get back to them.

Downstairs, the doorman told me that the cleaning lady had gone east and the others west. I walked to Riverside Drive but didn't see anyone. A gust off the river cut through my sweater, and I started walking in the direction I figured I would be walking if I were Peter, ruling out the park as too dark and desolate, although I admitted to myself that I was more likely walking in the direction that Peter would be walking if Peter were me and still nervous about empty sidewalks at night. Why should I still be the frightened one, I wondered, now that I had successfully identified our August assailants as members of the "magic syndicate," who surely bore me no grudge? The "magic syndicate"! Ridiculous. I still didn't see anyone on Riverside, so after hesitating briefly on the next corner, I forced myself to walk up the side street.

I would never know why Peter and I were attacked. The incident might have been a gay bashing or the men might indeed have been after Peter's bag, but they could also have jumped us as part of a drinking game or some club's rite of initiation. Or the answer I was looking for could be *None of the above*, and it was time for me to move on to questions I could answer. Did I honestly think that knowing *why* would eradicate all sense of vulnerability?

I thought back to the weeks after September eleventh, when I flipped between channels and clicked between Web sites, in search of more and more information. I was relieved to hear that the car bombs in Washington and the fire at the State Department were only rumors, and further relieved when the smoke cleared and I could see which buildings were standing. I felt safer when the hijackers were named, when their photos were broadcast, and the day itself was broken up minute by minute, but there was still, underneath it all, the dread that no matter how much the event was analyzed, there was a day in the future we could know nothing about. It had happened once; it could happen again.

I kept moving back and forth between Riverside and West End. Because I was listening carefully for cries of "Peter!" from any of the neighboring blocks, my hearing was more sensitive than usual to any sound in the shadows, and this kept me on edge. Was I going to jump, for the rest of my life, whenever someone came up from behind me? As I walked these blocks, strangers did approach from behind, and each time I felt my throat close. I clenched my fists and turned, planted my feet in a wide-open stance, in time to face innocent West Siders going about their business, many on their way to the next pub or party—some wore green plastic bowler hats and buttons that read *Kiss me, I'm Irish*. A few tipped their hats to me as they staggered by; the less inebriated ones crossed the street, reluctant to pass me on the same sidewalk. I gave up my search and returned to my aunt's building.

Back upstairs, I found Beth and Peter sitting in the living room. Peter had left without shoes and hadn't gone very far before she and Rod caught up with him. Beth told me Rod had gone home, and that she and Peter were having a private conversation about their engagement. I glanced up at the Pietà on the bookcase, making out from this perspective only Mary's face with its expression of helplessness—there was nothing she could have done to change what happened.

"Alone," Beth said. With an apology, I left the two of them and went into the kitchen, expecting to surprise my mother and Sonia. Empty. I wondered where they were. I noticed that many of the dishes had already been washed, dried, and put away. The sink, however, was still soaked, the faucet dripping. I rubbed the sticky residue from the Palmolive cap and spread the liquid soap between my fingers. I tried in vain to tighten the taps, wiped my fingers on my pants, and tried again.

I heard something behind me. The sound was coming from my mother's room, through my mother's door. The door wasn't completely closed, but it was closed enough that I held my breath as I faced it. What was on the other side? I quietly stepped over and gently touched the door as if feeling for the heat of a fire. Then slowly, with a deep breath, I pushed the door into the room. There, sitting on her bed, was my mother, and on the floor was Sonia, kneeling in front of her, her head in my mother's lap.

"*Cry . . . cry,*" my mother canted. She patted Sonia's head with her left hand. In her right hand she held what I knew to be a Red Cross relief check, now ripped neatly in half.

FOR THE FIRST TWO hundred miles of the drive in our rental car, Sonia and I did not discuss anything of substance. Annoyed at each other for what we considered outrageous behavior the previous evening, we kept quietly to our roles of driver and navigator, which added to the tension of an already overheated interior. I was also devising a business proposal to rental car companies, in which buses would shuttle New Yorkers to rural parking lots where their cars awaited them, because it was extremely hazardous for a New Yorker who hadn't driven a car in four years to reacquaint himself with a steering wheel and gas pedal in the middle of Manhattan, and then, after having survived midtown, taxis, and the tunnel, to find himself in the midst of the lunacy that is the New Jersey Turnpike—all this while having to endure Sonia's complaints about the heat of the car, how those bastards had given us a broken renter with no air, hotter inside than out. I nodded along with her rant but refused to return to the city for an exchange. Besides, she was in the passenger seat: the temperature and radio were her responsibilities, not mine. I was in charge of speed, changing lanes, avoiding accidents, keeping us alive. I was concentrating on the road. Somewhere in the farm country of Pennsylvania, the heat was unbearable.

I asked politely, quietly, "Could you please figure out the air conditioner?"

"It is on to the top!" she shouted.

"Then could I have some of it on my side? I don't feel any air from my vents." She furiously ran her hand in front of her vents to show that she had the same problem. "Well, what does the manual say?"

"Stupid, stupid things."

"It feels like the heat is on." The air coming through the open windows was cool, but we were both sweating.

"What kind of car is this?" Sonia suddenly asked.

"How would I know?"

Sonia screamed out the window, "I hate blue cars!"

"It's not the color of the car." I tried to reason with her. "It must be the leather interior. Leather holds heat." Why would anyone want a leather interior, I thought to myself. Finally, I had to stop the car. I pulled over to the side of the highway dominated by eighteen-wheelers, and we both jumped out of the car, fanning our sweating backs with our shirts. From behind a wooden fence a few yards down the embankment from the road, four cows chewed their cud and watched us at work.

"Where's that manual?" I asked. Sonia threw it at me and kicked the front tire. I compared the graphics on the dashboard with the graphics in the manual and, after several minutes, realized that the dials Sonia had turned to the top were the dials for the seat warmers.

"You've been baking our backs for two hundred miles," I accused her. She looked at the dashboard, consulted the manual she had been cursing for thirty minutes, and then she laughed. She couldn't stop laughing.

"Leather holds heat!" she quoted me in hysterics. I turned the seat warmers off and sat on the trunk of the car, my drenched back to the rumble of the trucks. I watched the cows, waiting for the seats to cool down. When Sonia at last caught her breath, she sat on the trunk with me.

"So last night, Sonia."

"Yes?"

"What happened in my mother's room? You ripped up the relief check?"

"Yes. This is what I did."

"What about your dreams of your CD?"

"Brad Willet will pay for my CD."

"There's no guarantee we're going to find him, and I doubt he's still a philanthropist. This might just be a long drive."

"Well, let us dream."

"What I don't understand about last night is that no matter how many times we talked about that check, I couldn't convince you to rip it up, but a few minutes alone with my mother and you're weeping in her lap?"

"And your mother is very special."

"Special? Did she quote verses at you? Did she tell you God

wanted you to get rid of the check? That there's a verse in Ezekiel 12 that says Sonia Obolensky . . ."

"Do not be nasty to her. How can I take money for CD when she gives in everything to help Peter and Ground Zero? She uses savings, she sells house, she quits job." She met my eyes. "How do you think she's here so long? She helps Peter pay."

"That's not true. His insurance pays."

"Ha, ha. Some. How does she help people for so long?"

"Her church in Maryland is sponsoring her work up here." It was the first time the idea sounded silly to me. The church in Maryland was made up of a small, humble congregation. It was possible she was supported by a larger organization with which the church was affiliated, but she had never mentioned that. She was never specific. This was why she sold the house?

"And you are not very good son. For months you stay in stinky apartment . . ."

"Oh, here we go!"

". . . and scare your mother and then you're better, you're crazy. Why do you hate what she believes? Why she is?"

"I don't."

"Yes, you do. You want the world to be like you. Believe in your God or not believe in your not-God. You want people to be very simple to you. To fit inside your world. But people are people." Then came a surprising condemnation. "You are very religiphobic."

"What?"

"We all have different religiality," she explained.

"Religiality is not a word."

"It is. And it is very, very complicated. You may think it is applying merely to kind of church . . ."

"What are you talking about?"

"But it is everything. One person *needs* to believe in God. A specific type of god. Jesus. Mohammad. Aliens. One person does not. And people who do not need this thing, do not need for many different reasons. And people who do, do for many different reasons. Are you in pain? Are you scared? Do you need God just for death? Do you want ritual? People in costume? Do you want nothing? Words only? Do you do religion because your parents do? Or do not because your parents do? Or don't? Or how do you see world and who you are? And some are liking organized and some are liking spirituality. Some are liking local, some are liking eastern. Where do you go? Fancy building? Plain building? And why do you go? Some read Bible to help people, and some do not. Some read it to selves and some read it loud, loud, loud. And for some it is hope and for some it is explanation and for some it is like story and for some it is 'to do.' And you tell me sex is bigger once. I agree. It is much bigger, yes. But religion too is big. Very, very. And everyone needs it different. So religiality. It is a word."

She hopped off the car and ambled down the embankment to the cows. Three of them turned and shuffled away, but the fourth stood at the fence and let Sonia approach her. I followed her down the embankment. I rested my arms on the fence and stared at her cow.

"Your mother tries to drown you, I know. I know this is not pretty. Last night we talked about this thing. But do you know why your mother did not succeed?"

"Do you?" How long was I outside the previous night? How was it possible that so much ground was covered in the limited time I allowed them to be alone in that apartment?

"You are not happy that the Christian man came by on that day?"

"I don't know. Anything. About a Christian man."

Although Sonia and my mother met only the night before, Sonia began telling me about the day in question, about how my mother carried me from room to room before going into the kitchen, but I asked her to stop. I was too tired to invent any more scenes unrecalled or unattended, weave my version into some form of order. I couldn't inhabit any more minds to make sense of my life. I just wanted to drive along the highway and dedicate myself to blinkers, road signs, and mileage. Without a word, I moved into the cooled driver's seat. Sonia joined me in the car.

"And that cow was hot," she said, laughing. "They say leather holds heat."

• • •

IF YOU BLINK, AND your navigator is snoring, you could miss Wheeling. If you've driven west on I-70, up and down and cutting through the mountains, with and against all the eighteen-wheelers driving in and out of the Bread Basket, leaving the relative flatness near the Atlantic but before entering the undeniable flatness of the Midwest, you've driven through Wheeling. When you leave Pennsylvania, it takes only eight minutes before you enter Ohio. In that stretch, you see billboards, many billboards, for Oglebay Park, for technical colleges, for the Festival of Lights, for car dealerships, and for banks. Then you drive under a mountain through a tunnel less than a half mile long, and unless you take the right lane immediately after that tunnel, you're on a steel bridge over the Ohio River, which we almost crossed at seven o'clock that evening after driving eight hours with scorched backs for a part of the trip.

The car's jolt to the right woke Sonia, who said, "Ah, we are here."

We turned left onto Main Street, an avenue running parallel to the river and lined with Victorian homes, which all seemed part of a deserted movie set. There were cars parked but no traffic at all. There was still the presence of stores and restaurants, though I couldn't discern what was real or merely façade, what was open for customers or long gone out of business. Many of the store windows were decorated not with goods for sale but with signs and mannequins advertising the institutions and stores that still existed, willing to revive a weary city. We drove past the Symphony Hall, which appeared active with an antiquated yet fully functional box office, past a deserted department store, and past an arena with up-to-date signage advertising concerts, a circus, and a hockey team. After driving up and down a few streets, we came across the theater Sonia recognized as the one where she sang at Christmas and where, presumably, she would sing on the Fourth, an old movie palace with a marquee and a future of live performances. I considered the city ideal for the Brad I used to know. There was the possibility for nightly shows, and there were the hills to run to if the authorities ever exited I-70. If Brad wanted to leave New York but retain an urban lifestyle, if he wanted to disappear from the here and now, the place and time of Wheeling seemed perfect. This was also a city he could help reinvigorate if he had brought enough of his foundation's money into his new life.

I stopped the car directly in front of the theater and we tried to look through the front doors. There were no lights on inside. We assumed that theaters in Wheeling, like New York, presented no shows on Mondays, so we drove on to find our hotel. I was going to check into our room and ask the people at the front desk and in the bar about the theater and any newcomers to town. Despite having no license, Sonia was going to drive the short distance to the house where she stayed during Christmas, and inform her host couple that she was stopping in town for a couple of days on her way to a gig in Chicago. I had suggested Columbus or Cleveland. While chatting with them, she would ask about the progress of the theater and about the person who wrote the newsletter. Then she was going to get directions to the house of Susan Hogan, the company manager as well as their daughter, and try the same. I wanted to drive with her in case she encountered Brad, but she thought, wisely, that if word got back to Brad that she was in town, it would scare him less if she was thought to be alone. I was still nervous. The last time Sonia had a conversation alone with Brad Willet, he had vanished into the night, and I feared that, left to her own devices, Sonia might send him farther west.

The clerk at the front desk was overly professional, courteous but laconic. He knew of the theater and gave me a brochure from the Chamber of Commerce about other venues of entertainment in Wheeling. He especially recommended Oglebay Park, which, he claimed, was one of the best maintained parks in the United States.

"I'll make sure I see it," I told him.

"They have a very nice zoo."

"Great."

"The last time I was there they had the albino alligator. It was all white, and you could watch them feeding it. They had that alligator right up front inside the main building. That was a surprise because you thought it would be somewhere outside, but then you remembered it couldn't be outside or it'd get sunburn." Now he was talking. I interrupted him and promised I would make sure I saw the albino alligator. "No, it's not there anymore. That was only a special attraction; it was on all the billboards, everywhere, but you can look through that brochure and see all kinds of things they're showing." He went on like this, but eventually handed over the key to my room.

On the other side of town, Sonia was welcomed into the living room of her holiday hosts, who reminded her of her grandparents. Their daughter, Susan Hogan, was there with them, having dinner. All were thrilled to see her and asked her about life in New York and most especially about her singing. She preferred the topic of Sonia the Singer to Sonia the Masseuse, and told dramatic stories about her upcoming gig in Chicago, where she was now headlining. The four of them then gathered around the piano and sang way too many songs before Sonia finally asked them her questions about the theater and who wrote the newsletter. A volunteer at the theater. "A fan of yours. A music lover." "Who?" "Michael Foley. He's new to Wheeling." "When new?" "He moved here last summer. Didn't you meet him at Christmas? He lives on the island. Right across the river from where you're staying." Sonia called me at the hotel to tell me her news about Michael Foley and to give a description of his house, by which point I was already convinced that Brad was living in one of those homes across the river.

Wheeling is home to the oldest long-span suspension bridge in the world. I could see it through my window. According to a brochure on the bedstand, the bridge was a key feature on the road to the West, spanning the main channel of the Ohio River to connect Wheeling proper with Wheeling Island. After the original bridge built in 1849 collapsed during an 1854 windstorm, this one was built and has withstood the winds since 1860. This bridge was the reason, I was sure, that Brad chose Wheeling: it reminded him of home, which may have been the same reason he arranged Sonia's invitation to the Christmas concert.

The Brooklyn Bridge is five or six times larger than the Wheeling Bridge—the mere approach to it is almost as long as Wheeling's entire span—and only three minutes after Sonia's call, I had left the hotel, turned the corner, passed the miniature anchorage, and was through the first tower. The roadway between the towers was a metal grating, and there were signs warning drivers to keep a distance between cars to keep the weight evenly distributed. I walked along the edge on a sidewalk bordered by a hip-high concrete wall. Off to my right was the steel-arch bridge carrying the busy traffic of I-70; there was no traffic on this one.

I stopped in the middle of the span, suddenly short of breath. I didn't know what I was doing here. The day before, in my short-lived period of confidence, this trip seemed like a great idea, but now I wondered. I watched a barge pushing nine massive containers of coal toward me. I decided to give it time to pass below, as my way of counting to ten, because the prospect of facing Brad, or Mike Foley, was making me nervous. Why was I here? Because I still wanted those answers. Because I felt that if I could understand my past, I could get on with my life. Learning what I'd learned so far, however, didn't make me feel any better; it turned me into a panicky control freak who destroyed dinner parties. What if Brad told me everything and I still couldn't move on? I had no choice, I told myself. When the barge was past, I began to walk, moving a little faster with each step until I was off the bridge and moving down the first street. I expected to catch a glimpse of Brad in a lit window or sitting on a porch listening to Gershwin or Noël Coward, but there was no such sign. I located the house, perfectly described by Sonia, and stepped up onto the porch. I stood there, staring at the front door—I didn't know what I would say or do if Brad opened it—but then my hand turned into a fist, and I knocked three times. Loudly.

The doorknob turned and there he was, holding a glass of red wine. Brad, the angel—the man who wore expensive suits and square-toed Italian shoes, whose smile and wink announced a fortunate upturn in your life, whether you were a dream-filled chanteuse or a tour guide without a Web site, and whom I had painted in mental portraits for months as a traitorous, self-involved, negligent, hypocritical, false, vain trust-fund ass, and then, with Rod's reframing, as a fearful and desperate white-collar, middle-class criminal making furtive dashes within New York City—was now standing in front of me with a goatee and wearing blue jeans and a white T-shirt from the Wheeling Jamboree. That perfect smile of his vanished.

"Andy." He gave a quick glance over my shoulder to see if law enforcement were moving in to seal off his escape.

"Mike," I said. I could hear music playing inside the house and the sound of voices laughing at a table. "Having a party?"

"Dinner," he said. He gave a glance over his own shoulder. "How did you find me?"

"Why else would Sonia be singing in Wheeling?"

"She never saw me."

"We figured it out anyway. Can I come in? I'm starving. You can tell them I'm an old friend."

Someone called from the table; Brad froze. He was not so suave. That had all been an act, a persona that could never fool me now. He begged me to leave and promised to come to wherever I was staying later in the evening or early the next morning.

"No way. Come outside."

"How can I leave my own dinner party?"

"You've accomplished more amazing feats than that." He shouted into the house that he'd be right back. He grabbed a coat from a closet next to the door and he joined me on the porch.

"Let's walk," he said, and the two of us made our way quickly up the street and onto the bridge. The coal barge was farther down the river. I heard Brad's voice behind me, keeping close to the stone archway. "We can't go too far out. They'll see us from the window." Headlights spilled over us as a car approached. Brad turned his face away until it rolled over the entire length. The bridge shook as the car slowly crossed. I remembered the singer from a year ago, who told me how lucky I was to have found Brad. I wished she were here, watching my Gandhi cower in the shadows. "Why are you here, Andy?"

"Why are you?" I asked belligerently. Brad mumbled something I couldn't make out. I recognized his confusion. He didn't know where to begin. He had no idea what I wanted to hear, so he had no idea what to say. I prompted him, "Why Wheeling?"

When Brad left New York panic-stricken in June, he followed whatever highway was busier and less likely to be blocked by construction or repair. A few days into his westward drive, his fear gave way to loneliness and anger. He thought Rod had broken their pact and he despised him for it. He now felt obligated to uncover what Rod had hidden, so, in a library in Tulsa, he started looking up articles on celebrities who had estranged children, missing European royalty, women who had changed their gender, and bank robberies. Finally, he hit upon unsolved murders, and, at the end of the second day, came across Michigan, 1982. He drove to Michigan, where he compiled more news clippings, interrogated townspeople, and even located and chatted with Rod's older brother who now owned a garage in Sterling Heights and was a father to three teenage boys. One of them worked in the shop, and Brad took a picture of father and son, which knocked the air out of Rod as it was intended to do. I let Brad talk on. On his way back to New York, in early July, Brad met a new boyfriend named Tommy at a truck stop, and so much for escorting Nan Kemper to the Philharmonic. They drove to Tommy's home in Wheeling, where Brad felt less lonely. He was not cut out for a solitary life on the road, buying coffee at gas stations and facing a future of painted white lines and green exit signs. A week in Wheeling was enough for him to see that he could make a home there, but he didn't know how to pass into a new life as fluidly as Rod had done. He returned to New York in August for an advanced degree in the fugitive arts and sciences.

"So how's Tommy?" I asked.

"He's good. He's just a friend now. Who thinks I grew up somewhere in Florida. It's not what we had."

"I don't even believe that, and I don't care. You left a note with your doorman."

"I didn't want anyone in my apartment. I panicked. I was also . . ." He searched for a word to describe a state, besides West Virginia, in which he'd never pictured himself. "Humiliated. When I found out you knew about me, I wanted to hide. I didn't understand why Rod told you or why you hadn't confronted me. I didn't know why you were playing games."

"I wasn't playing games. I didn't get the information you left me about Rod until the end of last month." He squinted, tried to read the lie in my face. "There's something else you should know. I had no idea about your day job." He seemed more tired than I was of trying to second-guess the world. Whom could he trust? "Rod never broke your confidence, Brad. There was no reason to leave the city. No one but Rod knew what you were doing."

"That night in the café, when we were deciding on the scholarships, you hinted that you knew the money wasn't mine."

"I wasn't hinting at anything."

Brad interrupted me. "That can't be true." He shook his head, refusing to believe what I was telling him. "Sonia knew."

"No, Brad. She didn't."

"Sonia knew, and she told me you knew."

"When?"

"In June," he said. He was referring to the night Sonia broke off with him by turning down his patronage in a bar. "That's when she told me you knew."

"That's impossible, because Sonia didn't know until yesterday that your money was . . . embezzled."

"It was never embezzled. The money all went to charity as it was supposed to. Some of it just went through my foundation."

"Well, Sonia didn't know and neither did I." We were both closing in on something bleak, the reason we were here on a bridge in Wheeling, the reason our entire year had become the year that it was.

"Sonia did know; she told me so. She was in tears. She sat me down, we ordered drinks, and she told me that you knew."

"She didn't. I didn't. We did not know."

"She quit me. She told me she didn't want my money."

"I know that, but what did she say exactly?"

"She said that you told her to step out. That it was dirty money. She had integrity, you had integrity, neither of you could take my money."

"Brad. Porfiry wanted Sonia to leave you. Porfiry! The dirty money she was talking about that night was the vague dirty money of anyone with a trust fund. You were rich, and he was political and critical . . ."

"No, but Sonia kept mentioning you by name."

"Impossible."

"She was saying over and over 'Andy knows this,' 'Andy says that.'"

"'*And he* knows this!'" I whispered. "'*And he* says that!' That is how Sonia talks! You know that! She starts her sentences with *And*."

Brad squeezed his head in his hands. "Oh, Andy. Andy. Andy."

"Don't call me Andy," I told him. "It's Andrew."

● ● ●

IT WAS THREE IN the morning. Sonia and I were drunk, staring up at the ceiling and sharing a room because it was cheaper. We had both gotten what we wanted from Brad.

"Okay. Now I'm ready. Tell me what she told you."

"Who?" Sonia's voice hiccuped from the other bed.

"My mother. Why did she do what she did and what stopped her?"

"Okay, so here it is."

I listened.

It was just shy of a month after my father's funeral. She had refused anybody who offered to stay with her, cook for her, care for me. Family and neighbors all asked if she needed help. She declined every gesture. It must be so hard with a child. Ruby didn't tell them that another one was on the way. Holding me, my mother entered one room of the house, walked its perimeter, and then progressed to the next one. She didn't remember why.

In the kitchen, she lay the baby on the countertop and placed her index fingers in his hands. He squeezed and smiled. Gurgled. She kissed the baby's soft lips, his small, wet tongue. She smelled the warm, soft, milky head. Hair had finally grown, sprayed from his bald scalp. She unsnapped the front of his pajamas, from the neck to the left foot. She slipped the arms out of the terrycloth sleeves, freed the fat legs. She pulled the soft jumper out from under him, dropped it to the floor. On the Formica, the baby lay in diapers, held his toes with his small hands. Ruby plugged up the sink and opened the taps. She was very careful, but this was a moment she doubted herself. Could she know what the water's temperature was? She felt icy herself and wondered if the water wasn't scalding her fingers as it poured and filled the sink. She scrutinized her hand, which was not red from heat or purple from cold. The bath was drawn just right. Warm and very deep. She stopped the water and turned to the baby, who had bent his neck and was looking above his head along the countertop at the cookie jar, a ceramic owl playing the guitar, next to the spice rack. Ruby ran her wet fingers down the middle of his chest, pressed her thumb against the tiny pink nipples, and then unclipped his diaper and lifted him to her face. She kissed his stomach, his two knees, and then lowered him into the water.

I floated, she told Sonia. Suspended, face up. She held me horizontally in the water, my ears beneath the surface. I looked up at her, resting in her hands which held me in my armpits, beneath my back. Her fingers slipped slowly from my body. My legs sunk. Ruby looked down at the baby waiting for her, trusting her, studying her face, staring into her eyes. Not a murmur of complaint, not a cry. Her hands were out of the water and her son was floating lifeless but alive. With three fingers, she touched his chest again. She pressed him into the water, pushing his face below the surface. The baby's eyes didn't close, but his mouth did. He held his breath. He looked up through the water. She pushed him farther, against the bottom of the sink and held him there. His eyes didn't close. She doubted herself again. She released his body and he floated to the surface.

My face popped out of the water, and I parted my lips. A small gasp. A tiny breath, a cough. I blinked my eyes. She pressed me down again, and just as before, I closed my mouth, held my breath, and peacefully regarded my mother through six inches of warm water. She held me down longer this time, her fingers against my chest, my shoulder blades against the metal basin of the kitchen sink. Nothing happened. She released me. I popped up for air. She was crying now, her eyes as wet as mine. She took a deep breath and thought she would hold me down until she passed out. Now holding me against the metal basin with two hands, she realized she could force the air from me. She slid both hands to the distended stomach and pressed her palms toward the drain. She forced my breath out of my body. The air was propelled through the water and into her face. She smelled jars of creamed carrots, bananas. Water splashed, there was movement, there were waves now. I thrashed, flailed, fought for some control over what was, after all, my life.

A knock at the door. There was a knock at the door.

Twice, three times? In the midst of it all, my mother pulled my body out of the sink. Her shirt and arms were drenched. She spun around the kitchen, looking for a place to hide the baby. A drawer, a jar, a closet. There was another knock on the door. Louder and firmer. She opened the refrigerator but thought it too cold for the screaming baby. She couldn't let go of the child. She raced to the living room and opened the door with me against her chest.

A stranger stood at the door. He was alarmed to hear the crying duet of the mother and naked child, but he was prepared to expect anything. He had heard of Ruby Green's loss, from his brother, the funeral home director. He himself was a deacon for a Baptist church, and he performed outreach on Saturdays. Like lawyers who chased ambulances, this deacon followed funerals. Having spoken with his brother and learned of Ruby Green's bereavement, he decided to drive to her house and tell her about Jesus. He calmed her, took me in his arms. They sat on barstools in the kitchen, and if he noticed, he didn't say anything about the absence of soap, towels, baby powder. He didn't mention the full sink or all the water that had splashed over the counter, cookie jar, spice rack.

"And why?" Sonia had asked my mother. "Why did you want to do that?" Sonia thought she'd say that it was some kind of chemical imbalance.

Instead, Ruby answered quickly and with a shrug: "To protect him."

Lying in bed in Wheeling, I reconsidered her lifetime struggles against the unplanned. Ruby Green wanted to regain her life after my father's death, manage her part of the world, control all the variables of every experience. She wanted to ensure that her son, for whom she alone was responsible, would never be hurt.

And then, thankfully, there was a knock on the door.

MAY 2002

ON THE DAY THAT the cleanup at Ground Zero officially comes to an end and the last girder is draped with a flag and trucked out of the city, I meet two students in a Manhattan restaurant. Both Karl Johnson and Angela Cho look much older and more cynical than when I first told them they were to be the recipients of the Andy Green Academic/Apologetic Scholarships. Both are curious when they approach my table; neither really smiles. For them, Andy Green is betrayal incarnate: someone offering substantial financial aid and delivering instead an empty graduation Hallmark; an illusionist holding out a deck of cards promising magic and then performing what is only a cheap trick; a candy of chocolate-covered earwax. The patience they exhibit humbles me, and I force myself to struggle out of my usual paralysis.

I opt against the small talk and immediately place on the table the two fat envelopes, labeled KARL and ANGELA, each filled with ten thousand dollars cash. I don't explain the logo for the First Wheeling Bank, but apologize and tell them that it has taken me longer than expected to raise the necessary funds. They don't ask any questions. The mood lightens, and we have an enjoyable conversation over lunch. I pay, and they secure their envelopes, Angela in her purse and Karl in a large pocket of his shorts. Hands are shaken and the two leave together. I stay to savor the euphoria over another iced coffee.

I am the only customer in the restaurant. The room is large, dim, heavily draped, because the sun at this time of day blinds anyone sitting near the tall windows. The owner and three of his children sit at a table near the door of the kitchen. His two- or three-year-old grandson looks around and then, hands in front of him, sprints against the door, which swings open into the kitchen where he stumbles and laughs hysterically. The door swings shut behind him. After a few moments, he pops back into the dining room with another laugh and then turns to push back into the kitchen. He doesn't laugh at the door closing behind him. He never deigns to turn to watch the sealing of the rooms. What he enjoys is hitting the door and entering new lights, new colors, new smells. Two entirely different worlds, separated by a panel of wood, and you can pass from one into the other, remaining the same person and yet experiencing slight, peculiar internal adjustments—a brief recollection of who you were in the old room as you adapt to your new surroundings. Back and forth he runs, into the kitchen, and back to us, in to the cooks, and back out to the dining room. Fearless. Over and over and over. The boy's laughter is contagious, and for the first time in months I'm joining in.

I empty the last few pieces of ice into my mouth and move toward the threshold between the tile floor and the concrete sidewalk, toward the sunlight on the other side of the heavy drapes. The exit is a set of double doors, so I use both hands to grip the bars and then fling them open, arms out, chest forward, head held high, and the boy is one hundred percent correct—moving in a split second from underneath a ceiling of tin ten feet above my head to one of whirling clouds much, much higher; with the traffic speeding uptown, down-town, crosstown; with the scowling statues covered by trees; with the people off to the movies, to the bookstores, off to work or back home; with awnings spattered, almost painted white with pigeon shit; with the flowers and the benches, the strollers and the traffic lights—it is absolutely exhilarating.

ACKNOWLEDGMENTS

FIRST OF ALL, THANKS to the many people who offered quiet places to write this novel when my upstairs neighbors began moving furniture to better practice their tumbling and clog dancing—to Audrey and Gerald Wolf for the use of their apartment in the Village, to the Meads for their top floor in Provincetown, and to the guys at Vice Versa who, no matter how crowded their restaurant was, always found me a spot to read or write.

Thanks to friends and family who read different drafts of this novel and provided valuable insight—to Julie Boyd, Andrea Burns, Shelley Delaney, Brian Fields, Peter Flynn, Wayne and Mia Heller, James Lecesne, Mike Nelson, Michael Paller, Kelly and Scott Proudfit, Trish Santini, Katy Terry, Amy Wolf, and, especially, Tessa Derfner and Marc Wolf, who were always available for "one last question."

ACKNOWLEDGMENTS

Thanks to my editors at HarperCollins—to Courtney Hodell and John Williams for their contributions, to Christopher Potter for his early belief in this book and his subsequent friendship, and to Rachel Safko whose dedication and enthusiasm were very much appreciated by this author during one particularly critical stage.

Thanks also to my Russians at Riverside Church—to Arkady, Alex, and Lina, who were supposed to teach me their language, but gave me something else.

And, finally, thanks and love to my parents.

About the author

About the book

Read on

Insights,
Interviews
& More...

Meet Robert Westfield

Kevin J. McCormick

ROBERT WESTFIELD was born on February 26, 1972, at the Bethesda Naval Hospital in Maryland. He spent his early years in Japan, Hawaii, and California. His father retired from the navy when Robert was eight years old—or as he says, "just as I was beginning to wonder why we were moving so much and who was telling us where to go."

The family drove cross-country, staying for a few months in Wheeling, West Virginia, a city in the Ohio Valley settled by their ancestors that has remained a family hub. While growing up Robert summered and holidayed there, staying with both sets of grandparents. His paternal grandparents were a unique source of thrills: their house was a four-level Victorian, full of hidden rooms and passageways. Providing particulars he adds, "It was also a funeral home complete with a hearse in the garage and an embalming room in the basement—a great place for hide-and-

> ❝ My paternal grandparents' house was also a funeral home complete with a hearse in the garage and an embalming room in the basement. ❞

seek, though very rarely did anyone hide in the embalming room."

There in the funeral home Robert endured what he genteelly calls his "first intimate encounters with death": his grandmother would lead his brother and him down to the open casket before anyone arrived to show them "how pretty the people were."

His family moved in 1980 to Bryans Road, Maryland, a one-stoplight community thirty miles south of Washington, DC. "There was no mayor or town hall, just a Burger King, gas stations, housing developments, a trailer park, liquor stores, and churches," he says. "The center of 'town' was where a country road intersected with Indian Head Highway. The highway terminated a few miles away at the Naval Surface Warfare Center, where they 'ensure operational readiness of United States and allied forces by providing the full spectrum of technical capabilities necessary to rapidly move any "energetics" product from concept through production to operational deployment,' and where my brother and I went swimming."

Following his naval career Robert's father worked at the Pentagon for a government communications contractor; his mother worked as a teacher's aide in an elementary school and also tutored children homebound by illness.

"My family was lower-middle-class and probably not as poor as I thought we were," ▶

> " I remember a childhood full of powdered milk, but my mother recently told me that we only drank it once. "

he says. "I remember a childhood full of powdered milk, but my mother recently told me that we only drank it once."

Fundamental to the family's quality of life, however, was the need to travel. "We sacrificed a lot at home," Robert reflects, "but we vacationed as a family through much of the United States and Europe . . . though we had to fly "space available" on military cargo planes. (It costs less than a hundred dollars for a retired serviceman to get a family of four to Germany as long as you go through air force bases in Delaware and Spain.)"

From an early age Robert felt pressured to land a full scholarship or attend a military academy. This pressure led to "several stupidly stressful, overachieving years packed with extracurricular activities." What kind of "stupidly stressful, overachieving years?" During his senior year alone he was editor-in-chief of the school newspaper, the drama club president, the lead in all of the plays, the student representative to the board of education, the captain of the quiz bowl team, the National Honor Society treasurer, the Latin club secretary, as well as the voice who gave the morning announcements over the public-address system.

Robert also began writing at an early age. His first efforts were very interactive; neighborhood kids played out his elaborate stories in which he cast himself "almost exclusively as the hero, certainly the guy with the most lines."

Happily, his writing found a natural outlet at school, where teachers invited him into creative writing programs and encouraged him to write plays for performance in class. "The short stories I read aloud almost always involved characters with names drawn from the audience," he says. "Classmates were tickled to hear their names . . . even though the characters more often than not came to unfortunate ends."

During the summer after his graduation from high school Robert went to work repairing jewelry for a local department store. "With only fifteen minutes of training, I was the teenager you could see in the window near the front door scratching bracelets and necklaces with sharp tools and wearing bloody Band-Aids on every single finger."

Robert left Maryland to attend Columbia University. His love affair with New York took flame almost immediately. "I tried to leave campus and explore the city as often as I could," he recalls. "I was overwhelmed and exhilarated by the cultural opportunities I had lacked growing up. I loved the idea that I could study a painting at school and then stand in front of the original at the Museum of Modern Art that afternoon, study an opera and buy standing-room tickets at the Met, or even study the architecture of medieval ▶

66 I was the teenager you could see in the window near the front door scratching bracelets and necklaces with sharp tools and wearing bloody Band-Aids on every single finger. 99

cathedrals and cross the street to visit Saint John the Divine."

His summers away from college, meanwhile, were passed in the employ of Naval Intelligence at Andrews Air Force Base. "I worked for three summers in a hangar near Air Force One as the assistant ACDUTRA coordinator at RIPO (Reserve Intelligence Program Office)," he divulges with a smart glance over his shoulder. "The week that Iraq invaded Kuwait my boss was on vacation. Since I was the only one who knew how to work the computer, I (a recent high school graduate) was responsible for processing the orders to deploy scores of reservists into the Persian Gulf. In the evenings I worked as a video store clerk, renting out copies of *Turner and Hooch*."

Throughout college Robert worked at the Hammerstein Center, showcase for the graduate program in theater studies. There he socialized with many of the grad students and fell in love with live performance. He became actively involved with as many shows as he could and worked in all aspects of the theater: acting, directing, writing, designing lights and sets, etc. He stage-managed several university shows, as well as performances by a modern dance troupe from South America. During his junior year he interned for the American Theatre Wing, working on events leading up to that year's Tony Awards.

There were other jobs during college. Stranger jobs. He worked as a librarian in the East Asian Library ("I couldn't read a damn book!"). He made hundreds of grilled cheese sandwiches "for a promotion where Kraft unveiled the 'world's largest grilled cheese sandwich.'" He taught a drawing workshop . . . notwithstanding a certain deficit of talent. ("I thought it was supposed to be an art history lecture. I was shocked when I saw the sketch pads.")

After college he worked for two and a half years as a waiter and bartender. The job required him to suit up in a polyester tux for weddings and bar mitzvahs and assured his presence at a number of remarkable events, among them the fiftieth-anniversary dinner for the United Nations, a buffet for nudists, and a going-away party for someone entering the Federal Witness Protection Program. He also worked a party at the home of Stephen Sondheim. "He was a legend I couldn't wait to meet," Robert says. "He joined me in the kitchen and told me that if he had to do what I was doing by hand (filling small phyllo cups with lobster salad) he would kill himself."

Robert began entering writing contests during his junior year, twice winning the college playwriting award. He also won the college fiction prize, along with a fellowship to write a play in Greece and Italy following graduation.

He spent his twenties writing for the

66 The waiter/bartender job assured his presence at a number of remarkable events, among them the fiftieth-anniversary dinner for the United Nations, a buffet for nudists, and a going-away party for someone entering the Federal Witness Protection Program. 99

theater. He was writer-in-residence for The Working Group and served as the dramaturge for Marc Wolf's award-winning one-man play *Another American,* a performance of interviews regarding the military's "Don't Ask, Don't Tell" policy. The play ran off Broadway and played in many cities across the country.

He describes his writing process thus: "When I'm drafting pages I have to work in the mornings and generally on a PC. I also like to take lots of walks. If I'm working on a scene I try to avoid crowds and prefer to stroll in a park. I've clocked many hours in the Brooklyn Botanic Garden, Central Park, and (most recently) Fort Tryon Park in Upper Manhattan. I walk, talk out loud to myself, and then sit and transcribe. I frequently work in The Cloisters, where I have a few favorite spots . . . the quietest one, unfortunately, becomes a crowded café during the warmer months."

Since 1997 Robert has conducted tours of New York City for corporate groups, diplomats, senior citizens, students, and families. He most recently traveled in Europe as tour manager for a singer/pianist. He has remained in New York since college, living in Brooklyn, the East Village, and (for seven years) Hell's Kitchen. He now resides in Upper Manhattan within walking distance of The Cloisters.

66 I've clocked many hours writing in the Brooklyn Botanic Garden, Central Park, and (most recently) Fort Tryon Park in Upper Manhattan. 99

A Conversation with Robert Westfield

SPOILER ALERT: Owing to the nature of this novel the reader is advised not to read the following conversation until completion of the book.

What inspired you to write Suspension, Robert?

Suspension was inspired by many of the events that took place during the period in which the novel is set: the attacks of September 11; the parade of corporate scandals beginning with Enron; Andrea Yates's murder of her five children; and the arrest of the funeral home director in Georgia, who instead of cremating bodies was just hiding them in his backyard. More accurately, the novel came out of an identification with the powerless: the passengers on the airplanes; the workers in the towers; those who lost their pensions because of corrupt accounting practices: the five children chased and drowned by their own mother; and the bodies in Georgia treated like garbage. It makes sense now, looking back on a time of instability when everyone around me was struggling in their own way to find their footing and adapt to a radically altered environment, that I was constantly drawn to stories of people whose lives were decided by others. ▶

> About the book

> **❝ The novel came out of an identification with the powerless. ❞**

A Conversation with Robert Westfield
(*continued*)

Given your proximity to the awful events of 9/11, it must have been terrifically hard to write a book.

At the time I wasn't expecting to write anything. I was in awe of writers who were able to pump out columns, stories, and plays within days or weeks of the eleventh. I had difficulty writing anything more elaborate than a check, and my journal from those few months is filled with drawings. I could read, however, and found solace in Dostoyevsky (for some reason) and in histories of New York.

Is that how you hit upon the story of Andrew Green—reading histories of New York?

Yes. In a scene that spoke to my sense of powerlessness, Andrew Green, known as the Father of New York for heading the consolidation of the boroughs in 1898, was accosted in front of his house by Cornelius Williams. Williams angrily demanded to know why Green had supported a woman slandering him. Green replied, "Go away from me. I do not know you." Williams had the wrong man, confusing this octogenarian for someone with a similar name. As Green turned to enter his vestibule, Williams shot him five times with a revolver. This disturbing encounter, both farcical and tragic, is at the heart of *Suspension*. Many months after reading that scene, I gave my protagonist the same name and began fabricating a plot that hinged on the mishearing of "Andy."

I enjoyed learning that the word for that kind of error serendipitously sounded a lot like the name of my hero. A "mondegreen" is a misinterpretation the ear makes of a spoken (or sung) line. The term is derived from part of a folk ballad—"They have slain the Earl of Moray / And laid him on the green"—which was misheard by Sylvia Wright (who coined the term) as "They have slain the Earl of Moray and Lady Mondegreen." I started recalling other examples. I once heard a man in a bar introduce himself to someone by saying "I'm a leather ninja," when in fact he was saying "I'm eleven inches." (A strange introduction in either case.) A friend of mine, having learned dance steps in seventh grade gym class, thought well into his twenties that "Do the Hustle!" was "Junior High School!" And another friend's mother, who grew up outside the church and heard religious terminology only at funerals, thought the Trinity was affirmed like so: "In the name of the Father, and the Son, in the hole he goes."

The mistakes themselves didn't interest me as much as the mental games we play in making sense of the blunders. Since we have no idea we've heard incorrectly, we accept ▶

> **I once heard a man in a bar introduce himself to someone by saying 'I'm a leather ninja,' when in fact he was saying 'I'm eleven inches.' (A strange introduction in either case.)**

what we think is true and can even rationalize it for anyone who asks. We blissfully go about our business singing the wrong lyrics without any shame (or expecting the boss with whom we're remodeling apartments in Brooklyn to make a joke every once in a while because we were told he was a comedian—a Canadian actually, which would explain the references to Toronto). What else do we all have wrong? Life is a comedy of disorientation about people who believe in, commit to, and act on the erroneous.

What informed your decision to write about a holed-up hero?

Besides the natural urge to hide away after a trauma, Andy's decision to withdraw from the world reflects a long literary tradition of heroes repudiating society and isolating themselves. These works usually end with the character in exile or about to turn their backs on the world. I wanted to begin a novel this way and document the protagonist's return to a community he mistakenly rejected. This was also tied to 9/11—in a world where our actions are so interconnected, I wondered if it was possible or moral to leave society? In literature there is something fulfilling in identifying with a character who steps outside of civilization or is removed from society by

> **❝ In literature there is something fulfilling in identifying with a character who steps outside of civilization or is removed from society by the author, but in the fall of 2001 I came to consider the rejection and retreat a simpleminded tactic of a reductive worldview. ❞**

the author ("Everyone's a phony," "Everyone's a racist," "Everyone's greedy," "Everyone's vile and stupid," or in my protagonist's rationale: "Everyone's violent and hate-filled."), but in the fall of 2001 I came to consider the rejection and retreat a simpleminded tactic of a reductive worldview. While justified (or at least satisfying) in literature, it seemed to me a flawed strategy for life, contributing to a depletion of empathy.

While writing the novel I became fascinated by the venting of recluses I found on the Internet, these people sitting in their homes expressing themselves in rants and vicious screeds that would not be tolerated face-to-face. I interact daily with people who no doubt vote differently than I do, but we still relate to one another. I give tours of New York to all kinds of people and it's part of my job to find a way to communicate with them. So many on the Internet seem the equivalent of people screaming obscenities on the subway. Are these fellow citizens psychopathic, or is it the context: does sitting alone and unobserved give them a license to group others into dehumanizing categories and address these groups with such vitriol? On the other hand, whenever I despair at how many appear to go out of their way to direct animosity toward complete strangers I always find examples of others reaching out and trying to make a ▶

A Conversation with Robert Westfield
(*continued*)

connection. After all, one of the most forwarded e-mails of September 2001, was the eerily appropriate Auden poem "September 1, 1939," in which the speaker sits in a dark bar in midtown Manhattan, fearing the new era and declaring the simple truth: "We must love one another or die."

Your novel unfolds from both first- and third-person points of view. How intentional was this?

It evolved out of the story. I was writing a first-person narrative about life being decided in other rooms, about communication being easily thwarted, about withdrawal and reengagement, and about a character undervaluing the people around him to justify his retreat. The novel became a narrative struggle wherein Andy Green must understand his story and life through the lives of others and accept a kind of "diminishing protagonism," a realization that he played a far smaller role in his own story than he originally thought.

I think this notion comes out of theatrical influences, particularly farce, that genre of slamming doors where all the characters are victims to some kind of cause-and-effect machinery and the universe seems to be conspiring against them. Imagine being a

66 Imagine being a character in a farce—every time you return to the stage something has transpired, something is slightly off, and you're not sure what it is or how it came to be. 99

character in a farce—every time you return to the stage something has transpired, something is slightly off, and you're not sure what it is or how it came to be (your suitcase is missing, a window is broken, a stranger is standing there without clothes). And then as you perform your little scene, other characters are offstage committing acts that will forever foil whatever plans you're in the process of making. The playwright David Ives recently wrote a brilliant essay in *The Dramatist* about translating a French farce by Georges Feydeau. Ives came to feel that the world of Feydeau was more frightening than the worlds of Beckett or Sartre because in Feydeau everything can be explained, everything has a reason—you just aren't privy to the information. If you think about it, there's really no art form more terrifying than farce. ∼

Author's Picks
Books About New York

Following is some background reading, era by era, on the grandest character in the novel:

1600s
The Island at the Center of the World: The Epic Story of Dutch Manhattan and the Forgotten Colony That Shaped America, by Russell Shorto

The Revolution and the Early Days of the Republic
Alexander Hamilton, by Ron Chernow

1820s
The Battle for Christmas, by Stephen Nissenbaum, traces the cultural history of a holiday that was outlawed by the Puritans in Massachusetts and reinvented by a group of New Yorkers in the early nineteenth century who married consumer capitalism with civic virtue and turned a raucous street holiday into a cozy, domestic celebration.

1830s
The Murder of Helen Jewett, by Patricia Cline Cohen, is a social history of a fascinating decade and the birth of sensationalist news.

1850s–1880s

Lincoln at Cooper Union: The Speech That Made Abraham Lincoln President, by Harold Holzer

Central Park, An American Masterpiece, by Sara Cedar Miller

The Park and the People, by Roy Rosenzweig and Elizabeth Blackmar

The Great Bridge, by David McCullough

New York 1880, by Robert A. M. Stern, Thomas Mellins, and David Fishman, is a study of the decade that gave us the Statue of Liberty, the Brooklyn Bridge, the rise of the office building, and the birth of many of New York's most renowned cultural institutions.

Before World War I

American Moderns: Bohemian New York and the Creation of a New Century, by Christine Stansell

Republic of Dreams, by Ross Wetzsteon, explores the history of the Village.

Between the Wars

The WPA Guide to New York City

Great Fortune: The Epic of Rockefeller Center, by Daniel Okrent

Author's Picks *(continued)*

After World War II
Here is New York, by E. B. White

The Power Broker, by Robert A. Caro

The Death and Life of Great American Cities,
by Jane Jacobs

Multiple Eras
Gotham, by Edwin G. Burrows and Mike
Wallace, is the incomparable history of
the city from the Ice Age until 1898.

New York, An Illustrated History, by Ric Burns
and James Sanders with Lisa Ades, is the
companion book to the PBS documentary.

Low Life, by Luc Sante

Waterfront: A Journey Around Manhattan,
by Phillip Lopate

Downtown, by Pete Hamill

Don't miss the next
book by your favorite
author. Sign up now for
AuthorTracker by visiting
www.AuthorTracker.com.